THE
MOONFIRE
BRIDE

THE
MOONFIRE
BRIDE

Cover design by Saint Jupiter

ALSO BY SYLVIA MERCEDES

Bride of the Shadow King
Bride of the Shadow King
Vow of the Shadow King
Heart of the Shadow King

Of Candlelight and Shadows
The Moonfire Bride
The Sunfire King
Of Wolves and Wardens

Prince of the Doomed City
Entranced
Entangled
Ensorcelled
Enslaved
Enthralled

The Scarred Mage of Roseward
Thief
Prisoner
Wraith

The Venatrix Chronicles
Daughter of Shades
Visions of Fate
Paths of Malice
Dance of Souls
Tears of Dust
Queen of Poison
Crown of Nightmares
Song of Shadows

See all books and learn more at
www.SylviaMercedesBooks.com

This book is for Emma, Tara, Stephanie, Clare,
Angela, Alisha, Kenley, and Sarah,
in honor of all our stolen brides.

1

Who are you?

I freeze with my comb partway through a tangle of hair. A shudder ripples down my spine, and I whirl around on the window seat to stare into the room, my heart racing.

No one is there.

Strange. I could have sworn that a voice—deep and dark as a moonless night—whispered directly into my ear. Even now I feel the tickle of warm breath raising gooseflesh on my neck. But no. The room is empty aside from a sagging rope-frame bed and a nearly vacant wardrobe. My work gown drapes over the back of a cane chair, but when my unsettled imagination tries to transform it into a menacing gray phantom, the flickering light from my candle shrinks it back into folds of limp gray muslin.

Cold seeps up through the floorboards to chill the soles of my bare feet. With a shiver, I tuck them up under my thin nightdress and sit cross-legged, hoping to warm my toes. The cushions under me are flat and threadbare now, their rich red velvet worn to a lusterless puce.

The whole room gives off an aura of "once upon a time."

Once upon a time beauty dwelt here.

Once upon a time this household rang with joyful laughter.

Once upon a time there was money enough to clothe us in better than thrice-turned castoffs, enough to keep our bellies full and our hearths warm.

"Once upon a time" feels so long ago now.

The candle in its clay chamberstick on the sill pops and sputters as I turn back to the window. Tallow candles are smelly and bothersome. But economical, I remind myself as its erratic light dances across my face reflected in the dark glass, my only mirror. I resume combing out my hair, unconsciously counting the strokes as Mama taught me to do when I was small. Few vanities remain to me these days—no jewels, no trinkets, no silks or perfumes. But my hair is glossy and thick, falling in gentle waves. If the idea ever occurs to him, Father will sell it in a heartbeat; wigmakers in town would give a good price for hair like mine. So far I've been spared that indignity. If worst comes to worst, however . . .

I twine a lock through my fingers and sigh. We don't face such dire straits yet. Seven gods willing, I'll be able to keep our heads above water.

Lifting my chin, I meet my gaze in the murky makeshift mirror. My eyes look hollow, spiritless. I'm bone-weary. My head is sore, and my hands are cramping after long hours of wielding a needle. Mistress Petren kept all of us stitch-girls late today, hoping to finish the new gown for Lady Leocan. I had crept home well after sunset only to discover the house empty, my father and sister gone, and the last morsel of oat bread in the larder reduced to mouse-nibbled crumbs.

No matter. I've gone to bed hungry often enough.

I set the comb on the windowsill beside my candle, then carefully separate my hair into three parts and begin plaiting. My tired eyes watch the crackling flame without really seeing it as it dances about.

Then, my eyes focus sharply and my brow creases. My fingers freeze, still threaded through my unfinished plait.

For an instant there—no more time than it took to blink twice in surprise—the candle flame looked *blue*.

I pause. I stare hard at the candle. It . . . no. It must have been my imagination again. Maybe I dozed off. I'm overtired. And hungry. That's all.

Hastily, I finish off the braid and pick up a discarded bit of remnant from Lady Leocan's last beribboned gown to secure the end. My idle gaze lifts to my blurry reflection one last time.

The distinct silhouette of a man stands just behind my right shoulder.

With a yelp, I drop the ribbon and spin about. One bare foot slides from under my nightdress to hit the floor, bracing to launch me from my seat. My heart pounds, and my hand instinctively fumbles for the wooden comb, the only thing remotely like a weapon in the room.

No one is there.

With my breath constricted in my chest, I force my gaze to travel slowly across the room. One of the wardrobe doors is partially open. My imagination instantly plagues me with dozens of ghouls and gremlins that might lurk within. Which is pure silliness! I refuse to fall prey to my own stupid fancies.

Knees trembling, I rise and cross the cold floor, brandishing my comb like a battle ax. I reach the wardrobe and, heart in my throat, fling the door wide.

It's empty.

Of course it is.

Forcing a wry chuckle from my throat, I step away from the wardrobe. Though it is undoubtedly ridiculous, I drop to my knees and peer under my bed. Just in case. Then I kick the folds of my work gown to check beneath the cane chair. My room is empty of all save shadows.

My frown deepens. "Foolish," I whisper and force my fingers to loosen their hold on the comb, to set it on the little bedside table. I return to the window seat and fetch my ribbon from the floor. Sitting quickly, my gaze darting about the room, I catch the loose ends of my braid, re-plait them, and tie off the end. I ought to go to bed. I ought to blow out my candle, climb onto that moldy old mattress, pull the covers up over my head, and try to huddle into a little ball of warmth. I ought to, but . . .

Footsteps sound on the stair. I recognize that tread, and my heart lightens. The steps continue along the outer passage to my door and stop. I hear a light, perfunctory tap, and the door cracks open. A pale little face set with a pair of enormous green eyes peeks inside.

"Vali! What are you doing still up?"

"Come in, Brielle. And shut the door." I snatch my candle from the sill on the way to my bed and set it beside my comb on the three-legged table. "You're late. Did the Trisdi children give you trouble at bedtime again?"

My sister obediently enters the room and shuts the door, then saunters over and climbs up to perch on the bed's footboard rather than the sagging mattress. Two thin plaits of brilliant red hair frame her pixie face, which is much too hollow and pinched for a girl her age. She clings to the bedpost like a squirrel and shrugs.

"Father's out," she says. "Probably won't be back until morning."

She didn't answer my question. My eyes narrow slightly. "You *did* go to work at the Trisdi's today, didn't you?"

My sister shrugs again and adjusts her seat, one foot swinging.

"We need the money, Brielle. How do you think we're going to buy bread tomorrow, hmmm? We can't afford to shirk our—"

"Don't you ever stop scolding?" Brielle rolls her eyes and swings around the bedpost, her braids flapping like two red flags. "Yes, I watched the Trisdi brats today. Yes, I brought home three sprells. Yes, I put them in the honey pot over the oven. And no, I don't think Father found them yet. I went out again after work, that's all."

"Where did you go?"

"Just . . . somewhere."

Wrapping a wool shawl around my shoulders, I sit on the bed. The frame ropes groan and the mattress dips, and if I weren't so used to it, I would fall to the middle in an awkward tumble. I catch my balance and level a glare at my sister.

"You went into Whispering Wood again." It's not a question. I know Brielle.

Her brow puckers slightly. "So what if I did?"

"It's after sunset!" The words burst out, and I hastily drop my voice. There's no one else in the house to hear me, only shadows. But tonight, the shadows feel . . . interested. "Do you have any idea how dangerous that is?"

Brielle has the grace to look ashamed at least. She is drawn to the wood like a forest creature, a wild thing I can never tame. If she could, she would spend her days loping through those green-cast shadows, foraging for wild berries and mushrooms. She would probably have disappeared into the wood long ago—either stolen by the fae or run off on her own, it hardly matters which—if not for me. She loves me. She knows how devastated I would be if she were to disappear.

But love won't be enough to keep her here forever. Someday I'll lose Brielle to the wood.

"Nothing happened," my sister growls. Her voice is petulant but underscored with a quaver that indicates at least some remorse.

I sigh and shake my head. Then, patting the bed beside me, I hold out one arm, opening the drape of my shawl.

Brielle swings from the bedpost, her lips pinched in a pout. "I'm not a baby anymore."

It's my turn to shrug. And I keep my arm extended.

With a roll of her eyes and a huff through her lips, Brielle hops off the footboard and joins me, tucking in close to my side. I wrap the shawl around her as her head rests comfortably on my shoulder. She's not the small bundle she was even a year ago. Bony, yes, but at eleven years old, Brielle is already beginning to show signs of young womanhood. It won't be long before she's too big to fit under my arm.

I close my eyes and press my cheek against the top of my sister's head. Seven years older, I've been a surrogate mother for Brielle since she was a baby. It's never been an easy task and will only get harder as the years go by. For now, I hug her close and try to pretend I can still protect her. A little longer at least.

"Why are you up so late?" Brielle asks after a bit, her tone less belligerent.

"You know I can't sleep until you're safely home."

"Where's Father?"

"He was out before I got home from Mistress Petren's."

Brielle snorts. "Won't be back till dawn, I trust. Think the fae might carry him off one of these nights?"

One can only hope. But one must also set an example for one's wayward little sister. I bite my tongue and plant a kiss on top of Brielle's head. When she looks up at me with a half-smile, giving me a clear view of her pinched face, my gaze fixes on one brown spot on her cheek. It's faintly heart shaped, a little larger than the rest of her freckles, and it's been with her since the morning of her birth. I remember Mother telling me it's a fairy kiss and means she's marked for great things one day.

When I was small, I thought the idea charming, exciting even. Now when I look at that spot, I can't help feeling a quiver of dread.

"It's cold," I say. "Want to sleep here tonight?"

"On this ratty old mattress?" Brielle extricates herself from my embrace and hops to the floor. "It'll fold up in the night and suffocate us both! I'll take my chances freezing on my own, thank you."

Yet another sign of my sister's growing independence. I nod sadly. Sometime in the last year she insisted on taking one of the other drafty, empty rooms in the Normas family home instead of sharing with me. Fighting her is useless. I've long since learned to pick my battles when it comes to Brielle.

"Good night then," I say.

Brielle tosses me a quick grin and skips to the door. Before opening it, she pauses and looks around the room. "There's a funny smell in here."

I frown. "Just the candle, I think."

"No, it's not tallow, it's . . ." Her lips pinch a moment in thought.

"Sweet," she says. "And sort of spicy. Like . . . I don't know. *Exotic*."

"I don't smell anything."

"Hmmmm." She shrugs one shoulder and raises both eyebrows. "Oh well. Happy dreams, Vali."

"Sleep well, Brielle."

When the door shuts behind my sister, the room is very still and full of shadows. I tuck my shawl tighter, pull my feet up onto the bed, and let my eyes roam . . . But, no, I won't let my imagination rule me. One can get into serious trouble that way, especially living this close to Whispering Wood.

I blow out my candle, lie down, and drag my blanket up to my chin, closing my eyes firmly. Tomorrow will come all too soon. I'll be up before dawn to scrape something together for Brielle's breakfast, all the while trying not to wake father from wherever his drunken stupor has left him sleeping in the house. Then I'll be off to Mistress Petren's to put the finishing touches on Lady Leocan's new gown. A day just like today was, and the day before that, and the day before that. Thus, life maintains its inescapable rhythm.

I squeeze my eyes tightly to force back the tears threatening to rise. I gave up on crying long ago. Only fine ladies have time enough on their hands to indulge in feeling sorry for themselves. I don't have that luxury. I must be strong. For my sister.

I release a long sigh that shudders a little at the end. Lying quite still, I let weariness overwhelm me, draw me toward sleep. The air is cold on my face.

Then suddenly it's warm. Warm like a breath.

My eyes flare open. For a moment I distinctly sense a body bent over me, a face hovering mere inches from mine. The impression is so strong, so unmistakable, that I press back into my pillow, shoving my blanket into my mouth to stifle a scream.

Only . . . nothing is there.

I blink hard, staring at the plaster ceiling overhead. I count to ten, then sit up and make myself look around the room. A thin band of moonlight creeps through the window, offering only faint illumination. The shadows are dense and dark, but . . . but empty. I'm sure they're empty.

I swallow hard. "Foolish," I whisper and again pull the blankets up over my shoulders, closing my eyes firmly. My heart is still beating too fast. It's some while before sleep steals up on me again. But I'm exhausted, so eventually I relax and slip into a half-dreaming state. My limbs are heavy, too heavy to move. In another few moments I'll be lost to dreams.

What is your name?

The whisper is there in my ear. Low, dark. More a feeling than a sound.

Will you tell me?

I frown. Then I open my lips and murmur, "Valera."

Valera.

The voice speaks slowly, as though tasting my name. Savoring.

I am pleased to make your acquaintance, Valera.

A jolt shoots through my heart and radiates out through every limb. I sit bolt upright in bed, eyes wide. Morning sunlight pours through the grimy window, bathing the window seat in a golden glow. Outside, birds sing in a joyful chorus not quite drowned out by the pounding on my door.

"Valera!" my father's voice bellows. "Valera, you lazy slattern, do you intend to sleep all day? Get your sorry hide out of bed and fetch me my breakfast!"

Seven gods have mercy, I've overslept! I'll be late for work if I don't hurry, and Mistress Petren offers zero tolerance to girls who show up even seconds past the seventh stroke of the chapel bell.

"Coming, Father!" I gasp and fall out of bed. Grabbing my dress and stockings, I throw them on in a flurry of haste. Father's voice still rings in my ears as I shake out my braid and stuff my hair up under a neat white cap. I slip on my shoes while simultaneously opening the door and hopping out into the passage, lose my balance, and almost crash into the far wall. Righting myself, I hurry down the narrow back stair to the kitchens.

Father is there. Still growling, still swearing. He stands precariously on a creaking chair, one hand groping along the top of a low-hung ceiling rafter. Just as I step through the door, his hand collides with the honey pot hidden up there.

"Father!" I cry. Too late.

The honey pot tilts, falls, and strikes Father in the face. With a roaring curse, he tumbles to the floor in a crash of broken pottery.

"What's all this noise?" Brielle appears at my elbow, peering into the room. She spots our father groaning on the floor and giggles. "Serves him right."

"Brielle!" I cast my sister a stern look before hurrying to Father's side. He's all right. He always is. A vapor of sour liquor clings to him, and he rolls over, hands searching among the honey-pot shards. "Careful, Father, you'll cut yourself," I say, taking hold of his arm and trying to draw his hand back.

"Get off me, little bitch," he snarls, his voice slurred. Before I can stop him, his meaty palm comes down on top of the three bright copper sprells Brielle had hidden in the jar. He grasps them tightly and, throwing my hand from his arm, sits up to brandish them in triumph. "Thought you could hide what's rightly mine from me, did you? Think again!"

"You're bleeding, Father," I say soothingly. "Why don't you sit up, and I'll—"

"Rightly yours?" Brielle's voice pipes from the doorway. Why can't the fool girl learn to hold her tongue? "Did *you* spend your day chasing after seven snot-nosed brats? For that matter, have you ever worked a single day in your gods-blighted life?"

"Brielle!" I flash a glare my sister's way. Then I'm falling back on my hands as Father shoves me roughly aside and surges to his feet. With a cry, I leap up, trying to catch his arm, to draw him back.

"Respect." Father's voice rumbles the word like a battle cry as he takes three lunging steps toward my sister. "You don't know the . . . the . . . the *meaning* of the word. *Respect.* But I'll teach you, all right. Mark me, girl!"

She's so small. Even smaller by daylight than she'd seemed last night. But she braces her bony body before our father's wrath, like a Serythian soldier facing the oncoming legions of the fae. Father draws back his fist, the fist clutching the sprells.

"No, Father!" I catch his wrist, yank it down. "She didn't mean anything by it. Let me have the money, please. I'll run out and buy us some eggs—"

Pain explodes in my temple. My hand flies to my face, and I choke on the cry trying to escape my throat. It was a glancing blow; Father's too bleary this early in the day to aim properly. But there's power enough in his arm to send me reeling back until my hipbone cracks against the edge of the kitchen table. I bend double as sparks fill my vision, interspersed with bursts of darkness. It's all I can do to press one hand to the tabletop, to keep myself upright.

"Vali!" Brielle's shrill voice bursts in my ear, jagged with tears. "Vali, are you all right?"

"I'm . . . I'm fine." I lower my hand from my head and search the room through the haze of dimming sparks. The kitchen door stands open. Father is already gone. Off to the nearest alehouse, no doubt, if he can find one open at this hour.

I shake my head and blink down into Brielle's face, so pinched with worry and rage. She gently touches my head, and I wince. "Sorry!" she says quickly, then bares her teeth. "I'll kill him," she growls. "I swear by Tanyl's bow, I'll kill him one of these days."

Heaving a sigh, I slip one arm around her and draw her close. Her bright little head tucks under my chin, and her body trembles with the power of her rage. I close my eyes, wishing I could protect her from these feelings the way I usually manage to protect her from Father's blows. "He's not worth it," I whisper.

"Once he's done battering us black and blue, he'll see us starved and on the streets!" Brielle hugs me, squeezing tight. "I hate him."

"Don't say that. Don't hate him." Tears threaten, but I force them back. Brielle doesn't need my tears; she needs my strength. "Your hatred only poisons you, sweetheart. It doesn't touch him."

A loud sniff. Then Brielle pulls back. Her eyes gleam a little too bright, and her expression is hard. Harder than I've ever seen it. I glimpse the shadow of the woman she's swiftly becoming—and the vision frightens me.

"I'm going to be late for work," she says.

"Me too." I fetch my faded blue cloak from the peg by the door and pass a slightly less faded green one to Brielle. "Come on, then. I'll see if I can get Mistress Petren to pay me a day early. If so, I'll bring a midday meal to the Trisdi's on my break. All right?"

Brielle pulls the hood of her cloak over her pinned-up crown of braids, nodding mutely. I wrap an arm around her skinny shoulders and lead her out the open back door. I'm not entirely certain why

I bother to shut and lock the door behind us. Nothing left inside is worth a thief's attention. Maybe I like the sense of control, false though it may be.

Slipping the key into the pocket of my gown, I turn toward the back gate and stop short.

"What's wrong?" Brielle looks at me, then follows my gaze. "Oh!" she gasps.

A stumpy figure stands at the gate, leaning on a gnarled staff. Her gown is a hodge-podge of patches from so many other garments that its original color and style can't be discerned—the sight of it makes my skin crawl. A peaked black hat perches on top of her gray, frizzled hair. I can barely discern the face peering out from beneath its broad brim. A pair of glittering eyes set in a densely wrinkled face watch us with keen interest.

Mother Ulla. The Witch of the Ward. I know her on sight, though we've never exchanged more than a few polite words in passing.

"What in the gods-blazes does she want?" Brielle muttered.

"Language!" I snap, jabbing an elbow into her ribs. "She's probably just stopped a moment to catch her breath. She's quite old, after all. Don't stare!"

"She's not *that* old," Brielle mutters but allows me to escort her down the narrow path to our gate. She drags on my arm as we approach the witch, but I lift my chin, put back my shoulders, and force a pleasant smile. My head stabs with pain where Father's blow landed, but I ignore it.

"Good morrow, Mother Ulla," I say. "May I be of service? My

sister and I are just on our way out, but if you need a place to rest awhile, I'll let you into our kitchen. There's still a little kindling for the fire, and—"

The old woman hocks loudly and spits, startling me so much I nearly yelp. The spittle plops on the ground just in front of my feet. I jump back a half step.

"Blazes!" Brielle hisses, and I pinch her arm.

Mother Ulla tilts her face, one eye opening a little wider than the other, the wrinkles parting to let a gleam of blue shine through. She peers up at me, then opens her mouth, revealing three strong white teeth in all that remains of what might once have been a ferocious snarl. "Here now," she says, and points a quivering finger at my nose. "Here now, what you been up to, girl?"

I frown, uneasy under that cold stare. I can feel the minutes slipping past. The chapel bell will toll seven soon, and if I don't hurry, I'll face Mistress Petren's wrath. "I'm sorry, good mother, I'm not sure what you—"

"There's magic all around this house." The witch waves the end of her staff. "Strong magic. You girls been playing at spell casting?" Her one visible eye swivels from me to Brielle and back again.

"Spell casting?" I shake my head. I've been told there's magic in our blood from Mother's side of the family. Father, when in a more conversational drunken state, likes to tell us how Mother was the daughter of a witch who'd kept her trapped in a tower all her life. When Father rescued her and carried her off, our grandmother put a curse on him, and all the wealth of our once great family vanished like faerie gold.

I know some girls who indulge in little spell-casting attempts on full-moon nights. Love potions, beauty spells, and the like. But Brielle and I are forbidden to so much as *think* about magic. It's caused our family too much pain.

"No, Mother Ulla," I say, careful to maintain a respectful tone. "There's been no magic around here."

"Hmmph." The ward witch sucks loudly on one of her teeth and slides her long fingers along her staff. "Don't think I don't know me own business. If I says there's magic abouts, then there's magic abouts."

I tip my chin demurely. "Of course." The last thing I need is to offend a witch. "I only mean that neither my sister nor I have had any hand in magic doings. Now, if you'll pray excuse us, we really must be off."

"Hmmph," the witch grunts again, but she steps away from the gate, allowing us through. Brielle watches her with silent, wide-eyed wariness, and the witch pulls a face at her, making her start. "Be off with you," she says, waving a hand. "Go on, get out of here."

I pull Brielle several paces after me. Before we've gone far, however, Mother Ulla's voice barks behind us: "And be wary of shadows!"

A shiver ripples through my heart. I pause and slowly look back over my shoulder. But the ward witch is waddling away down the street, the end of her staff *thunking* loudly on the cobblestones with every step she takes.

"Vali? What's wrong?" Brielle tugs at my cloak. "You look

awfully pale."

"Nothing's wrong." I give my head a little shake and offer my sister a swift smile. "Come on, we've got to hurry."

I set out at a trot, not quite a run, dragging my sister after me. I refuse to glance at the shadows cast by the buildings we pass. Or to search in those shadows for another shadow, deeper and darker still.

3

My eyes blur as I bring the hem closer to my face to study the line of stitches. For the most part they're neat and even, but the last few have gone a little too long. Customers wouldn't be likely to notice, but Mistress Petren is certain to inspect and find fault.

Sighing softly, I unthread my needle and stick it into my cuff for safekeeping while I carefully pull out the last few stitches. The fabric is pink samite, soft and delicate to the touch. But it pulls easily, and a wrong stitch can leave unsightly holes if the fabric isn't worked with proper delicacy. I bend over my work, my brow furrowed, determined to avoid harming the lovely cloth.

"Normas!"

I look up, startled by the sound of my surname so sharply

spoken. Mistress Petren stands in the doorway of the stitch room, her face square, her jaw as stern as a general's. Her appearance makes every stitch-girl in the room sit up straighter, like soldiers coming to attention.

"Lady Leocan has arrived. I need you up front."

I nod and set my work aside. I'd like to protest. Like the other five stitch-girls employed at Petren's, I have a quota of hems and buttonholes to fulfill each day. But Mistress Petren long ago discovered my eye for cut and drape and, happy to make use of a resource, often drags me to the shop front to help with pinning and fitting, chalking and cutting. Proper seamstress tasks, for which I've had no official training.

But I'm good at it. I don't mean to boast; it's simply a fact. Working here these last few years has only improved my natural abilities.

Mistress Petren knows I need this job so badly that I'll do anything asked of me without complaint and still fulfill my quota at the end of each day. I sometimes stay on well after the other stitch-girls have left, working by the light of a single candle.

My limbs stiff, my hands cramping, I rise from my seat and cross the room, weaving between the other stitch-girls at their stations. I've already been at work four hours. Long enough for the sameness of the tasks to dull my mind to the morning's events— both Father's brutality and Mother Ulla's oddness. Just one more hour until midday break. Maybe, if I can please Lady Leocan, Mistress Petren will agree to give me half my week's pay early. Then I can buy a meal for Brielle . . . and myself, for that matter.

I press a hand to my hollow stomach, bereft of too many meals in a row. I'm slightly lightheaded as I follow Mistress Petren to the front of the building, into the brightly lit receiving room where Lady Leocan stands on the fitting block, already stripped to her small clothes. She's a slight, pretty little thing, but her dainty frame is oddly off kilter due to the swell of her hugely pregnant belly.

"Valera!" she trills sweetly when I enter the room. "There you are! Oh, my dear, have you hurt yourself?" She touches her own cheek, her eyes rounding.

Self-conscious, I touch the sensitive skin over my cheekbone, feeling how swollen it is. Father's blow is no doubt darkening to an ugly purple. "Just a little clumsy this morning," I say, offering a quick smile. "I'm well though, thank you, your ladyship. How may I help you today?"

Easily worried but just as easily soothed, Lady Leocan answers my smile with a brilliant one of her own and tosses a hand to indicate a pile of rich gold brocade draped over a nearby rack. "I've gone and grown again, you see! The new dress simply won't fit. Petren here says you're the one who can save the day, and I do hope you can, for my beloved Leocan needs me to be quite radiant tonight, as he's hosting the company from Wimborne, you see, and . . ."

She rattles on like this with hardly a breath. I nod, still smiling, and accept pins from Petren and one of the other seamstresses. There's no point in trying to answer. No one could interrupt that stream of chatter. I like Lady Leocan, though. She always calls me by my first name, never *Normas*. Some might consider the informality rude, but I like to think of it as companionable.

By rights, we should be peers, after all. If Father hadn't lost every penny we ever had . . .

I shake this thought away and focus on my work, draping the lovely gold gown over tiny Lady Leocan, who has indeed grown significantly around the middle since her last fitting. It seems a bit foolish to order an elaborate, expensive gown that will no longer fit as soon as the child is born. But Lady Leocan is grimly determined to keep up with the ever-changing currents of fashion.

Pins in my mouth, I set about reconstructing the front of the gown. A pleat here, a tuck there, and a swath of creamy, shimmering fabric, and soon Lady Leocan is cooing with delight as she turns to catch sight of herself in the mirror. I smile, pleased with my efforts. If I'm honest, these moments in the front of the store are my favorites. I delight in finding solutions of fit and style for even the most difficult body types and shapes. If I had the money, I would purchase an apprenticeship and become a proper seamstress. Then someday I might open a shop of my own.

But someone like me has no business wasting time on daydreams.

"And when Lady Torric sees this gown, I know for a fact that she's going to— Oh!"

Crouched on the floor to pin up the hem, I look up as Lady Leocan's voice cuts off sharply. The young mother presses a hand to her lips, her eyes rounding. "What's wrong, my lady?" I ask around my mouthful of pins.

"N-nothing." She shakes her head, dark curls bouncing. "I-I'm just a little faint. The baby, you know . . ."

Mistress Petren steps forward at once, hand outstretched. "Would you like to sit, your ladyship?" she asks as Lady Leocan steps down from the fitting block. "Normas, you kept our guest standing too long! Where are your manners, girl?"

"No, no, don't trouble Valera." Lady Leocan shakes her head, trying to smile. One dainty hand presses against her swollen middle. She casts another uneasy glance my way but averts her eyes again swiftly. "I-I do think I would like to sit. Thank you, Petren."

"But the hem!" The protest blurts from my mouth as I watch the fabric of the unfinished gown drag on the floor. "May I just—"

"You may not," Mistress Petren snaps. "You've done enough here, Normas. Get back to your proper work. Quick now!"

Trying not to bristle at the totally unfair implication, I spit pins from my mouth and drop them on a side table. I cast a last look Lady Leocan's way, but the pretty girl won't meet my eye. She sits on a chair Petren offers and simply rubs her belly, looking uneasy, her coppery skin oddly pale.

Oh well. I slip between displays of lustrous fabric, heading for the back room. Maybe the young wife is having early contractions. Best not to take offense where most likely none was meant. Lady Leocan is innocent enough. I step back into the stitch-girls' room, which feels close and stuffy and uninspiring. I pick my way between the other girls, careful not to step on the mounds of cloth spilling from their laps, resume my seat, and take up the samite gown.

I'm picking out the last few crooked stitches when I become

uncomfortably aware of eyes on me. Looking up, I find the five other stitch-girls all staring at me, their work dropped in their laps, their hands, still holding glinting little needles, frozen.

I blink, then frown. One hand creeps up to the bruise on my cheek. Has it gotten worse? It does feel awfully swollen and must look a sight. Still, it doesn't warrant such rude staring. A flush heats my cheeks. "I'm sorry," I begin, "but is there something—"

The girl nearest me screams.

It's such a sudden, sharp, terrified sound that I let out a yelp of my own and nearly fall from my chair. As though a dam had burst, the other girls take up the scream as well, and several of them bolt from their chairs. The nearest girl points, and through the noise of the others I can just discern her words: "The Shadow of Death! She's cursed! The Shadow has found her!"

A cold fist grips my heart, and I twist in my seat to stare into the space behind me where the girl is pointing. I see nothing but empty wall.

Yet the stitch-girls are still screaming. The first girl collapses in a swoon, and the others flee to the door. Mistress Petren shouts furiously in the front room, and I hear Lady Leocan's voice rising in a thin wail. "I saw it too! It's an omen, a wicked omen! Oh, my poor baby!"

I rise. The unfinished pink gown falls from my hands to land in a pile on the floor. I'm numb, somehow, as though I've stepped outside of myself, as though my body no longer belongs to me. My gaze travels around the room, into the corners, into the deepest shadows, searching for . . . for what?

Something flicks on the edge of my vision.

With a thin cry on my lips, I turn. Instead of trying to flee through the open door into the front of the house, I make for the back door that opens into the alley. At first it's a relief to leave behind the screaming and terror, but within three paces I realize my mistake. The alley is painfully narrow, the tall buildings at either hand crowd close, blocking out the sun. Here, the shadows are deep as midnight.

Little caring that I left my cloak behind, I gather my skirts, duck my head, and run. The end of the alley seems so far away, and the gathered shadows make it feel like the mouth of a monster slowly closing even as I struggle to climb back up its throat.

I burst out into the open street under the brilliant sun, gasping for breath. I stagger, then whirl to look back the way I came. The screams are distant now, and the alley no longer seems quite so dark and threatening. Why was I so frightened? And what did those girls see to make them lose their heads like that? It doesn't make sense . . . and I'm so cold!

I take a step, half wondering if I ought to speak to Mistress Petren, apologize for whatever trouble I've caused. I pause, bite my lip, turn to look back over my shoulder . . . and choke on a gasp of surprise.

Mother Ulla stands just behind me. Her ugly face peers at me from under the brim of her hat, and one bristly brow slowly rises, mounding wrinkles as it goes.

"Tell me, girl," she says without preamble, "have you given your name away recently?"

"What?" I blink stupidly, my mouth opening and closing. "My . . . my name? What are you—"

"Don't bat your eyes at me! It's a simple enough question. Have you given anyone your name recently? Last night, for example."

For a moment I can make no sense of the words. It's as though they're the wrong shape and won't fit into the slots of my brain.

Then memory flares.

"Yes," I breathe. "Last night."

That deep dark voice speaking in my ear. Like a dream but not a dream.

I am pleased to make your acquaintance, Valera . . .

The ward witch growls, closes her eyes, and shakes her head. The pointed tip of her hat flops dolefully. "I thought as much. You've brought trouble down on your head now, ain't you? Come on, quick." She grabs hold of my wrist, turns, and hastens down the street, moving surprisingly fast for her age.

"What's going on?" I try to yank out of the witch's grasp, but it's like trying to pull free from the clutching roots of an oak. "Where are you taking me?"

"Home, girl," Mother Ulla says. "I'm taking you back home, and there I hope to keep you, if the gods are with us."

"Home? Why?" I look back. For the briefest possible instant, I think I see something move in the mouth of the alley. A tall, slender figure without feature or solid form. A man.

I shudder and look away quickly, my skin crawling. "What's happening?"

"What's happening is you've gone and gotten yourself halfway married," Mother Ulla says, giving my arm a vicious tug. "And if you ain't careful, you're going to finish the job and be a bride, like it or not. Don't gawp like that, and don't drag your feet! We ain't gots no time to waste."

4

Mother Ulla drags me back through town. At first I try to ask a question or two, but I can't seem to make my lips shape coherent words. It doesn't matter; the old witch isn't likely to answer anyway. I duck my head and concentrate on trying not to see the shadows closing in all around. It's midday . . . at least, I think it is. Clouds pass over the sun, and if I didn't know better, I'd almost believe evening was closing in.

At my own back gate Mother Ulla stops, crouches, and plants her palm in a patch of scuffed dirt. I watch her, both curious and disconcerted, but can't for the life of me discern what she's about. But Mother Ulla grunts with satisfaction. Then, uttering a groan loud enough to wake the dead, she hauls herself upright, using her staff for support. "Ward's still in place," she says. "We might undo this tangle yet. Quickly, girl!"

She ushers me through the gate, and I obey without a word. At the kitchen door I stop and fumble for my key, nearly dropping it three times before I manage to shove it into the lock. The door swings open so quickly that I stumble inside, prodded in the back by the end of the ward witch's staff. Mother Ulla slams the door so hard behind us, it threatens to rattle off its hinges.

"Give me some space now," she says, tossing the words over her shoulder.

I back away and watch in bemused silence. The old woman begins tapping out strange rhythms on the floor with one end of her staff and scratching marks on the door and walls with the other end. There doesn't seem to be any purpose behind it. The marks on the wall are strange shapes, more like a child's scribbles than anything else.

Witch's work. It must be. But though I strain every sense, I can't detect any magic. Then again, despite all Father's assertions that witch blood runs in my veins, I'm not particularly attuned to magic. Even enchanted nights like Glorandal and Winter Solstice tend to roll past me without so much as prickling my skin.

"There. That's done." Mother Ulla turns from the door, stumps across the room, pulls out a chair from the table, and sits, all her fat flesh sagging comfortably. "That spell will spread over the rest of the house. I'll check the front door in a bit to make certain it's properly covered, but we should be safe enough now."

"Safe enough?" I try to swallow, but my throat is much too dry.

"Mother Ulla, forgive me, but I don't understand what's happening. You said something about a . . . a . . ." I can barely force the word out. It's too bizarre. "About a marriage."

Mother Ulla nods. She hikes her skirts, revealing one gnarled foot and a decent amount of fat, veiny calf, and props her heel on the other kitchen chair, leaving me to stand. "Got a drop of something to offer your guests, girl? Your mother ought to have trained you right."

"Oh. Yes." I move to fetch a cup of water. There's nothing else in the house. Father drank up the fine stores in the cellars long ago, and by the end of the month there's never enough money for tea. So, water it is. At least it's cool and clean, drawn from the well yesterday, twice-boiled and thrice-strained.

Mother Ulla curls a lip at the offering but accepts the cup and tosses back its contents without a word. I wait until she's finished before pressing, "Did I hear you correctly? Did you really say I've gotten myself . . . halfway married?"

"If I'm reading the signs right, yes." Setting aside the cup, the ward witch grabs her other leg and, grunting, hauls it up so she can cross her ankles on the chair. Her toes splay and curl comfortably, rather like a cat settling in for a nice long nap. "I told you this morning there were magic doings at work on this house. Took me a bit to work it out, but I think I've pinpointed it right enough. Tell me, was there a blue light in your room last night?"

I nod mutely, remembering the flashing blue candle.

"Thought as much." The old woman sucks thoughtfully on a

tooth. "I've never bothered much with your family. You're Granny Dorrel's granddaughters, after all. A witch don't like to mess with the progeny of another witch. T'aint respectful and often leads to trouble. But since the day your dearly departed mother moved into this house, I been keepin' a watchful eye on the doings here. Bad luck tends to dog the footsteps of those what cross Granny, and I had the lot of you earmarked for trouble. Been quiet enough round here though, I must say. Sure, your pappy may be cursed, and you girls've had your share of hard times, but . . ." she shrugs. "I've got my business. Watch over my ward. Do what I can to keep fae folk out of human affairs. A curse or two ain't my business."

"My father really *is* cursed, then?" I ask softly.

"What? Course he is! Don't take no magic eye to see it! But that don't *pertain*." Mother Ulla taps the tabletop with one long fingernail. "You gots troubles of your own now, girl, make no mistake. There was blue light in your room last night. Moonfire, that is. Lunulyrian magic. That's the Moon Kingdom, if you didn't know. Faerieland. They gots their own strange ways of doing things over there. I don't have dealings with them if I can help it, and by and large they don't care much for humans anyway. But when a Lunulyrian fae sets his sights on young mortal flesh, the signs are clear enough."

The witch leans back in her seat, idly twirling her gnarled staff and sucking her tooth again. "You gots a bridegroom on your heels, girl. And you've already given him your name when he asked it. Did you even try to get around it?"

"No." A shiver flutters down my spine. I plant one hand on the tabletop to steady myself.

"Didn't try to give him a false name or pass off your middle name or something of the kind?"

I shake my head.

"Right. He asked, and you just gave it. Typical!" The ward witch rolls her tiny eyes and snorts. "Well, that's that. Moonfire light. An asking and a giving of a name. And tonight is the new moon. Mark my words, girl! You're halfway married now, and there's not much you can do about it. But if we're clever, we can keep you from getting all the way married."

My knees feel weak. Since Mother Ulla's feet occupy the other chair, I hop up to sit on the kitchen table, the toes of my shoes dangling several inches from the floor. "How?" I ask bleakly. "How do I keep from . . . from getting married?"

"You just gots to stay inside tonight. From sunset to sunup, you can't cross the threshold of your father's house. If you can manage that, the bond will be broken, and you'll be free."

Hope warms my breast. That's all? Just stay inside overnight? I never venture out after sunset anyway. I run my hands down my face, pulling at the skin under my suddenly tired, aching eyes. Strands of long dark hair escape from my cap, and I push them back into place with trembling fingers. Silly that I should tremble so. The danger is past now. Now that I'm inside and the ward witch has placed her spells all around the house.

An image flashes through my mind—that tall dark shadow

shaped like a man, standing just at my back in the window's reflection. I shiver again and wrap my arms around my middle, trying to still the uncomfortable twisting in my gut.

"At Mistress Petren's," I say, glancing sidelong at the ward witch, "the girls saw something. They said something about . . . about the Shadow of Death."

Mother Ulla snorts. "Dramatics."

"What did they see?" I press. "Do you know?"

"I'd guess they caught a glimpse of your bridegroom. Probably a projection spell allowing him to see you without physically traveling into the mortal world. Lunulyrian magic, I told you." The old woman looks up, catches my questioning stare, and snorts again. "You don't gots to worry yourself! From what I can gather, some fae has taken a fancy to you for reasons of his own—reasons which no doubt make sense to his twisted fae mind—and he's sent a projection to watch you go about your day. You've halfway married him according to his laws and his thinking, and he probably wants to make sure nothing happens to you until he can send his people to claim you tonight."

I'm going to be sick. My stomach somersaults, and I tighten my hold around my middle, trying to hold myself together. How hungry I am! Hollow inside like a burned-out tree. There's no food in the house, so I hop down from the table and fetch a cup of water from the basin. While there, I look down at my dim reflection in the water. My gaze shifts to the empty space over my right shoulder. No dark featureless figure stands there.

I shiver even so and take a hasty gulp of water.

Suddenly my eyes widen. I whirl to face the witch again, splashing droplets on my hands and dress. "Brielle! She's out there, out at work!"

"The little one?" Mother Ulla adjusts her seat. "She's fine. Nobody's earmarked that knobby-kneed mite for a bride."

"But can she get through the protections? The spells you put on the house? And what about Father? What if he comes home and can't get through the door?"

"Don't seem like you should be breaking your heart over *that*." The witch sniffs. But after a second glance my way, she adds quickly, "Relax, girl! So long as your sister's inside before sunset, you don't gots nothing to worry about. The wards will let humans in up to that point. After the sun goes down, ain't nothing getting through that door until dawn."

I nod, trying to take heart. But something about the witch's words leaves me feeling unsettled. "Can't you make a spell so that no one can *leave* the house until morning as well?"

A funny look passes over her face, impossible to read through her mask of wrinkles. "For the marriage bargain to be properly broken, you gots to properly break it. That means you gots to *choose* not to leave the house. If I take away the choice, you'll still be half married, and your bridegroom might try again to claim you next new moon. No, no." She shakes her head, pursing her lips in a firm line. "It's best we take care of this tonight. I gots more than enough dealings to keep me busy in my wardship

47

without scampering back here every month or so to make certain you stay unmarried!"

I take another, slower sip from my cup. My hands still tremble, and the water swirls uncomfortably in my gut. I glance out the window. The day, which was already strangely dark, has darkened still more since we stepped inside. How much longer until sundown?

"Well now," Mother Ulla says, plopping her bare feet back down on the stone floor. She stands, groaning so loudly I have to wonder if it's more for effect than any real aches or pains. "Gots to check that front door of yours now, and all the lower windows as well. You might want to nip upstairs for a bit of rest, girl. You've got a long night ahead of you."

"A long night?"

The witch gives me a look. "You didn't think you was just gonna go to bed and sleep 'til morning, did you? No, girl. You've got to stay up and *choose* not to leave. Them's the rules."

Muttering something about the senselessness of the young, Mother Ulla shuffles past me into the passages beyond. I continue to stand by the water basin, slowly turning my cup in my fingers. My mind spins with thoughts I hadn't dared to face until this moment. First of all, my job . . . Would Mistress Petren take me back after such a disturbance in front of her wealthiest customer? If not, I'll have a long, hard search to find another job somewhere. I'll be lucky to find something that allows me to use my sewing skills. Most likely, I'll end up scrubbing floors at the local inn. Or worse.

But these thoughts, though worrying, are nowhere near so

dreadful as those lurking just below the surface of my mind. I close my eyes and see again that shadowy image, hear again that dark deep whisper in my ear. A fae! A fae is trying to stake a claim on me! But why? What could I possibly have done to attract such attention? Brielle is the one to worry about—Brielle, who dashes off into Whispering Wood at the drop of a hat, who all but dares the fae folk to come out and play. Reckless, wild, madcap Brielle has always seemed destined for danger. While I live my life walking the road between home and work and home again. Day after tedious day.

Yet somehow, with no idea how I managed it . . . I've gotten myself entangled with the fae. I'm halfway married to one!

It's too much. I'm suddenly too tired, too utterly bone-weary to deal with one moment more of this nonsense. Setting my cup down with a clang, I leave the kitchen, climbing the back stair up to my room. If Mother Ulla is right, and I'll have to spend the night sitting up and *choosing,* I might as well snatch whatever sleep possible ahead of time. I fall into the bed, asleep almost before my head hits the pillow.

A voice whispers. Just beyond the edge of hearing. Just beyond the range of perception.

Valera . . . Valera . . . Valera . . .

I drift off into uneasy dreams.

5

I jolt awake to the sound of vicious shouting below stairs. At first I can't think, my exhausted mind all a-tumble. Is it the fae? Have they broken through Mother Ulla's spells, come to steal me away to their strange world?

Blinking hard, I shake my head, the strings of my white cap wafting across my shoulders. I press the heel of my hands into both eyes, trying to press some sense back into my head. Only after I lower my hands do I recognize one of the two voices downstairs: Father, cursing by as many of the seven gods as he can remember. And the answering voice—the creaky squawk that sounds like an old gate opening and shutting in high wind—must be Mother Ulla.

I yank the cap from my head, letting my hair tumble freely down my back as I climb from the bed and rush back downstairs to the kitchen. Father's voice rings loud enough to bring showers of dust raining from the rafters. His words clarify as I approach the door, "I won't have witches under my roof! Never again, do you hear? I've stomached enough of witches and witchcraft to last me a lifetime. Out, hag! Out!"

His words are crisp, clear. Which means he isn't drunk yet. Or not very drunk, anyway.

I carefully peer into the room. The day has lengthened, darkness is settling fast, but a fire burns bright on the kitchen hearth. I take a second glance. A fire without fuel, glowing faintly purple! Mother Ulla's work, no doubt.

By its light I see Father screaming into the ward witch's face. He looms large, his eyes swollen and puffy with sleep, his cheeks and neck many days unshaven, his shirt unfastened to reveal the thick black hair on his chest. He isn't a tall man, but he has to stoop to stand nose-to-nose with tiny Mother Ulla, who blinks up into his red-faced fury, sucking her tooth with bored disinterest.

I can almost see the rage roiling inside my father. When I was a child, when Mother was alive, he would at least attempt to control the bad feelings that plagued him. These days, he doesn't bother. At the least disturbance to his tenuous equilibrium, he opens wide the floodgates of passion and lets the torrent overwhelm everything in his path. There's no reasoning with him in such a state. I learned that the hard way, long ago.

I watch in horror as Father draws back a clenched fist, aimed straight at Mother Ulla's hooked nose. "No, Father!" I cry and lunge for him, catching hold of his upraised arm.

He turns to me, surprised. For half an instant, he almost looks ashamed of being caught on the verge of striking a little old woman. The shame vanishes in a blink, however. His face, bathed in that weird, purplish glow of firelight, is like a monster's mask.

"You!" he snarls, rounding on me. He wrenches hard, trying to free his arm, but I hold on tight. When he gets free, he'll strike. "You let her in here, didn't you! Always knew you were a little witch, just like your slattern grandmother before you. I'm cursed with witches wherever I go! But I'll show you. I'll teach you what happens to those who cast the evil eye on me."

He shoves me to the floor, breaking my grasp. Then his other arm rises, prepared to swing a vicious backhand at my already bruised face. I cry out, flinging up my arms to catch the blow.

It doesn't fall.

Slowly I lower my arms, peering up at Father's face. It hovers above me, his features twisted in that savage snarl I know too well. But his eyes flick back and forth in their sockets, full of shock and fear. His arm, caught mid-swing, trembles as it struggles to follow through on the action his brain commands. But he can't move.

"That's better." Mother Ulla taps the end of her staff smartly against the stone floor, then bends slightly, peering around Father's bulk to cast me a wry, wrinkly look. "Have a good rest, girl? How about some tea?"

I look from the witch to my father and back again. Knees shaking, I rise from my defensive crouch and straighten my skirts.

Father remains immobile. Wrath fairly oozes from his pores, but other than his eyes, he can't stir a muscle. I sidle away and move to the table, fumbling to pull out a chair. I sit down hard, as though all the strength has suddenly gone from my body.

"Here." Mother Ulla sets one of my own plain wooden cups in front of me. "Drink that, why don't you."

I lift the cup to my lips and sip. A sharp, bitter flavor flows over my tongue, and I nearly cough in surprise. But as the warm liquid trickles down my throat, I feel some of the spiking fear ease out of my body, and my breathing resumes a normal rhythm.

I glance up at Mother Ulla, who's watching me closely. "Where . . . where did you find tea?" It's an odd question perhaps, considering my father is standing frozen just a few steps away. But for some reason it seems a reasonable thing to ask in the moment. "Our larder is empty."

"Ain't it just!" Mother Ulla sticks her hand into a pocket of striped fabric at her hip and pulls out a small silk packet. "I never goes nowhere without it. Never know when you'll find yourself stuck somewhere overnight and wanting a nice cuppa."

She takes a seat in the other kitchen chair, uttering another of her bone-chilling groans as she settles. Then she leans back and eyes me again. "You gots more spunk to you than I would have credited."

I hastily swallow a second mouthful of tea. "I beg your pardon?"

"You looks like a little wisp of a thing, all pale and bony with those big doe eyes of yours. I'd expect you to flutter away altogether under the next big gale to blow through. Then you goes and throws yourself at a man three times your size, knowing full well he's going to turn and hit you a good one. Judging by the color on your cheek there, he's walloped you often enough. And I'm sittin' here wondering how often you takes the hit so another person don't has to."

I drop my gaze and watch how the dark water swirls in my cup. I don't answer. What can I say? I'm not brave. If I were brave, properly brave, I would have packed up Brielle and fled this house years ago.

But Mother Ulla clicks her tongue thoughtfully, shaking her head. She's taken her broad-brimmed hat off, and her hair is a frizzy cloud of tight curls in the firelight. "*Valera*," she says softly. "Maybe it suits you after all." Then she sits up suddenly, her eyes opening wide behind her wrinkles. "Ah! It's starting."

The ward witch groans mightily as she lurches to her feet, then waddles to the kitchen window, where she stands on her toes with her nose close to the dim glass. My stomach turns over. I quickly set my cup down before my trembling fingers spill it.

"Sunset," the old witch says. "And . . . yup. They're here all right."

I hasten to the window and peer over Mother Ulla's shoulder. I see only the familiar kitchen garden: weed-grown upraised beds; fruit trees, now hardly more than twigs with a few mold-blighted leaves clinging to thin branches; and the narrow path leading down to the little gate that lists on its hinges, only just managing to stay shut. It all appears normal to my eye, cast in the gloom of swiftly deepening twilight.

Then a gasp escapes my lips. Are my eyes playing tricks on me?

Did my overtired, overstrained mind invent the huddled shape, no bigger than a groundhog, that scuttled swiftly past the gate, just visible through the slats? A shape like a small bent man with ears like a bat's wings?

"Goblins." Mother Ulla growls the word like a curse and spits on the floor. "Nasty little blighters."

I back away from the window, my breath tight in my chest. Then my eyes widen. "Brielle! Did she come home?"

My heart shudders with dread as the ward witch shakes her head. "Don't you be worrying about her," Mother Ulla says, still craning her neck to stare into the darker reaches of the kitchen garden.

"She's still out there?" I take two steps toward the door before stopping short. I can't see or feel the protection spells Mother Ulla has placed. But somehow I feel as though I've hit a barrier—not a magic barrier, but the wall of my own cowardice. What might happen if I dare to take hold of the doorlatch, if I pull the door open, if I look outside? Would I be carried off by goblins? It seems too fantastical to be believed, and yet . . . I can't deny that awful little shape I've just seen. Goblins are out tonight.

And my prospective bridegroom? Is he one of their number?

See, I tell myself bitterly, my upraised hand dropping away from the door handle. *Mother Ulla is wrong. You're not brave. Not even a little.*

But, Brielle . . .

I become aware of the witch's gaze on the side of my face. Glancing sideways, I meet the old woman's contemplative stare.

Mother Ulla's left eyebrow rises slightly, and her eyes glint in the magicked firelight. Then she grunts and waddles back to the kitchen table.

"The fae folk don't gots no interest in your sister tonight," she says, easing herself back into her seat. "They might torment her a bit for the sport of it, but the Pledge protects her from any real harm. At worst she'll have a fright and come home in the morning a bit footsore and hungry." She leans an elbow on the table and nods toward the other kitchen chair. "Sit down, girl. You wants to be sure she's got a sister to come home to tomorrow, don't you?"

I draw a long breath and let it out slowly. I look back at the door and then, with a frustrated hiss through my teeth, wrench myself around and perch on the edge of the chair. I feel Father's eyes on me again and cast him a swift glance, unwilling to meet his gaze.

So begins the long night. The night of choosing. I drain my cup to the bitter dregs, and a short while later Mother Ulla refills it from a copper kettle hung over her purple fire. Outside, twilight deepens into night. And still Brielle does not come.

Father, standing with his arm upraised in mid-swing, groans now and then, a wrenching, rasping sound. Mother Ulla casts him a vicious glare and growls, "None of your tantrums, you sad little man! I gots no patience for you tonight."

I shake my head sharply and press my hands to my face. "Please, Mother Ulla. Please, let him go." The witch gives me such a look, I'm almost ashamed. But I straighten my spine and speak again more firmly. "He won't cause any harm, I promise. You won't, will you, Father?" I add, looking his way.

He swivels his eyes and groans again.

"Eh. You's too softhearted for your own good," Mother Ulla mutters. But she twitches the end of her staff. Father's arm finishes its arc, and the momentum sends his whole body tumbling to the floor. He lies there, groaning more loudly than before and occasionally twitching. I start to rise, to go to him, but at a sharp word from the witch, sit back down again. "He's fine," she says, sneering at the prone man. "Just a little spell-stiffness wearing off. Leave him be." She eyes me again, her face distinctly disapproving. "You do know he don't deserve your compassion, don't you?"

I open my mouth to speak, but my tongue feels oddly numb. I shake my head and look down at my hands folded in my lap. "I . . . I don't think compassion is a matter of *deserving*, Mother Ulla."

The witch snorts. She opens her mouth, but before she can utter another word, there's a sudden scratching at the door. A frisson of terror ripples down my spine. I sit bolt upright in my seat, staring at Mother Ulla.

"Don't worry, girl," she says and rises again. This time, I note, there is no groaning or stiffness. The old woman moves as smoothly as a cat, creeping to the door. She carries her staff along but doesn't let its end tap on the floor. The scratching continues, getting louder. Mother Ulla turns her head, listening.

Then she clunks the gnarly top of her staff hard against the door. There's a shriek on the other side, a sound of scrabbling. "That's right!" Mother Ulla cries, her voice pitchy with glee. "That's what you get for messing with my wards! Little garbage-grubbing blighters." She chuckles merrily, waddles back to the table, and plops into her chair, grinning. "How about another spot of tea, girl?" She fetches the packet from her pocket and tosses it to the table between us. "There's a lot of night left to go."

Without a word, I rise and fill the kettle from the water basin, then hook its handle over the crane and swing it back over the magicked fire. As I work, I keep an eye on Father. He's pulled himself into a heap of limbs and sits with his back against the wall, his shoulders hunched, his eyes glittering with malice. He shows his teeth at me in a silent snarl and looks as though he might speak. But at a sharp glance from Mother Ulla, he bites his tongue and hangs his head.

I stand near the fire, rubbing my arms and watching the flames as I wait for the water to boil. I try not to let my gaze slide to the door. But it . . . *calls* to me somehow. The urge to look out into the night is intense, and though I know I ought not to give in to the impulse even for a moment, I find myself almost unconsciously moving to the window. The glass is bright with the glow of the fire at my back, but I lean in, cupping my hands, and peer through into the kitchen yard.

My heart thuds in my throat, choking a scream.

The yard is crawling with movement. Indistinct figures hurry and scurry between clumps of weeds, climbing through branches. And between the trees, tall, long-limbed humanoid figures stand perfectly still save for the faint movement of what might be antennae protruding from their foreheads.

A horse waits at the gate—a huge black beast with hooves the circumference of dinner plates and eyes that gleam red in the darkness. The silver decorations on its tack glow even though there is no moon in the sky to shine upon it. It tosses its head and puffs a stream of vapor like smoke, and I would not have been at all surprised to see sparks shoot from its nostrils.

Suddenly, a figure appears right in front of the glass. A creature with a strange, perfectly oval face and eyes so large and dark that no trace of whites can be seen. It blinks hugely at me and holds up something bright and glittering: a necklace of shining stones.

I leap back from the window. My heart drops back into place in my breast and makes up for lost time, beating fast. The glare from the fireplace reflects off the window glass, blocking out the apparition.

"It don't pay to look, you know." Mother Ulla appears at my elbow. Startled, I look down into her upturned face. "Make your tea. Take your seat. Don't let them tempt you."

"Tempt me?" Was that what the creature was trying to do, offering me jewelry like the bait in a snare? It's almost insulting. So, was that big-eyed, blinking creature my bridegroom? I shudder.

"Go on, girl. Sit." Mother Ulla nods back at the table. Then she shrugs. "Or not. Just as you choose. Tonight is about your choosing after all."

My hands curl into fists. Behind me, I hear the kettle boil over, water sputtering and sizzling from its spout. But I can't quite bring myself to care. "Brielle," I whisper. "Brielle is—"

'Hush!" Mother Ulla springs up, one fat arm thrusting out as she claps a hand over my mouth. "Don't say her name so loud! If *they* get ahold of it, there's no telling what they might do! Your sister's safe enough tonight, but *you* are another matter."

The scratching at the door starts up again before I finish drinking my next cup of tea. I close my eyes, trying not to hear it, trying to concentrate on other things. Father sitting against the wall, muttering under his breath. Mother Ulla's strange, tuneless humming. The crackle of the fire merrily burning nothing.

But the scratching continues. Soft, rhythmic. Insistent. It will drive me mad.

A voice whispers through the crack under the door: "We have gold. So much gold."

My eyes open. I stare across at Mother Ulla, but the witch is looking at Father on the floor.

"If she chooses us, we'll give it all to you. Your curse will be broken. Your house will be wealthy once more."

Father sits upright. His head tips to one side. His eyes are bright, brighter than I remember ever seeing them before. They seem to shimmer with an inner glow. His body slowly unfolds itself in awkward, jerking movements as he clambers to his feet. He sways unsteadily in place.

"Valera." His voice emerges from his throat as though echoing up from some hollow cavern. "You could save us."

I stare at him. I feel frozen in my seat.

His gaze turns to me, unseeing and too bright. "You could save us, sweet child!" he says. "You could undo this curse that's on me!"

"Don't listen to him," Mother Ulla growls softly from her seat. "*They* don't have no control over the curse he's under. Any gold they give him will melt right through his fingers, just like your whole family fortune did."

"You don't know that, witch!" Father snarls. Then he turns to me again and, to my horror, drops to his knees. "Please, girl!" he cries. "Please, do this for me. It's not my fault, you know. It's not my fault your wicked grandmother cursed me. I loved your mother. I loved her like my own soul, and now she's gone, and I'm left with nothing, nothing! Nothing but this old, empty, gutted house!"

I stare down into his face, unable to speak. I feel as though he's reaching down inside me to grab my heart and squeeze it, squeeze until it bursts.

"Shut your mouth, fool man." Mother Ulla angles her staff to point it at his chest. "Shut your mouth, or I'll seal it shut for you."

The voices outside start up again. A whole chorus of them this time.

"Gold!"

"Gold!"

"We have so much gold!"

"Gold for you!"

"Gold for yours!"

"If she so chooses!"

"The bridegroom will pay handsomely for his bride!"

"Gold!"

"Gold!"

"Gold!"

Father clutches the hair at his temples, his mouth dropping open in an inarticulate cry. Then he leaps up and grabs me by the hands. I scream, but he doesn't hurt me, merely holds on tight, gazing urgently into my face. "Please, daughter!" he cries. "If not for me, for your sister's sake!"

The voices outside go still. Suddenly. Abruptly.

Father's plea seems to echo through the kitchen, bouncing off the stones around us, then fading away. I gaze into his eyes, into that expression of desperate hope, desperate fear. My ears roar with silence and blood pounding in my veins.

Mother Ulla blows out a breath and curses softly. "Now you've done it."

The voices outside start up again in a murmur like a swelling storm. No words at first, or none that I can discern. Maybe they speak another language, talking excitedly to one another.

Then one of them speaks, sounding close to the door: "We have your sister."

My stomach drops.

"It's a lie, girl," Mother Ulla says. She reaches across the table as though to take my hand, but Father still has a firm grip on me. "Don't listen to them."

"She's a pretty little playmate," the voice says.

Another voice chimes in: "Such bright, pretty hair!"

"We love to dance with her!"

"We love to play with her!"

"She is so sweet!"

"So sweet!"

"So sweet!"

There's no threat in what they say. No bargain. Nothing. There doesn't need to be.

I stand. I pull free of Father's hands and turn toward the door.

"I told you," Mother Ulla says, jumping up from her seat and stepping in front of me. "They can't hurt her! They don't gots her name, and the Pledge will keep her safe. Even *they* don't dare break the Pledge!"

I grimace. I try to swallow, but my throat is dry as dust.

Brielle . . .

I push past the witch and approach the door. The voices outside chitter and whisper, then redouble their efforts.

"We love your little sister! We love her so!"

"She is so sweet, so sweet!"

I touch the door latch, then hesitate. This is a trick. I know it is. They're manipulating me. They're luring me into their waiting arms. I don't have to play their game. I can choose to turn around right now, to take my seat, to wait out the night.

But what if it isn't a trick?

A wild, terrified scream splits the night.

I throw my hands over my ears, backing away from the door. Echoes of the scream resound in my head, paralyzing my limbs.

Though I strain my ears, strain every sense I possess, I don't hear a second one.

"It ain't her." Mother Ulla stands at my elbow. "It can't be."

I lower my hands and clutch my skirts. Slowly I turn my gaze to look down at the old witch. "Are you ever wrong?"

She hesitates a mere fraction of an instant. Then, "No."

But it isn't the truth. And if she's wrong this time . . .

I step forward, reaching for the latch again.

"I'm warning you, girl," Mother Ulla says at my back, "you cross that threshold, there ain't nothing I can do for you. You're on your own, at the mercy of the fae. But it's your choice!"

"My choice," I whisper. I close my eyes and tuck my chin, leaning my forehead against the door. Lips parted, I draw a long, long breath.

Brielle.

I turn the latch, pull the door open, and step out over the threshold.

"Very well!" I cry, my voice ringing across the darkened yard. "It's my choice. And I choose this."

For a moment, I'm blind. My eyes struggle to adjust to the dark of a moonless night after the glow of the purple fire. I feel tension in the air around me, feel the sudden intake of many breaths.

My vision clarifies. Just for an instant, I see them all around me. The little creeping ones, the tall willowy ones. And at the end of the path, beyond the garden gate, that massive black horse with its flaming eyes.

A jubilant cry goes up all around me. Terror thrills through my heart, and I half step back, instinct telling me to flinch, to flee.

Then everything goes black.

faintly pulsing blue light fills my head.

I open my eyes a crack—then shut them again right away. It doesn't matter. Even with my eyes squeezed tight, I know I'm not home in my sagging old bed. Everything about the atmosphere is strange, different. I'm not achingly cold, for one thing. For another, the air doesn't smell of moldy feathers but is gently perfumed with a floral scent. Something sweet and a little spicy.

I've smelled that scent before. Last night. When my candle glowed blue.

I wrench my eyes open. A tall white candle in a stick of delicately wrought silver flickers before my gaze. The blue flame sways gently on the wick like a lazy dance of heat and light. A halo of tiny sparks radiates from the flame, spinning softly, glinting pink, gold, orange, and green as they spread and dissipate into darkness.

I stare at the candle, hypnotized by its gentle, pulsing aura. I can't even feel properly afraid.

Then, with a growl, I tear my gaze away and sit upright. My head spins. The perfumed air is too strong, too cloying, and my stomach pitches in rebellion. The sensation passes, however. My innards settle, my head levels out. I open my eyes and take another look at my surroundings.

I'm sitting in a bed. A huge bed like a sleigh carved from black stone. The blue candlelight sparks on white flecks in the stone, making it look like a star-studded sky. The bedding itself is pale fur, softer than velvet, softer than silk, softer than any of the fine fabrics or trimmings I've ever handled in Mistress Petren's shop.

I look down. I'm still wearing my rough work gown of faded wool. It feels grimy and wrong in this setting. I touch the bedding again, running my fingers back and forth to make the fur stand up and lie down. What if I were to strip out of these itchy old sagging garments? Stretch out on that fur, luxuriate in the sensation of that softness against my skin—

No!

My eyes widen, and I scramble out of the bed, almost falling over the edge. It's much taller than I anticipated, and I land hard, jarring my bones. I grip the side of the bed to pull myself upright, my heart pounding. Where had that shocking thought come from? Was something in the air, in the candle's scent? Some drug meant to lure me into complacency? I shake my head, clenching my teeth as I warily scan the room, half expecting some monstrous bridegroom to spring from the deepest shadows at any moment.

The candlelight reveals fine furnishings. Much finer than I've ever seen before—an elegant lounge rich with scrollwork, a tall looking glass etched around the edges with delicate designs, and a massive chest, its lid opened to reveal mounds of fabrics and laces, their colors indeterminable in this light. A fireplace adorns one wall, its mantel a large block of stone decorated with various ornaments, and flickering blue flames rise from a little pile of pulsing white stones on the hearth. Near the fire, where the light can fully shine on it, stands a table displaying a bountiful array of jewels—tiaras, bracelets, brooches, chokers, and earrings dripping with sparkling gemstones that must dangle all the way to the shoulders.

My gaze passes over these to a wall hung with heavy curtains of richly embroidered fabric. A window? I spring across the room, grab the fabric, and yank it back to find leaded-glass panes rising to at least twice my height. Pressing my face to the panes, I try to gain an impression of the world outside. But it's too dark. I can't see anything. My hands run over the glass, searching for some latch or catch. If there is one, it must be too high up for me to reach.

No way out.

I draw a steadying breath. Right. No use in panicking. I seem to be alone, which means there's time to get my mind in order, time to make a plan of sorts.

Behind me, I hear a soft sound like the creak of an opening door.

I whirl in place, pulse jumping, to see an opening in the wall on the far side of the bed. An opening I'm almost certain wasn't there before. I wait, staring, expecting any moment to see one of those strange, oddly elongated figures appear. But the opening merely reveals a glow of light from the chamber beyond.

"It's a trap," I whisper.

And maybe it is. But what am I supposed to do? Stand here beside this huge bed and wait for my so-called bridegroom to arrive? I clench my fists, set my jaw. I'm not some meek little lamb waiting for the slaughter.

Moving with caution, I creep to the doorway and peer through. My eyes the sight of another room—a huge circular space with an enormous pool in its center. Lovely painted tiles line the pool, creating a pattern of moons, stars, and planets. Light emanates from the water, and a closer look reveals three glowing white orbs floating near the bottom. Living things? Or candles caught in some sort of magical baubles? I can't say for sure.

The air is cool, but steam rises invitingly from the surface of the pool along with more of that lovely, exotic scent. A little table stands to one side, laid out with bottles of ointments, fine soaps, little combs, and brushes. A shimmering white gown drapes over a chair.

So. My bridegroom expects me to strip down, bathe, and dress myself for his pleasure.

I back away from the door, my lip curling. I may have chosen to step across my father's threshold. That doesn't mean I'll give in easily.

I return to the bedchamber and stand in its center, turning slowly in place. What can I do? There must be some way to escape, but . . . how? And where to? I don't even know where I am. Did the goblins carry me through Whispering Wood and away to Faerieland? I shiver, remembering what Mother Ulla had said. *Lunulyr*. The Moon Kingdom.

At least that made sense. I'd expect a Moon Kingdom to be gloomy like this. And if I ever get out of this room, if I manage to escape this house, this prison, will I find myself lost in the middle of a moonlit landscape, prey to whatever beasts lurk and hunt in the shadows?

Terror tries to rise and flood my veins. I tamp it down hard. This is no time for panic. I must be reasonable, rational. I will think through my options . . . such as they are.

My eyes flick toward the table of jewels to focus on one particularly large brooch, and I hasten over to pick it up: polished metal of some kind, beautifully wrought into a scarab inlaid with gleaming jewels. I can't determine their color in this lighting. Maybe red. Maybe violet.

I turn it over and undo the clasp. The pin is a spike the length of my index finger. I tap its point daintily, wince, and stick my finger in my mouth. A taste of iron spills across my tongue, my own blood. Popping my finger out again, I grimace. But it will do. It will have to.

Now what?

I pace the periphery of the room, feeling the walls, trying to figure out where there might be a door. But the only door I find is the open one leading to the bathing pool. That's no good: I intend to wait by the wall and stab my bridegroom in the back as he enters the room. My hand trembles at this thought, and for a moment I fear I'll be sick. Can I actually stab someone in cold blood like that?

If I must. Yes.

I continue to pace, feeling more and more like the caged bear I once glimpsed passing through town with a carnival. Gods above, why did I step through the door, why did I cross the threshold? I'm a fool, such a fool!

"Brielle," I whisper.

My sister's name brings burning tears to my eyes. I worked so hard to hold them back, but it's no use. They burst free, coursing down my cheeks in steady streams. Did the fae folk really get Brielle? Or was it just a trick? Did she go out larking in Whispering Wood again, never once dreaming of the torments I experienced for her sake? Is she safely home now? Oh, please the gods, let her be safely home!

Exhausted, I sink into an upholstered chair near the fireplace. I try to sit upright, my back straight, but my body seems to melt around me, slumping into the cushions until my head rests on the pillowy back. I clutch the scarab brooch in both hands, turning it over and over, careful not to prick my finger on the pin again. Though fear still bubbles in the back of my brain, fatigue creeps through my limbs until I feel nothing else. My eyelids grow heavy, and the sweet scent from the candle and the fireplace lull me as gently as soft music.

I return to myself with a jolt. Did I fall asleep? The candle is out, and the fire on the hearth burns low, only a dull glow from the pulsing white stones. The washroom doorway is shut, but another is open on the opposite side of the room. A faint light gleams through it.

For an instant, I think I see the silhouette of a tall, broad man. I blink.

And the image is gone. As is the lighted doorway. Did I imagine it? All is dark and still. So dark that I can't see the bed across the room. So still that I can't hear my own tight breathing.

I slowly, carefully emerge from the chair, holding the scarab brooch out in front of me. My eyes strain into the shadows. Without fully expecting an answer, I whisper, "Is someone there?"

"Yes."

I scream and whirl in place, swinging the brooch like a knife. I hit something—I feel the point of the pin plunge into fabric, hear a rip, a grunt. My grip fumbles, and the brooch lands on the ground with a loud thump even as I stagger back, encounter the chair, and flop into its cushions.

I wait. Poised. Hands gripping the chair arms. Blood races in my veins, and my stomach feels like I swallowed a swarm of hornets.

Movement. A shifting of feet, a rustle of fabric.

"I trust your journey here was comfortable?"

The voice is as deep and warm as a summer night. A rough growl edges each *r*, causing the skin on the back of my neck to prickle. I know that voice—I've heard it before, whispering into my ear.

My throat thickens. I can't answer. Not even if I wished to. I can only grip the chair's armrests as tightly as I can, every muscle tensed for flight. Only there's nowhere to flee.

"My servants tell me you slept much of the way. I trust you are rested?"

Rested for what? I swallow and shake my head, still mute.

Something moves in the darkness. The dim firelight catches the edge of a long, flowing garment. I can gain no further impression of the person standing before me.

"I don't intend to hurt you," that deep, dark voice rumbles from somewhere above. "I realize this must all seem very . . . strange to you. But allow me to set your mind at ease. Your comfort and wellbeing are of utmost importance to me. My servants are under strict orders to provide you with anything you desire. You need only ask. What they cannot get for you, they will tell me, and I shall endeavor to procure it."

For a time, I hear only sounds of shifting feet and robes. Then: "Is there anything you wish for, Valera?"

I draw a shuddering breath. "My . . . my freedom," I whisper. The words come out so small, so thin, I doubt he will hear them.

Another long silence follows.

"Yes," the voice answers at last. "Yes, of course. Come dawn, every door of this house shall be opened to you. You may come and go as you please through the halls and every room. You need only speak your will, and it shall be done. As my lawful bride, you are mistress of this house. You may lay claim to all you see and order my servants according to your wishes and needs. Does this please you?"

"That's not . . ." I swallow and drop my gaze to my lap. The effort to discern some shape in the darkness is making my eyes hurt. "That's not what I meant."

The figure moves. I gain an impression of a tall form, taller than any man I've ever seen. But he's broader by far than the willowy figures I'd glimpsed in the kitchen garden back home. Is he not the same sort of being then? The hem of a long garment flicks into the firelight and out again. I hear something scrape like a chair being drawn across the floor, followed by the creak of a body settling into place.

"You meant," the voice says, speaking with something of a sigh, "that you wish to return to your own world. Your own kind."

"I wish not to be a prisoner," I answer sharply.

"Of course." Is that a shadowy hand I see upraised as though in defense? Maybe not. It's impossible to tell. "You must indeed feel imprisoned under these circumstances. I . . . I understand."

It sounds as though the thought hadn't occurred to him before now. As though he struggled to put himself in my shoes and, having done so, finds them an uncomfortable fit. I wait, breath held, perched on the edge of my seat. I don't know what to expect next.

"I do not intend to keep you," the voice says after a musing silence. "Neither to keep you nor to harm you. But the laws binding our marriage require you to remain with me for a year and a day. When that time is up, I shall return you to your father's house."

My whole body shivers, and I can't keep it from affecting my voice when I whisper, "Why?"

"I must have a wife. For reasons I cannot now reveal. Let us leave it at this simple understanding: I require a wife, and you fulfill that requirement. You are mine according to the Lunulyrian laws of Claiming and Choosing. Beyond that, there need be nothing more between us. Merely your patience, as it were."

What can I possibly say? I can't stop shivering. Nevertheless, hope, faint but eager, flutters in my heart. Perhaps I won't have to face the terrors my imagination has conjured since the moment I woke in that bed. My fingers dig into the arms of the chair, my knuckles standing out white.

"One simple rule will govern our marriage," the stranger continues. "You will remain here in my house for the term stated, and in that time you must never see my face. This is important, Valera. Do you understand? We will meet only in darkness, after your fire has burned down to coals. While you abide by this rule, you will live in great comfort here in my house, treated with all the respect and courtesy due the wife of Lord Dymaris of Orican. You will have jewels and gowns, sweetmeats and fruits, delicacies from across Eledria—whatever your fancy desires. I intend that you will never regret the time you spend in my home."

My chin quivers despite every effort to stop it. I try to speak but feel the sob threatening to break if I do, so I quickly swallow my words. With an effort, I pull my shoulders back, look up, and face the darkness from which the disembodied voice came.

"Why me?" The question comes out in a short blurt. I hate myself for sounding so fearful.

Is that a gleam of eyes in the shadows? Or is my tired mind imagining things again?

"I saw your face." His voice is soft; the underscoring growl seems softened to a mere purr. "In the Starglass Mirror. I paid a great price for the chance to look within the scrying waters and discover the woman who would be my bride. And I saw you, seated before a window. Running a comb through your hair. Your back was to me, but I could see your face reflected clearly enough. A human." A rumbling chuckle makes my stomach knot. "Not at all what I expected."

I grimace. "Well, I never expected to be lured into marriage with a shadow. Life is full of disappointments."

Another pause. Another gleam like yellow cat's eyes in the darkness.

Then: "I did not say I was disappointed."

I don't want to be a frightened little mouse, but my next question emerges in a thin squeak: "But it's not a real marriage?"

"It is real according to the Laws of Claiming and—"

"Yes, yes!" I hold up a hand. "The Laws of Claiming and Choosing. You said as much. What I mean is, you don't intend to . . . That is, as a husband, you won't . . . I will return to my father's house just as I am?"

"Yes." A thoughtful silence, then, "Though I shall, of course, provide you with a handsome separation gift."

"I don't care about that. I just want your word that you won't touch me."

"You have my word."

"But how can I trust it? You're . . . you're a fae. I know about your kind. I've heard the stories. What assurance do I have that you won't cheat me somehow? Or that you won't simply change your mind?"

The shadow across from me moves, stands. I shrink back into the chair, pressing my back into the upholstery. My pulse thrums frantically, and it's all I can do to quell a rising scream.

But the stranger says, "You are right."

I blink up at him, at the shadow where a face ought to be.

"It is not fair," he continues, "that I should hold unequal power over you. Not when you do me such a service."

The sound of a heavy step. I can almost see the outline of broad shoulders above me, can almost get the impression of a hooded head.

"Valera, you are my wife by Claim and by Choice. As my wife, you are owed all that I own, my property, my title . . . and my name. My true name. The name my mother spoke over my cradle on the morning of my birth. The name that has not been spoken by a living soul since that day, for it is a powerful thing. Too powerful and too dangerous to be given lightly. But I give it to you now, along with my assurance that when you leave my house at the end of the stated term, you will be untouched and unharmed."

Another shifting of movement as the unseen figure kneels before me. I cannot make out his features, but his silhouette is starkly outlined by the moonfire glow. Even as he kneels, his head is as high as mine. Long fingers catch my hands, prying them free from the chair arms and pressing them close. His touch is cold, and each hand is large enough to cover both of mine at once. Is that the scrape of long nails—talons? A thrill of dread races up my arms.

He leans toward me. I feel breath against my face, just as I did the night before when I lay upon my pillow. My eyes struggle to discern something of his features, but his head blocks out the blue-glowing embers. I can see nothing at all.

"My name," he says, "is Erolas. I am your husband, Valera."

Something touches my forehead. I realize with shock that it's a pair of lips planting a kiss on my brow. Before I can move or react, the sensation passes, but a second kiss touches my cheek, feather-light so that I almost miss it, then a third kiss on my other cheek.

I utter a strangled cry, yank my hands free, and push wildly at the darkness in front of me. I feel what might be a nose, and one of my fingers strikes something sharp—a tooth?—while another pokes into an eye. I don't care. I push with everything I have, then spring up from the chair and whip around behind it, grabbing the back of it with both hands like a shield.

"Liar!" I gasp. "You said you wouldn't touch me! What is all this performance, giving me a false name? Why bother if you're only going to do as you please the next moment?"

The shadowy form stands, and I almost think I see him shaking his head as he backs away. "Forgive me," he says quickly. "I did not lie. The ceremony of name-giving is an ancient custom. The three kisses are part of the traditional Eledrian wedding night. I must give you my name before I may kiss you thrice. And then I must wait until you ask me to kiss you a fourth time. It is our way. I meant no offence."

I'm panting, my fingers tensing and relaxing and tensing again. My lips move, and I try out the shape of the name: "*Erolas.*" I have no gift for magic, and yet . . . and yet I sense something as the word vibrates off my tongue. Something in the air as it escapes. Is it possible that he has given me his true name? Is it possible that I now possess it, that I wield a certain measure of power over him? Over a fae?

"Erolas," I say, then hesitate. But why not try? Why not see just how far this power extends? "I wish to go home."

"I understand, Valera," he replies. "And I will take you home. In a year and a day. I swear it."

There it is again, that unnamable *something* in the atmosphere. A sensation of power and . . . and certainty. I don't know how else to describe it. I clench my teeth, resisting the feeling.

But I believe him. Against all reason, against the throbbing pulse of anger and fear in my heart, I believe him.

"I wish to go home *now*," I say, leaning into that power. I feel a tremble of sorts, like the shudder of a soul.

"I cannot do that," he replies. "There are too many . . . I cannot."

"Why not?"

"I cannot tell you."

"Why not?"

He doesn't answer.

More fae games, no doubt. More tricks. More deceptions.

"All right, then," I say slowly, drawing myself up as tall as I can. "If that is the only answer you can give, then we can have nothing more to say to one another. I bid you good night."

I wait, tense with terror. Will he leave? Will the power his name has given me hold sway? Have I any authority, any autonomy in this situation?

The shadow shifts. I gain the impression of a large figure bowing. "M'lady," the deep voice says, no longer warm but hard as stone.

Then the sound of retreating footsteps. The doorway opens in the wall again, and I glimpse a male form standing in silhouette for half an instant. The next moment, he's gone.

The door shuts behind him.

I stand there for I don't know how long, holding onto the back of the chair, breathing in and out, long, labored breaths. My knees buckle, and I nearly fall to the floor, only just managing to hold myself upright. I glance over at the enormous bed with its luxurious furs but shiver and look away again quickly. I'm not certain my trembling legs can carry me that far anyway.

Instead, I step around the chair and sink back into its cushioned seat. My body sags, all strength draining from my limbs. I let my head drop back on the headrest, close my eyes, and exhale a long sigh.

"Brielle," I whisper. "Brielle, I'm . . . I'm so sorry. I'm sorry I'm not there for you."

Sobs overwhelm me, painful in their violence. I lean on the arm of the chair, bury my face in the crook of my elbow, and give way to the onslaught of feeling, weeping until my tears run dry. Then I rest my head on my arm and gaze dully at the glowing white stones on the hearth, watching them fade one by one until the whole room is lost in darkness.

7

I wake with a crick in my neck and sunlight pouring into my face. Groaning, I try to shift into a more comfortable position and nearly fall out of the chair. Startled into complete wakefulness, I sit bolt upright, terrified and confused. By the seven secret names, where am I?

Memories flood in.

Right. My bridal chamber.

I shiver and peer around the room, which looks less austere and forbidding by daylight. The bed is carved from blue stone, not black, and marbled with shades of gray, teal, lavender, and even red. The chair beneath me is richly upholstered in a fabric I don't recognize, embellished with dainty silver threads in an elaborate pattern of flowers and leaves and strange two-headed birds.

"Well," I whisper, stretching my stiff back and shoulders, "at least it isn't permanently dark here." Maybe I wasn't stolen away to the Moon Kingdom after all. Maybe . . .

I spring from the chair, all stiffness forgotten, and hurry to the window. The panes are brightly colored, depicting some sort of garden scene, but I don't take time to look at it. Instead, I press my nose against a pane of bright pink glass, trying to glimpse the world beyond. Are those trees? I can't tell. The glass is too murky.

It isn't a night-bound world, however. Of that I'm certain. For the first time in what feels like forever, my spirits lift.

Now, if I can just find a way out of this room . . .

I turn toward the wall my shadowy visitor passed through last night. A shiver creeps up my spine at the memory, but I shake it off. He said he wouldn't hurt me. I don't exactly believe him, not completely at least. But he didn't hurt me last night, and that's something. Perhaps I can find my way out of here before he changes his mind.

The wall, however, proves impassable. Though I feel up and down and along the floors from side to side, I can't find even a hairline crack to indicate where an opening might be. I start to tremble. Sweat beads my brow. Am I trapped? Entombed? No, there must be a way out. There must be!

What was it my dark bridegroom said last night?

"Speak your will, and it shall be done," I whisper. Taking a step back, I contemplate the wall, chewing the inside of my cheek, then back up a few paces, eyes narrowing. Could it really be so simple?

"Open!" I say, my voice quavering only slightly.

At once the door slides open. I don't see how it's done. There's no ripple in the stone, scarcely a creak. One moment there's a solid wall in front of me, the next, a door.

I let out a short breath. Incredible! Yet also terrible somehow. I don't feel any magic in my blood, yet magic responded to my voice, my command. It's a strange sensation.

Is it because I possess his name?

"Erolas." I speak silently, forming the word with my lips but uttering no sound. Once more I feel that shimmering power in the air around me, that sense of strength I don't understand but cannot deny. This knowledge is powerful indeed. And dangerous.

Could I use it against him? Could I leverage it in my favor? Maybe, but . . . how?

Shelving that thought for future consideration, I step into the doorway and peer out. A white stone passage awaits. Tall, color-stained windows line the far wall, and doors line the other. The windows are as elaborate as the one in my room, depicting scenes—men and women, lords and ladies, monsters, seas, castles, clouds. Far too much to take in with a single glance.

I step from my room into the passage, wrapping my arms around my middle. The doors and windows are so tall, I feel altogether dwarfed in comparison. My clothes are poor and thin, my feet bare. If anyone were to catch me creeping around in a place like this, they'd mistake me for a sneak thief for sure!

The passage seems just as long in both directions, so I turn to the right and set off at a trot. The doors along the wall are all shut fast, and I don't bother trying to open them. Funny that I can see them on this side of the wall. Once inside the chambers, do these doors vanish into the wall like in my own room?

The corridor ends abruptly at an arch hung with diaphanous curtains. Pulling these gently aside, I look out into an open courtyard surrounded by a pillared colonnade. The walls all around are three stories high at least, but bright sky vaults overhead, its blue unimpeded by any canopy. Little white clouds trail into my line of vision.

A huge table stretches down the center of the courtyard, lined with dozens of chairs, each elaborately carved from a single block of stone and set with plump cushions. The table itself is shaped like a huge beast with monstrous legs and great clawed feet that seem to plunge into the ground itself, gripping fast. I wouldn't be surprised to see it suddenly rear up and roar!

I hesitate, half hiding behind a pillar. Something tickles my nose—a delicious aroma. Turning my head, I see that the far end of the table is set with gold flatware. Tall footed platters hold elaborate displays of fruits I don't recognize. But the smell is one I know quite well: fresh-baked bread.

My stomach growls, its rumble unexpectedly loud in that open space. I wince and suck in both lips, biting down hard. Gods above, how hungry I am! How long has it been now since I last ate? Is this meal intended for my shadowy bridegroom? I glance up and down the courtyard, searching for a glimpse of him. But no . . . he said I couldn't see him. For some mysterious reason of his own. Does this mean he won't be joining me for meals? A small comfort under the circumstances, but I'm grateful anyway.

Perhaps this meal is meant for me.

I take one step from behind the pillar. Then I jump back, startled, when a strange figure appears at the other end of the courtyard. It's a woman—unmistakably a woman: She's completely naked from head to toe, and completely green except for a creamy stripe from her chin down between her small breasts, to her navel. Her skin's texture appears rather leathery. Her body is shaped like those weird, elongated forms I glimpsed last night, with arms that reach below her knees.

She moves with a fluid grace, long antennae wafting gently from her head amid of a cloud of thick dark-green curls, like the tendrils of a vine. In one hand she carries a covered platter, which she balances over her head as she glides silkily to the end of the table where the meal is set. She places her platter among the others and lifts the lid.

A ululating cry of rage bursts from her lips.

The lid drops from her fingers and hits the floor with a ringing clang. I give a start and duck back behind the curtain but peer out again the next moment as the green woman's cries echo about the courtyard.

A little creature lies in the center of her tray. Long, twiggy fingers hold up what looks like a stuffed pastry, which it brings daintily to its lips, taking tiny, precise bites with huge brown buck teeth. Like the green woman, he is utterly naked, every bit of his scrawny manhood shamelessly displayed for all to see. His ears are huge and pointed like two batwings, and his nose is nearly as long as one of his bony little arms.

He blinks large eyes up at the green woman and takes another unhurried bite. She shrieks and takes a swipe at him. Somehow he contrives to go from a lounging sprawl to an upward spring with no discernible transition, dodging the blow and cackling with delight. The green woman hisses, displaying a ferocious set of sharp white teeth. Snatching the now empty platter off the table, she swings it at the little man. He dodges this just as easily, lands on the table, and bounds down the length of it, hopping like a rabbit rather than running. The green woman pursues him, her yodeling voice echoing among the pillars. The two of them disappear between the columns at the far end of the courtyard, swishing through another set of curtains.

I clutch the pillar, my eyes so wide they're stinging. At least now I know I'm not alone in this house with my shadowy bridegroom. What are these folk exactly? His servants?

Were they among the people who stole me away last night?

My gaze drifts back to the food, and my stomach grumbles again. I feel hollow inside, weak. Could I safely dart out and snatch some of that bread or one of those strange fruits before the weird folk return? Almost unconsciously my muscles tense, my feet bracing for a quick sprint.

But what if it's a trap?

I stop. My hands tighten on the pillar. I've heard stories, of course. So many stories of human girls whisked away by mad fae lovers, lost in the depths of Faerieland, only to return to their families decades later, unaged and dripping with jewels. It doesn't happen often these days. Not since the signing of the Pledge established peace between humans and fae. But the stories linger on.

I've never paid much attention. My life offers no time for stories, either horrible or fantastic. I rise before dawn to labor through the long day, then collapse soon after sunset with barely enough energy between times to provide a little comfort for Brielle. I have never attended the village dances or joined the throng in the village square when a traveling storyteller passed through.

Nevertheless, I seem to recall a detail, something that had worked its way into my subconscious: To eat from the bounty of a fae lord's table always spelled disaster for the unwary maid. Somehow, accepting his food meant accepting the fae himself. Many a maid lost her freedom and virtue because she could not control her appetites . . .

I place a hand across my cavernously hollow stomach. Who can say whether such stories are history or fancy or something in between? Best not to risk it. I must find a way out of here.

Something moves across the courtyard.

I turn quickly, half retreating behind the pillar again. Is it the green woman and the little man returning from their chase? No, the courtyard is still and silent other than a distant sound of running water coming from somewhere unseen. There seems to be no one about.

Then a shadow peels away from the deeper shadows cast by the pillars across from me. For an instant I see the dark silhouette of a tall, broad-shouldered man. My heart lurches. Has my bridegroom come for his meal?

The shadow vanishes and reappears farther down the courtyard, flashing against pillars and disappearing between them. It moves away from me.

I frown, caught in a moment of indecision.

Then, though I'm not entirely certain why, I creep out from behind the curtains and hurry after the shadow, skirting the table and following at a distance of ten yards. My bare feet make no sound on the cool tiles, and I take care that not even a loud breath gives me away. My eyes search carefully, swiveling among the pillars and over the long table, but I spy no sign of who might actually cast this shadow, only the shadow itself.

It leads to the far end of the courtyard and slips under the colonnade. Another curtained arch waits there, and the curtains waft gently. Stirred by a breeze? Or did the shadow disturb them when it passed through?

I firm my jaw and hurry after, parting the curtains carefully.

A huge space spreads before my view. At first it seems so large, I wonder if I've stepped outside. On second glance, I see that walls frame a large hall lined with windows and sheltered by an arched ceiling high overhead, painted in fantastical images of clouds and gods and airy beings. The floor is inlaid with precious and semiprecious stones—lapis lazuli and garnet and jasper and others I don't recognize—forming stunning floral patterns that branch from each other in ever more complex displays.

Tall statues line either side of the space. Four times the size of even the tallest man, they are carved with such lifelike precision, one almost expects them to step down from their pedestals and move and speak together. There are seven in total: three on one side, three on the other. The seventh and final statue stands at the far end of the hall.

I draw a sharp breath. In my world, it's considered blasphemous to create graven images of the gods. Yet I would recognize these holy figures anywhere. Tanator and Tanyl, Elawynn and Lamruil, Nornala and Uyrm . . . I name them by turn. And the Great Goddess. Aneirin, Mother of All.

It's a chapel. This magnificent space, so lofty, so light, is a chapel to the gods. My gods. It's strange somehow to realize that the fae—or this fae, at least, this Lord Dymaris—worships the same gods I do. He's so strange, so other, his world so removed from mine.

But are we really that different after all?

The sight of those beautiful faces carved in red stone is almost too much, too overwhelming. My head swims, and I want to draw back from the arch, back into the courtyard. I have the ridiculous fear that any movement of mine will draw those hard stone eyes my way, so I stay where I am, frozen.

Then my eye lands on a shadow before the altar of the Great Goddess.

At first it seems insignificant, and I almost turn away. Then it moves, and I fix my gaze on it to better discern what is there. But there's nothing to discern. Just a shadow. A tall shadow with no body to cast it. It kneels before the altar. As I watch, two arms lift as though in supplication. Then the shadow doubles over as though crumpling onto its face.

Something about that sight is so horrible, so abject . . .

Suddenly finding my will to move, I let the curtain fall and leave behind the magnificent chapel. My heart thuds painfully, and I clench my fists, my brow tightening into a frown. What did I just witness in there?

I shake my head and turn away. I need to get out of here, need to find my way home somehow. That should be—must be—my only concern.

My pulse is jumpy, and my skin prickles with nerves. I half expect strange figures to appear from behind the pillars as I retreat. I don't want to return to my own rooms, so I choose at random another passage leading from the courtyard. It too is lined with doors on one side and windows on the other, but at the end I see an open window not paned with colored glass. I hasten toward it, hoping to at last have a look at the world beyond the walls of this great house.

A fresh wind blows in my face as I draw near, and the sound of running water intensifies. I slow, suddenly afraid of what I'll see on the other side. Perhaps I don't want to know. But what good will cowardice do me now? I shake my head, clench my teeth, and make myself continue, make myself look out.

My vision swims.

The house stands atop a huge block of stone many stories above churning white water. The water flows swiftly, pouring out over the brink of a massive cliff. From this vantage, I can't see the end of the waterfall, only mist. But beyond the brink a vast expanse of wide, wild landscape stretches out before me, so far away it might belong to another world entirely.

Though a midday sun shines overhead, that faraway land is bathed in silvery moonlight.

The wind blows cold spray into my face. I unconsciously wipe it away and continue to stare. Horror slowly swells inside me, and I can't stop it. I'm not sure I want to. Finally, I pry my fingers free of the stone sill and back away from the window.

The truth slams into me like a blow from behind, buckling my knees. I sag, sink to the floor, and only just manage to catch myself, to keep from falling flat on my face. There's no denying it. No resisting reality.

I'm trapped. Trapped in this house. Trapped in this world. Far from everything and everyone I've ever known. And there's no way out.

Not until my monster bridegroom decides to let me go.

How long I remain sitting in the middle of that corridor I can't say.

My body is numb, my mind immobile.

At some point, the naked green woman finds me. Long large-jointed fingers wrap around my shoulders from behind, and a crooning, burbling voice speaks softly in my ear. I sniff loudly and turn to look into that odd face with its flickering antennae and those huge black eyes. It's a horrible sight. Like something out of a nightmare, and yet . . . and yet the expression is tender despite its strangeness. Gentle and full of concern. The voice burbling through those thin lips and sharp teeth sounds almost maternal.

"I don't understand you," I say when the voice speaks something that ends with a questioning lilt. "Don't you speak my language? No, you must." My stomach twists, bitter bile churning in my gut. "I heard you and the others. Last night. Outside my door. You promised gold and you . . . you . . ." I grimace and shoot a glare at the woman from under my lowered brows. "You said you had my sister."

The green woman tilts her head, the motion sharp and birdlike. Her dark eyes blink slowly, one after the other. Then she burbles some more and tugs at my shoulders, urging me to rise. There's subtle power in that grasp. I suspect she could pick me up and toss me over her shoulder with hardly a thought if she so desires.

Not wishing to see this theory proven, I scramble to my feet, straightening my skirts. The green woman chirrups happily and waves an arm, gesturing down the hall. It's either do as I'm told or be forced like a prisoner.

I turn and walk purposefully back the way I came. I stop when

I reach the courtyard, not because I don't know where to go, but because I don't relish the idea of returning to my room. But where else can I go? What else can I do?

Beckoning with hands and antennae alike, the green woman urges me toward the head of the table where the meal is still set. I plant my feet and shake my head. "No. I will . . . I will rest now."

She pauses. Then, with a gesture that might have been a shrug, she motions again. I follow her around the table and back through the curtained arch. We walk down the hall of windows, stepping through pools of colored light cast on the floor, the fae woman's skin transforming from green to purple to red to gold by turns. She keeps up a steady stream of burbling chatter all the way. I don't bother trying to understand.

At last we reach what must be my door. The green woman waves her hand, and it opens. I look inside, see the huge sleigh bed, the upholstered chair, the fireplace. My room. *My* room.

I shudder. I don't want anything about this house to be *mine*.

"Thank you," I say stiffly and step inside. When the green woman makes as though to follow, I put up a quick hand. "I wish to be alone."

The antennae twitch, rubbing against one another thoughtfully as the woman tilts her head from one side to the other. With a last burble, she sweeps a graceful bow and glides off up the corridor, casting several looks over her shoulder as she goes. I wait until she's out of sight.

Then I back into the room, look at the wall, and say quietly, "Close."

The door shuts. The wall becomes solid stone.

I'm closed into my tomb. My nice, safe tomb.

On unsteady legs, I move to the chair by the hearth and sink into it. My heart is heavy, my spirits, numb. I'm right back where I started that morning. Only now with the added knowledge that I'm farther from home than I'd ever imagined possible. With no hope of escape.

I close my eyes, leaning back against the chair. For some while I can do nothing but sit there, seeing the darkness inside my head. Then an image seems to form, drawing my attention, my thoughts, piquing my curiosity.

It's the image of a shadow kneeling in abject despair and humiliation, arms upraised to the impervious face of a goddess in stone.

8

The day passes slowly.

Exhausted by the ebb and flow of fear and despair, I drift in and out of restless sleep. Occasionally I rise from the chair and take a turn about the room. Once I even stop and look into the bathing chamber, eyeing the gently steaming, aromatic water. By day, sunlight pours through a skylight overhead, gleaming off the white walls and colorful tiles. The little globes of light float along the bottom of the pool, their brilliance dulled in the sunlight. I still can't decide whether or not they're living.

I take a closer look at the silky white gown presented on the chair. The fabric is smooth beneath my fingertips, its folds shimmering with an unexpected iridescence. Professional curiosity aroused, I turn it inside out to examine the stitching but can't find a seam.

The gown may have simply sprung into being fully formed. It's exquisite. And it looks as though it would fit me rather well.

I drop it on the floor and return to the bedroom, refusing to so much as look into the bathing chamber again. I'm not going to be won over by gifts and luxuries. The lord of this house can tempt me all he likes—it won't make me any less his prisoner.

Eventually the light cast through the window's colorful panes dims. The shadows deepen, and soon the room will be quite dark indeed. I sit in my chair, staring into the empty hearth where last night a fire had burned. How am I supposed to light a blaze? Simply speak it into being?

I lean forward in my seat and whisper softly, "Light."

Immediately, shining white stones appear and blue flames erupt around them, flickering bright and filling the room with a pale glow like moonlight. I settle back in my seat again, watching them burn.

More time passes. Still, I sit here.

The flames burn down eventually. Perhaps I should light them again, keep the fire going all night. Would it be enough to keep my bridegroom from visiting? He said I couldn't see him, after all, that we couldn't meet save at night when my fire was low. Could it be that simple to ward him off?

Maybe, but . . . I tighten my grip on the chair arms. If I'm going to survive my time here, I need to show him that I won't be cowed. I can't hide. I can't shrink and tremble. I must face the master of this house and then . . . and then . . .

"And then what?" I whisper.

My resolve wavers.

Before I can think of a suitable answer, the door opens. I look up, see a dark silhouette, and look down again quickly, staring at the burning white stones. My heart races, and I struggle to maintain steady, rhythmic breathing. His sharp fae ears will certainly hear it if my breath catches, and I won't give him the satisfaction of knowing how badly he frightens me. Not if I can help it.

"Good evening, m'lady," rumbles the deep voice of my unseen groom.

I clench my teeth hard and stare more intently into the blaze.

A long pause. Then a soft murmur of, "Close." I hear the swish of the door shutting. The wall is solid once more.

Ears pricked, I listen to the sound of his footsteps and the drag of heavy robes as he crosses the room. From the tail of my eye, I glimpse an indistinct form pausing at the little table where the jewels are displayed. Another silence follows.

"Do you not like my gifts?" he says at last.

I almost flash a glare his way. But no. I won't look at him. I won't speak to him. Not until I'm ready.

He waits a polite interval. Then I hear a little wordless grunt followed by a jumbled noise, as though he's pushing the jewels off to one side. Several of them land with small *thunks* on the floor. After that, a clatter, a vaguely familiar sound. Like porcelain and silver.

The next moment, a smell washes over me—a hearty, meaty,

savory smell that makes my traitorous stomach growl. I slap a hand against my middle as though I can physically make it stop. This . . . is going to be harder than I thought.

"My servants tell me you have not eaten."

I listen intently to another series of gentle clattering sounds. Is he serving up something? Despite my efforts to resist, my gaze swivels slightly to one side, and I spy a bowl, a ladle, a spoon. My mouth waters.

The shadowy figure turns, and a shallow gilt-edged bowl slides into my line of view. Cuts of meat still on the bone lay in an elegant display, drizzled with dark sauce and garnished with leafy herbs and slices of some sweet-smelling fruit I don't recognize. It's beautiful, a feast for the eye. And the smells rising to tickle my nostrils make me dizzy with hunger.

I set my jaw and grip my hands tightly in my lap. "I'm not hungry."

Unseen eyes watch me closely. I can almost feel them narrowing. "Is the meal not to your liking?"

I shake my head. "I won't eat."

"I instructed my people to prepare dishes similar to those you would find in your own world. They may have struggled somewhat to fulfill the order, but I will speak to them if you wish. They desire to please, even if they—"

"I said I won't eat." I flick a glance up to the figure holding out the platter. He stands in such a way that I cannot even see his hand. When he said I couldn't see him, did he truly mean not so much as a fingernail? I store that thought away for later consideration and direct a glare up at the dark space where a head might be. "I'm not a simpleton. I know the games you people play. I won't fall so easily."

A long, contemplative silence follows. Then the plate withdraws from the firelight, and the shadowy form returns to the table. I listen to the clatter of spoons and bowls, see a cover being lowered. It blocks off some of the smell, much to my relief. It was going to drive me mad with hunger.

Then my dark bridegroom moves to the place across the hearth from me. He takes a seat in the empty chair. I feel him watching me, and I look back, determined not to drop my gaze.

"The food is not poisoned," he says at last. "Neither is it enchanted. You are my wife. You may safely partake of all that I own, for it is yours. My servants are instructed to treat you with the utmost courtesy and respect, as is due the Lady of Orican."

I swallow painfully. "I am *not* the Lady of . . . of Orican. And I am not your wife."

"According to the laws of Claiming and Choosing—"

"Yes, yes, you went over all that last night. But I don't see how even your fae laws can govern in this instance. Coercion and choice are *not* the same, after all."

"Coercion?"

"Yes! What else would you call it? When your people stood outside my door and told me they had my sister in their clutches? What else was I to do, what choice did I have, but to step through my door?"

"Did they . . ." A pause, then I hear a noise like a throat clearing. "Pardon me for asking, but did my people *threaten* your sister?"

I open my mouth. Shut it again. My memories of that horrible evening are a bit clouded. I remember the many voices telling me how sweet my sister was, how they loved to dance with her, how pretty they thought she was. And there had been a scream. But I can recall no actual threat being spoken.

A sick sensation coils in my stomach. I sag suddenly back in my chair, feeling weak. "No," I whisper at last. "No, they didn't threaten her. Not . . . not overtly."

"And they made no bargain with you? Set no terms for her release?"

I shake my head numbly.

I hear a long intake and slow release of breath. "In that case, the terms of the Claiming and Choosing are still honored. So long as they made no threat and offered no bargain, your choice to cross the threshold, by law, constitutes a choice."

I drop my chin. For the first time in a very long while, I taste a foul word rising in my throat, struggling to get out. Mother always said that expletives are a coward's way of expressing emotion, so I swallow it back. I'm no coward. "I was still tricked," I say instead, my voice thick.

"Yes." There's a dangerous rumble in the darkness, like a growl. "Yes, you were. And for that, I shall have words with my people. I swear it. They will suffer for their insolence."

I shoot a quick glance at the shadow. In my mind's eye, I see again the green woman, burbling and gentle, leading me back through the baffling corridors of this massive house. "I don't want anyone hurt," I say at length. "After all, I suppose they were only trying to fulfill your orders."

Another long silence follows this. Then a little huff, a sound of surprise. "You are a strange one, m'lady." There's surprise in his voice. He doesn't sound displeased, merely baffled. "I had not known humans were like you."

I blink and duck my head again. "Like me? What do you mean?"

"I mean . . ." He hesitates as though struggling to find the right words. "I suppose I mean . . . *kind*. Even now, angry as you are, you take no opportunity to give vent to your anger. But then again, perhaps you do not yet understand."

The shadow shifts. I get the impression he's leaning toward me.

"Whatever you ask of me, if it is within my power, I shall do for you. Command me to punish my people for their trickery, and they shall suffer the direst of consequences. Command me to flay their hides with iron rods, and it shall be done. Command me to make them apologize, and I shall send them to grovel before you on their bellies, to plead your forgiveness. Such is the power you have over me as my wife. Do you understand?"

The darkness of the chamber seems suddenly so much deeper. And colder. Until that moment I hadn't realized just how menacing that voice was or how carefully its owner modulated its tones to make them gentle, palatable to my ears. I'd always known the fae were dangerous, but until now I hadn't grasped exactly what that danger meant.

Now, listening to my unseen bridegroom's voice, I feel as though I hear the voice of a tiger. Not cruel exactly—a tiger is not cruel as it follows the impulses of its nature. Yet it is utterly dangerous. An apex predator of the night.

"I don't want anyone hurt." I repeat, speaking softly lest he hear my trembling. "And I don't want any groveling. I . . . I only want to go home."

I watch the shadow shift as he leans back in his seat. "You will go home. The first day of our marriage term is now complete. One year from now, I shall personally deliver you to your father's door."

I close my eyes, determined not to let hot tears slip through my lashes. When I'm certain I have control over my voice, I say, "In that case, there is something else I want."

"Name it." He sounds relieved, as though the very hope of being able to grant some wish of mine removes a burden from his shoulders.

I clench my jaw and speak through grinding teeth. "I want to know that my sister is unharmed."

"My people would not hurt her. They honor the Pledge."

"Are you certain of that?" I lift my head, staring into the darkness where he sits. "You didn't even know what means they used to lure me from my home. Are you so sure of your people or your control over them?"

My words hang in the air between us, ringing a little too loud and a little too vicious. I twist a fold of my skirt between my hands but refuse to drop my gaze. Let the monster snarl, let him rage at me for my insolence! I won't back down. I've lived in the same house as a monster all my life. A monster who beat me, who despised me, who treated me like less than nothing. And over the years, I learned just how strong I could be, how deep the wellspring of my courage ran.

The shadow stands. I choke back a startled yelp as he moves suddenly, his cloak sweeping to block out the light of the fire. Then he is on his knees before me as he was the night before, when he held my hands between his, whispered his name, and kissed me softly three times. I try to stand, but he catches my hands again now, and I freeze at his touch.

"Valera," he says, my name soft on his lips. "I swear to you, I will find your sister and ensure her wellbeing."

I draw a careful breath. "I want proof."

"I will bring proof."

"Proof I can believe. Something only she can give me."

"You shall have it."

"I want your vow that you won't trick me."

The shadow of his head bows. "Speak my name."

"What?"

"Speak my name. Use it to command me. You will feel the power go out from you into me. You'll know that your command will be honored to the utmost of my ability."

I swallow. An odd sort of reluctance twists my heart. I don't want to possess his name. I don't want either the power or the intimacy such possession means. I don't want there to be anything shared between us.

But just now I need every weapon available to me. And this, I know without a doubt, is a weapon unlike any other.

"Erolas," I whisper.

His hands clasped around mine tense. I feel the edge of long nails and have to stop myself from flinching and pulling away.

"Erolas," I say again with more force this time. "I command you to find my sister and bring back proof that she is all right. And . . . and . . ." My mind spins with all the things I suddenly wish I could communicate to Brielle. All the warnings, all the injunctions. All the advice and love and wishes. I suck in both lips and taste the salt of my own tears. "Let her know that I am well. That she must not try to find me. That she must . . . she must wait for me."

My voice gives out in a sob. Yanking free of his grasp, I cover my face, pressing the heels of both hands into my eyes in a vain attempt to stop the flow of tears. He remains kneeling before me, a huge, solid presence. Several times I think he tries to speak, but each time he stops himself.

At last, he stands. "You have my word, Valera. Do you believe me? Do you feel the truth between us?"

I shudder. But when I search, I feel an odd . . . something. A sensation like a trembling wire anchored down inside of me, stretching across the void between souls. Am I right to believe that a second anchor sinks deep into the heart of this dark, terrible being standing before me? That the wire stretches between us, a profoundly real if utterly inexplicable bond?

"Erolas." I speak the name silently, my lips moving without

sound. The sensation quickens, the invisible connecting wire vibrating slightly. Perhaps it's my imagination, but . . . no. I don't think I could imagine something like that. "I believe you." I lift my head, my face damp with tears, and blink into the darkness where his face should be. "I believe you, and . . . and now I want you to go."

He stands and bows. I hear the movement of his robes and feel the grace of the gesture I cannot see. "M'lady," he murmurs.

The next moment, his footsteps sound on the hard floor as he crosses the room. The door in the wall opens, and he is visible there in silhouette, huge and inscrutable. I watch the outline of a hand reach up to grip the doorway.

"The food is safe for you to eat." I watch his head turn, catch a glimpse of a hard profile, but only for a moment. "I understand that you do not trust me. I cannot blame you. But I hope you will eat even so."

With this, he steps from the room. The door closes behind him. For a time I sit huddled in my chair, my arms wrapped tight around my middle, trying to stop my body from trembling.

Then with a growled, "Fine then!" I spring up and cross to the little table. I fumble in the dark, find the lid, and lift it, breathing deep as a cloud of delicious steam rises to my nose.

Perhaps the meal is enchanted. Perhaps it's poisoned. Perhaps I'll regret it come dawn.

I eat every last bite anyway.

9

It's difficult to determine the passage of time in this new world. When I come groggily awake in my chair, my stomach still knotted and tight after my large meal of the night before, I guess it's already several hours past dawn, but the daylight shines through so much colored glass that I can't be certain.

I sit up, feeling dull and stupid. But less frightened; that's something. My fear is still there, coiled into a little knot and tucked down deep in my gut where I can find it if I prod at it. Otherwise, I'm more tired than anything.

Hearing a tentative knock, I sit bolt upright, blinking hard to drive lingering sleepiness from my eyes. "Who's there?" I call. Is it my so-called husband? No, he wouldn't come in daylight . . . would he? Besides, he promised he would find Brielle. Surely that endeavor will take him away from this house for a while at least.

A lilting burble reaches my ear, muffled through the wall. I get up and cross the room. Putting my ear against the wall, I listen to that voice climb up and down the scales as it rattles on in its strange, fluid language. It ends on a questioning lilt.

I chew the inside of my cheek. The green woman hadn't seemed at all threatening yesterday. And it's awfully quiet and lonely in this room by myself.

I step back from the wall. "Open," I say.

The wall obeys, and the door slides back. The naked willowy woman stands in the doorway, a covered tray in her hands. She smiles at me, displaying an overabundance of sharp teeth. I have to wonder if smiles are a natural expression of fae women of her kind, or if she's trying to make herself more approachable to a human. The little antennae wobble uncertainly, and the woman lifts her tray.

"Oh. Yes, come in." I step back, ushering the woman through. I indicate the table of jewels and the tray containing the remains of last night's meal. "I . . . I suppose you can put that down there."

The woman trills and chirrups. Shifting her tray to one hand, she uses the other to tidy up the table with quick, graceful movements. She's so swift and efficient, I wonder if she's using a sort of magic. She also gathers up the little necklaces and bracelets tumbled on the floor and adds them to the pile on the other side of the table. Then she sets down her tray and turns another toothy smile my way.

"Yes. Thank you." I approach a little timidly. I'm not used to being waited on like this. Certainly not by someone quite so odd. And naked.

The woman waggles her antennae and says something else in her strange voice while lifting the lid. I blink and take a step back, startled. The green woman, her smile vanishing, flips the lid over and looks down at the tray.

A little bat-eared man sits in the middle of an empty bowl, licking his fingers with a long purple tongue. A dab of what looks like porridge sits on his head like a white, soppy hat, and his belly is fat and distended between his two scrawny legs. He grins up at the green woman and wiggles his ears at her before sending me a sly wink.

The green woman shrieks, throws the lid and the tray of empty dishes down on the floor in a terrible clatter of scattered and broken dishware, and lunges for the little man. He dodges but isn't quite fast enough. The green woman catches him by one huge ear, and he hollers a stream of squeaky, garbled words. I don't need to understand the language to recognize expletives when I hear them. Enraged, the green woman wraps her long fingers around the little man's throat, turns him upside down, and begins smashing his head into the table. The jewels on one end jump and fall in a stream of glittering stones, and the platter with the empty bowl tips and smashes on the floor, adding broken shards of porcelain to the overall mess.

"Seven gods!" I cry, leaping at the green woman and grabbing her arm. "Oh, seven gods save us, what are you *doing?* Don't kill him! It's just porridge!"

The green woman hisses, her antennae sticking up straight and quivering with rage. The little man, gripped upside down in her fist, shakes his head, blinks goggly eyes up at me, then spits out another expletive and waggles his ears again. The green woman, driven to new extremes of rage, whirls on her toes and nimbly springs to the wall where she resumes beating the creature's head in.

"Stop!" I take a step, pause, then draw myself up tall. "I command you to stop!"

The green woman freezes, her arm in mid-swing. She looks back at me, her black eyes narrow and resentful. The little man sticks out his long purple tongue and wiggles it at her, making her hiss again.

"Put him down," I say. "Gently!"

The last word comes out too late. The green woman merely uncurls her fingers and lets the man drop headfirst onto the hard floor. For a moment he lies spread-eagle, stunned.

Then he pops upright, twirls in place, and offers an elaborate bow to me, made all the more ridiculous by the sight of his bare, bony little bottom sticking up in the air. He rights himself and dances a jig before dashing into the fireplace. He's up the chimney and out of sight in a wink.

The green woman looks sadly at the broken dishes. Little mewling noises vibrate in her throat. Is she crying?

"Don't worry," I say, putting out a reassuring hand but not quite daring to touch her leathery green arm. "I wasn't really hungry. But if you want to help me, I could use a wash."

The woman tilts her head, antennae twisting. I pluck at the front of my dress, which is rather grimy now after several days without changing. "You know. Wash?" I frown slightly. "I could've sworn I heard you and your friends speaking my language outside that night. Or was that a spell you cast to make me *think* I heard you? I'd like some water, please. Clean water." I mime washing my face.

At this, the green woman's antennae perk up. She takes hold of my hand and, burbling cheerfully, leads me across the room. I guess where we're going even before the door to the bathing chamber opens. "Oh no!" I pull my hand free. "No, I have no desire to . . . to submerge myself! A wash basin and a cloth will be fine."

The woman either doesn't hear or doesn't understand. She dances into the bathing chamber, beckoning enthusiastically. I creep reluctantly to the doorway and look inside, watching how the green woman moves about the space, picking up and setting down the various bottles of ointments, the combs and brushes, the woven cloths. She finds the white gown dropped on the floor and plucks it up, clucking and shaking her head.

Then she tosses the garment across the empty chair and, much to my surprise, dives into the pool. She whisks around under the water, nimble as a fish, swimming the whole circumference three times before coming up for air. She tosses her little tendril ringlets back from her dark eyes and chitters her teeth happily, beckoning me.

"Um." I step into the room and peer cautiously over the edge of the pool. "I, um . . . My kind don't bathe in groups as a rule."

The woman blinks at me and chitters again. Her own nakedness bothers her so little that she must find my modesty both baffling and amusing. When I firmly shake my head, however, she slides up out of the water, shakes herself off, and pads dripping to the table of bottles and soaps. She selects one, unstoppers the bottle, and holds it under my nose.

It smells heavenly. Sweeter than roses. Deep and somehow plumy. I can't repress a sigh of approval. Pleased, the woman chortles and proceeds to pour the contents of the bottle into the bath. The water foams and bubbles, filing the air with more of that delicious aroma. Beneath the bubbles, the water turns a vivid purple.

I pinch my lips together and glance at the green woman. She nods and waves her antennae encouragingly. "Oh, all right!" I cry, pulling at the fastenings of my gown. "All right, you win."

The bath is beautiful. Absolutely beautiful. Seven gods! How long has it been since I'd bothered to drag the old copper tub onto the kitchen hearth back home, fill it with water that all too soon went from scalding to tepid, and crammed myself into it? I can't remember. And it's been positively years since I used the last of the hidden stash of mother's soft, scented soaps. Years since I'd resorted to rubbing my skin down with hard lumps of lye soap or simply scraping it with a pumice stone.

This is pure bliss by comparison.

The pool is deepest at its center, almost reaching my chin, but is shallow enough for me to sit down along the edges. I glide around it, wading through the aromatic bubbles. Several times the glowing baubles under the water bump against my feet. They are unexpectedly slimy and a bit squishy, and I yelp the first time. But I get used to them quickly enough. If they are living creatures, they're gentle and seem happy to trail around behind me in the water, like a trio of spherical glowing puppies.

After I've splashed a while, I catch the green woman's eye. She sits with her legs dangling in the pool and motions me to her, holding up a comb and another bottle of ointment. I obey and allow the green woman to work the comb through the knots and tangles of my hair then massage sweet-smelling oil into my scalp.

It's strange to be waited on. But I could get used to it.

At last, combed, oiled, and smelling of exotic flowers, I climb from the bath, wrap my body in a soft towel the green woman hands to me, and look around for my dress. It's a shame to put that dirty old thing on while my skin feels so silky and clean, but . . . but . . .

I frown. "Where is it?"

The green woman blinks at me and burbles questioningly.

"Don't play coy." I wrap the towel a little tighter around myself. "Where is my dress? What did you do with it?"

With a wave of one hand, as though motioning me to wait,

the green woman darts around the pool. She returns, holding the shimmering white garment in both hands and offers another of her disconcerting, toothy grins.

I look at the gown. It's beautiful. Undeniably beautiful. And it would feel so much better to put on something lovely and clean like that rather than to struggle into my old rags. But it feels wrong. Wrong to indulge in these luxuries, to enjoy these comforts. Like . . . giving up.

"No." I shake my head, then hesitate. Issuing commands makes me feel uncomfortable, as if I'm playing at being someone I'm not. But what else can I do? "Bring me *my* dress. Now. If you please."

The green woman's eyes narrow, an expression of displeasure. With a little sniff through her slitted nostrils, she flounces out of the bathing chamber, returning soon after with my old dress draped over her arm. It's been washed, I note at once; washed and pressed, and a little tear in the seam of the right sleeve is mended with stitches so tiny, they look as though they've been woven into the warp and weft of the fabric itself. The under gown is pristine, whiter than it was the day I first wore it.

"Thank you," I say, and clothe myself under the green woman's resentful gaze. Once I'm clad, I allow her to style my hair in an elaborate arrangement of coils and braids. This seems to please her, and when she's through, she leads me to a tall etched mirror standing against one wall in the bedchamber.

I look. My somber reflection blinks back at me. The same hollow-eyed, scrawny, sallow-skinned girl I've always been. Only now there's a slight flush to my cheeks that hasn't been there in a long while. My hair, though far too elegantly styled to go with my simple dress, looks shiny and healthy, one coiling strand escaping to fall across my shoulder in a calculatedly fetching manner.

The green woman knows what she's doing, that's for sure.

"Very well," I say softly, meeting my own gaze in the glass. "You're here for a year. A year." My stomach pitches, but I tighten my jaw and speak firmly. "You're going to make the best of it. And maybe . . . maybe you can find a way home sooner. If you're careful."

The green woman appears in the glass, peering over my shoulder. She blinks innocently. Did she understand what I just said? It's hard to guess.

"I'm hungry," I tell her firmly.

The green woman flashes her teeth and takes my hand. She leads me to the door in the wall, which opens at no command that I can discern. We step out into the corridor, and the woman turns right, tugging me after her, leading me through the patches of colored light on the floor. I look up at the windows as we pass them. Yesterday I'd not taken time to notice the images rendered in glass and lead. Now I catch only brief glimpses of figures—men, women, and monsters. Fantastic landscapes of mountains and valleys, majestic palaces. I think I spot the image of the same man appearing in each of the windows, but I'm not certain. Perhaps there's a story being told here, spread down the length of the corridor. Perhaps I should take the time to look at it . . .

Later. For now, my attention is diverted as the green woman sweeps back the curtains at the end of the corridor and leads me out into the courtyard. The long feasting table crawls with movement. My eyes widen in surprise. Dozens and dozens of little naked men with enormous ears run up and down, bouncing from chair to chair, shrieking and swearing and singing in their odd little squeaky voices.

The green woman roars at the sight and, dropping my hand, throws herself at the creatures, swiping at them with her long-fingered hands. She catches several of them with good sound slaps and sends them flying through the air. Others dodge and dance around her feet, leaping to the height of her head to stick their long tongues out at her and flap their ears.

It isn't long before several of the little men catch sight of me hanging back behind the curtains. A cry goes up among them, and they swarm my way. I don't have time to react before they're surrounding me, pulling at the edges of my skirt, linking arms and dancing in circles around me. Several of them leap up to my eye level, offering me pastries and fruits.

"Thank you!" I gasp and hold out a hand. A delighted little man drops his offering into my palm, while the others shriek and seethe with jealousy before redoubling their efforts. They spring like grasshoppers, up and down, shoving delicacies at me. One intrepid fellow tries to stuff a whole pastry into my open mouth.

"All right, all right, settle down!" I cry. The unintentional command works like magic. The little men scatter, vanishing under the table like scuttling bugs. The green woman stomps her foot down hard on one, which lets out an angry bleat. When she lifts her foot, it pops right back up and keeps on running, none the worse for wear, vanishing with the others. Soon the whole courtyard is still and silent. If I didn't know any better, I'd believe the green woman and I were the only living creatures in the whole massive house.

"Well!" I exclaim. There seems to be nothing else to say, so I shake my head and say it again. "Well!"

The green woman ushers me to a chair. Despite the madness and mayhem, the table still holds a fine display of pastries and fine fruits, breads, and cheeses. The green woman pours a large serving of red wine into a jewel-edged goblet, but I opt to drink only water. I also choose the simplest of the foods presented to me—a bit of cheese, a bite of bread, a fruit that looks at least similar to an apple, though its flavor is more sour than sweet.

When I've finished eating, I'm surprised to realize that the green woman is gone. I didn't know when she'd silently slipped away. An oppressive silence hangs over the courtyard, interrupted only by the distant murmur of water.

I rise and stand a moment, uncertain. The fear still coiled tight in my gut begins to stir, to uncurl. No! I have no time for fear. I must be sensible about things and try to take charge of my circumstances.

"You need to learn," I whisper, looking up and down the buildings looming around the courtyard, their high walls and arched windows. "Learn about where you are. Find out why you're here. There must be a reason!"

Otherwise, why would *he* go through all this trouble? To make me his bride? It doesn't seem as though he intends to take me to his bed. He's neither tormented nor made sport of me. But there must be a reason. Hadn't he said something about paying a great price to find me? I can't remember everything he told me that first night, but I recall something about a scrying pool.

Some mystery is going on here. If I can figure out the right questions to ask, perhaps I can piece it together.

I look past the length of the table to the far end of the courtyard, the way the shadow led me yesterday into that enormous chapel, but I can't quite bring myself to venture back under the eyes of those cold, stern gods. Instead, I return to the corridor of stained-glass windows. For the first time, I stand near the opposite wall and properly study the images in those windows, starting with the one at this end, nearest the courtyard. I frown, backing up until my shoulders press into the wall, and tip my head back, trying to see the whole of the image at once.

It's very strange.

There's a woman—a tall, pale woman. A queen, I think, for she wears a crown on her head. A black band wraps around her throat, set with a blood-red stone. She stands over a large block on which lies a naked man. Dusky purple glass forms his skin, but the glass depicting his hair is black, so black that no sun can shine through. He lies on the block with his head thrown back, his throat exposed, and the woman . . . the queen . . .

She plunges a knife into his neck with both hands. Brilliant drops of red glass cascade down his skin, over the stone, and seem to fall to the bottom of the window where many panes of red fill the space like a rising flood.

My stomach clenches. I turn away, suddenly wishing I hadn't eaten so much. Seven gods, this corridor had seemed so lovely just moments ago! It shouldn't surprise me, though. It makes sense that a vicious kidnapping fae lord would choose to decorate his home with scenes of murder.

I move on to the next window, intending to give it no more than a quick glance and hurry on to my room. But what I see stops me in my tracks. I look more closely.

There's that woman again. The pale queen in her crown, still wearing that black choker set with the red stone. The dark-skinned man is with her, resplendent in gold robes, and he holds her in a close embrace. The passion of the pose is palpable, even depicted in glass and lead. Over their heads is a pattern of alternating suns and moons, three of each. Three days and three nights?

I move on to the next window, where the relationship between the pale queen and the dark man has fluctuated from passion back to violence. Here he is shown fleeing through some dark landscape of jagged rocks and pitted ground. He's small and naked, and she looms over him, a giantess of tremendous power, disastrously beautiful. She brandishes her crooked dagger like a lightning bolt. The sun shines directly through the red glass of her choker gem, making it blaze like hellfire.

I shiver and turn away quickly. I've seen enough. I don't like this story, whatever it is. I don't like it and certainly don't want to understand it.

Gathering my skirts, I hasten along the passage, taking care not to look at the windows again. I find my room easily enough, and the door opens as I approach, as though anticipating my return. But suddenly the idea of spending another day in there makes me sick. So, I continue along the passage in the direction I haven't yet explored. Might as well see where it takes me.

It ends in a garden.

I emerge between two great pillar supports, my mouth dropping open at the sight, at the sweeping view. I can scarcely believe it. Once upon a time, the Normas family garden was tended and formal, a lovely retreat in which ladies could take their leisure. Back before the curse on my father stripped everything away and both house and grounds fell into ruin.

But even at its height of glory, Normas House had nothing on the grandeur now before me. From this elevated vantage, I can see down multiple tiers to a long reflecting pool lined with graceful flowering trees. At the end of the pool stands a towering fountain wrought with elaborate gold figures—horses and men and monsters. Water springs from dozens of heads to fall into a wide basin. From this central point, paths diverge into long, rambling walks of shady trees, flowering shrubs, and formal beds full of bounteous blooms the like of which I've never seen. Birds flit among the branches, trailing plumage richer and more varied in color than a queen's royal train. Their voices fill the air with sweet songs that blend in intricate natural harmonies.

Seeing it like this, all at once, is dazzling. Overwhelming. Almost sickening. I can't take it in.

And it's . . . Is it . . . *mine?*

"No!" I growl, clenching my fists until my nails drive into my palms. "It's a prison. *He* can say what he likes, but it changes nothing. You're trapped here at his pleasure."

My knees tremble. Suddenly I see what my first dazzled glance failed to recognize—surrounding the garden, standing tall and white and utterly impassible, is a huge stone wall.

My legs give out. I sit down hard in the circle of my skirt and remain there for some time, just in the shadow of the corridor. Part of me longs to venture among those flowers and fountains, to walk amid those inviting shades. But I can't. I can't find the strength even to rise and return to my room. Not yet. I simply sit there.

At some point, I realize I'm not alone.

"I know you're there." I shudder and rub my arms, though the air is pleasantly warm. "I don't care for your lurking. Come out in the open." My voice sounds strangely commanding in my own ears. Funny, how quickly one can grow used to issuing commands.

Movement on my right catches my eye. With a fleeting glance I see the faint image of a shadow, almost imperceptible beneath the full light of the sun. I face forward again, determined not to look more closely.

"M'lord," I say softly. "It *is* you, isn't it?"

No answer.

I glance again. The shadow is still there, insubstantial, almost invisible. But present. I draw a long breath, hold it for a count of ten, then let it out slowly. "Can you speak?"

Still nothing. I take that for an answer.

"Well. I suppose I shouldn't be surprised. Shadows are by their very nature silent, aren't they?" I swallow and bite my dry lips to moisten them. "So, you're a shadow by day and solid by night. That's . . . interesting. I suppose. Is it normal? For your kind, I mean? No, never mind." I wave a dismissive hand. "I know you can't answer. I'm merely . . . trying to understand it myself. That's all. I don't know where I am, you see. This place, this house, this garden . . . On one side of the house, we seem to overlook a cliff, but then this side is this grand garden, and I don't understand how it all fits together. I suppose we must be in Faerieland. Beyond that, I have no idea."

The shadow shifts. I shiver at the movement but refuse to look his way again.

"Mother Ulla said that the magic used on my house was . . . I forget the word. Something from the Moon Kingdom. But this hardly looks like a Moon Kingdom to me. Was she wrong then?" I bow my head, rubbing my temple with two fingers of one hand. "It's all a bit much. I'm confused and . . . and frightened. I suppose I may as well admit it."

Giving my shoulders a quick shake, I sit upright again and fold my hands in my lap. "What are you doing here anyway? Did you forget your promise? To bring back proof that my sister is well, that your people did not do her harm? Or was that another one of your tricks?"

The shadow is still. When I glance at it again, it seems to have faded slightly. Perhaps maintaining even this amount of visibility under direct sunlight is a strain.

Then it turns, and I glimpse a flashing glitter of eyes before it takes two steps toward me. It holds out one hand.

My stomach flips inside me. I stare at that hand, so insubstantial I can see right through it just like an ordinary shadow, save that it floats in the air before me rather than cast on the ground or wall.

"What do you expect me to do?" I whisper, lifting my gaze to the dark blot against the sky that may be a head, a face. "Take your hand? Shake and be friends?" I harden my jaw. "I won't."

The shadow continues to stand there, hand outstretched.

"What if this is another fae trick? What if by taking your hand I'm inadvertently agreeing to something I shouldn't? What if . . ." My throat tightens. "I don't trust you. I can't."

He takes a half-step nearer. I shrink back, my eyes widening. Then something appears suddenly in the air, fluttering between his hand and my lap. It lands on my skirts, and I stare down at it, momentarily unable to make my brain recognize what it is.

Then I gasp.

It's paper. A folded piece of parchment edged with delicate gold leaves. My mother's stationery. After she died, I hid some of it under my mattress, and only one other person besides me knows where it is.

With a glad cry, I snatch it up and clutch it to my breast. I lift my head, my mouth open to speak to the shadow, to demand how he'd come by it, if it was real. But the shadow is gone.

Surely not even a very powerful fae could forge Brielle's terrible, scratchy penmanship, complete with its telltale blots and bad spellings.

Seated in the privacy of my room once more, my chair pulled close to the colored window where the best light can fall through on the page, I pore over the missive, desperately searching for some sign of falsehood. But it seems, so far as I can discern, genuine.

Deer Vali—it reads—*Mother Ula seys youv bin takin bye the fae and ar now a brid and this od litle man showd up t'daye and seys Im to writ youe a letr and tell you Im fyne. I am fyne, Vali. I didt no you wer in troble that nite or I would hav bin ther to saev you. I will saev you, I promys.*

Your afecshonate sistr,

B.

I sniff and press a hand to my quivering mouth. Oh, Brielle! It sounds like her all right. My brave, foolish little sister, who always chooses to be brave, never realizing how her thoughtless courage might put others at risk. Will she try to follow through on this promise? Will she go plunging into Whispering Wood, chasing the fae who took me, only to be lost forever in Faerieland?

"I've got to write to her," I whisper. "I've got to tell her not to do anything stupid!" I spring up from my seat and begin a search of the room. Surely there must be parchment and writing utensils somewhere!

But wait . . . I pause in the middle of digging through an ornate clothes chest, pushing aside piles of silks and satins and velvets to rummage at the bottom. Sitting back on my heels, I grip the edge of the chest tightly. The fae don't write. I can't remember where I learned that, but it's common knowledge. The fae can neither read nor write, do not understand the magic of making marks on paper to capture words and ideas. I won't find writing utensils in the house of a fae.

I stand and drop the lid of the chest before turning to face into the room. Brielle's letter lies on the table piled with jewels, far more precious to me than any of those sparkling trinkets. I move to the table, pick up the note, and read it again and again. It is a form of magic in a way I've never before considered—a piece of my sister's soul caught in physical form. Something I can have and hold even though she is worlds away.

"He'll deliver a message for me. He must." I breathe in and out, steadying my head, steadying my soul. I must get some sort of assurance to Brielle before the fool girl tries to follow through on her promise.

I have to lie.

I gaze down at the letter, which flutters in my trembling hands. Would an answering letter be enough? Brielle isn't a girl for written words. Besides, she simply won't believe anything I write.

There must be another way.

I don't venture out of my rooms again that day. The green woman visits me in the evening, trying to coax me out to the courtyard and a meal, but I staunchly refuse. I sit before my quiet hearth, and when the sun begins to set and the multicolored light cast through the panes of my window travel up the wall and fades, I don't call the blue flames to life. The room darkens and darkens, and my eyes struggle to adjust to the gloom.

But it works. Sooner rather than later, the door to my room opens. I look up and see the dark silhouette of my bridegroom standing there. Even from this distance, he feels more solid, more real than the shadow I encountered at the top of the garden.

"Come in," I say, sitting up straighter in my chair.

Something about the dark shape seems surprised. After a moment's hesitation, he steps into the room and closes the door before crossing to the seat across from mine at the hearth. He does not sit right away but stands, a huge, heavy presence. I can hear his breathing, deep and full.

"Good evening, m'lady," he says at last.

"Good evening, m'lord." I wave a hand, indicating the chair. "You may sit."

He obeys. I wait until the sound of creaking and rustling fabric settles. Then I wait a little longer, my hands folded, my face calm even as my heart gallops in my breast.

"Did you find your sister's letter satisfactory?"

I flick a gaze across the space to him, forgetting that it's pointless in the darkness. "Yes," I say. "I . . . I believe it is genuine."

"It is."

I grimace but bite back a sharp retort. What is the point in reiterating my distrust? "I need to speak to her," I say instead. "Is there any way you can make this happen?"

He is silent for some moments, considering. I wait in terrible suspense, hoping and fearing by turns. Finally, he says, "If I were to find pen and parchment for you, could you write a response?"

"Yes."

"Would that satisfy your needs?"

I think a moment, then shake my head. "No. No, Brielle might think I was being forced to write it. I need to speak to her."

"You cannot."

My stomach twists. I clench my fists tight, forcing my voice to remain calm. "Why not?"

"I . . . cannot tell you. Only that it is important. But a year from now—"

"Yes, I know." The words come out in a bitter snarl. "A year from now you'll take me home. But a year will be too late for my sister. She'll come looking for me, and then she'll be lost in Faerieland. By the time you take me home, there will be nothing left for me to come home to!"

The air rings with the echo of my voice until the shadows close in tight, drowning it out. I sit staring at my hands in my lap, scarcely able to discern them in the gloom. I feel my so-called husband's gaze rest on me, feel the intensity of his scrutiny. In that moment, I think I might hate him, truly hate him.

"I will ponder this problem," he says at last, breaking the silence. "I promise, I will find a solution that will suit both your needs and mine. Please, m'lady, don't think I dismiss your worries out of hand. However, there are other concerns at play here of which you do not know."

"Yes. That's true." I grind the words between my teeth. "I *don't* know. I don't know *anything*. I don't know why you stole me, why you insist on this false marriage—"

"It isn't false."

"It isn't a marriage! Not by any stretch of the word! I would understand better if you had taken me for your bed. To bear your children, or merely for your sport, to satisfy your pleasures."

"Is that what you want?"

"No!" I bark. I hardly recognize my own voice, so sharp and angry. It sounds more like Father's than I ever believed possible. I shiver and draw back into my chair. "I don't want anything like that. I'm merely saying I would *understand* your motive then. But this?" I wave a hand vaguely in the dark. "I don't understand any of it. And I . . . I don't like being made to feel helpless."

Another terrible silence stretches out between us. I take the opportunity to close my eyes, to breathe deeply and compose myself. What nonsense have I been spouting anyway? It was hardly wise to bring up the marriage-bed question while sitting alone in this dark room with this strange man, this strange *being*. Then again, trying to ignore the reality of that fear won't make it any less potent.

"Valera."

I shiver as his dark, deep voice rolls over my senses. I squeeze my eyes tighter, every muscle tensing with dread.

"I will explain what I safely can," he says. "As for the rest . . . You don't need to trust me. But I have my reasons for silence, reasons I would express to you if I dared. Believe me or doubt me or even hate me, just as you will."

He pauses again, and I sit in agonized suspense, waiting for him to continue. At last, his voice reaches out to me across the space between us. "You want to know where we are. Whether or not I have brought you to Faerieland. The answer is both *yes* and *no*. This house—Orican—is my ancestral home. My family, the House Dymaris, presides over the land from the Nesterin Mountains across the Valley of Rora. For many ages, we were one of the foremost families in the Kingdom of Lunulyr, respected throughout the worlds and realms of Eledria."

As he speaks, his voice seems to glow, warming the darkness with a proud light. But then his words trail off, and darkness closes in.

"This part of Orican in which we now live and move is *not* in Lunulyr," he continues. "Or at least, not fully. It is a . . . I'm not sure how to describe it. Consider you take a piece of cloth and fold it in half. It remains the same cloth, one and whole. Yet the folds are now on two separate parallel plains. Orican has been *folded*, as it were. One fold of reality remains in Lunulyr, but there are other folds as well. This fold on which we now live and move is many times removed from Lunulyr but simultaneously still connected. From various windows and doors you can still catch glimpses of the original reality. But you cannot reach it."

I stare mutely into the darkness, struggling to follow what he says. Perhaps it would make sense to someone like Mother Ulla, who breathed magic every day. Even Brielle would better understand after all the time she's spent in the strange glades and paths of Whispering Wood. But my life has been singularly devoid of magic until now.

"Wh-why?" I ask after a few moments. "Why would you . . . *fold* your reality like this?"

He doesn't answer.

"Ah." I pinch my lips together and nod. "I see. Something else you cannot tell me."

"I am sorry."

"Yes. So you've said."

"I would—"

"Tell me if you could. I know." I shake my head slowly. "Is there nothing else you can say? No reason you can offer for why I am here?"

"I needed a wife."

"Seven gods above, I *know* that! But *why?* No, no." I fling up both hands in a sharp, angry gesture. "Don't tell me again. You can't answer and you won't. Just . . . promise you'll find a way for me to speak to my sister. Promise me that. Please."

"I promise to . . . try."

I sag in my seat. "Go away." The words fall dully from my lips. I lean my head on my hand, my elbow propped on the arm of the chair. "Go away. I can't bear to be around you. Go."

He stands at once. I don't look up—it doesn't matter anyway since I can see nothing. But I hear the movement of fabric as he bows. "Goodnight, m'lady," he says.

I grit my teeth and turn my head to one side. Ears pricked, I listen to his footsteps retreat across the room, the door open and shut. Only then do I let out a long, shuddering sigh.

"Damn," I whisper.

It doesn't make me feel any better.

11

The next day I throw open the lid of the huge clothing chest and pull out five gowns. I spread them out on the floor around me, studying them closely. They're magnificent, undoubtedly. One is gold velvet, another a green brocade richly embroidered with silver threads. Another sports layer upon layer of what looks like Vaalyun lace. Expensive.

They're all human-made gowns, I note with interest. Not like the seamless white garment in the bathing room. These are styles and fashions I recognize, a little outdated, certainly, but no less beautiful for that. They're fit for a princess.

"Well, my dears," I say, raising an eyebrow as I survey the garments, "I fear I am no princess. And I have need of your services."

The green woman, responding to my request, finds and fetches a pair of shears, chalk, a bright silver needle, several spools of thread, and a little box of pins. She looks confused as she presses them into my hand, waving her antennae and looking about at the gowns spread on the floor.

"They are *my* gowns, aren't they?" I say, offering the woman a determined smile. "I suppose I may do with them as I please, mayn't I? Don't look so offended. I'll take care, I promise."

The green woman burbles uncertainly and perches on the back of the upholstered chair, sitting with her knees up, her hands and toes gripping the headrest. I try to ignore her black-eyed scrutiny as I kneel beside the gold-velvet gown and, using the chalk, begin marking out lines on the huge expanse of skirts. The green woman says nothing through all this, though every time I glance up at her, her antennae wave as though in quiet alarm.

But when I take the shears and begin cutting, the green woman lets out a yodeling yelp of surprise and springs from the back of the chair. She tries to gather up the gown, but I brandish my shears at her. "No! Don't touch it! You'll spoil the marks!"

The green woman rattles off a stream of chirrups and squawks utterly incomprehensible to my ears. I shake my head and point firmly. "If you're going to stay in here, sit. If you please," I add in a gentler tone.

A few more angry chirps and an aggressively disapproving rattle of antennae, and the green woman lets go of the gown. Instead of the chair, she moves to the sleigh bed, where she takes up the same frog-like perch on the curved stone footboard. Not unlike Brielle,

I think with a smile—hanging around in my room of an evening, swinging from bedpost to bedpost.

My smile falters and threatens to dissolve into tears. But that won't do! I need to keep myself busy, keep my mind active. I can't indulge in self-pity and despair if I hope to survive this coming year.

So, dashing the back of my hand quickly across my face, I concentrate on the task at hand. I cut, pin, try pieces against my body, adjust the pins, tack a seam here and there, and try it again. Eventually the green woman slips from the room only to return a short while later with food and drink. I pause to refresh myself, all the while silently studying the pieces of gold fabric spread around me. It's a jumble, a terrible mess of cuttings and trimmings and thread and pins. But I know my work. I know this mess is merely the thundershower heralding a sudden break in the clouds when all will become suddenly clear.

I finish eating and set to work again under the watchful eyes of the green woman. As the day wears on, I catch myself unconsciously talking over my work: "This fabric is exceptionally good, you know. The nicest velvet I've ever seen! Mistress Petren imports her velvets from Sumina, but they're not so rich as this, and they tend to pull easily. What Lady Leocan would give for a gown made of such cloth! It's a shame, really, to waste it."

I cast a glance up at the green woman, who blinks at me.

"I don't suppose you have any idea what I'm doing here. You don't look as though clothing is . . . well, much of a concern to you.

Do you never wear anything?"

The woman tilts her head to one side and chirrups.

"Maybe you simply haven't had opportunity. We'll have to do something about that." I bend over my work, running a line of tiny stitches neatly along one seam. "I wish I knew your name. It feels very strange talking to you when we haven't been properly introduced. I don't suppose you would tell me, would you?" I look up again, eyebrows upraised.

The green woman's slitted nostrils flare slightly. Then, with a flash of sharp teeth, she says, *"Ylylylyly."*

I frown. "Is that your name?"

"Ylylylyly."

"I'm not sure I can say it properly." I clear my throat and make an attempt. It comes out all wrong, harsh, not at all the bright, liquid trill the woman made. The green woman, hearing my attempt, tosses back her head and utters a chortling sound that is unmistakably a laugh.

I chuckle and roll my eyes, bowing over my work again. "Fine, make fun all you like! I can't help it if my tongue isn't so nimble as yours." After a little while, I add, "I think I'll call you Ellie. Is that close enough? Ellie?"

The green woman tilts her head again, first to one side then the other. Her hands flutter, palms up, a gesture communicating the same indifferent acceptance as a shrug.

"All right then, Ellie." I stand and shake out my work, hanging it in front of me. "What do you think? Do you like it?"

With a little chirp, the green woman hops down from her perch and circles me. Her long fingers pluck at the fabric here and there, and she shakes her head, antennae wafting curiously. She croaks then, a loud *gawarp!* that makes me jump.

"Well!" I pull the dress out of her grasp. "That's certainly a strong opinion. Let's see if you think differently when it's on."

It's the work of a few moments to shimmy out of my work dress and slide into the new golden gown. I designed it to lace up the front so that I can easily manage it myself, and it fits quite nicely across my bosom and my thin waist. The skirt flares just enough to allow for good range of motion but not so much as to be flashy. The little tucks and gathers accentuate my figure gracefully. I also added a tiny touch of lace from the Vaalyun gown along the rounded neckline.

The overall effect when I stand and look at my reflection in the mirror is . . . lovely. I smile, a glow of professional satisfaction warming my heart. Yes, it's a lovely gown. Simple, to be sure, hardly more elaborate than my work dress. But the fabric is so rich and the little details of fit and cut so subtly elegant that even Lady Leocan would jump at the chance to wear such a garment.

My gaze drifts from my reflection to the other dresses still on the floor, bundled off to the side to allow room for my work. What might I create out of them? Their colors and old-fashioned cuts fill my mind with interesting ideas, concepts I'd never had opportunity to indulge while working as Mistress Petren's stitch-girl. Would it be wrong to take this opportunity to explore the possibilities of my skill? Would it be wrong to indulge my creative curiosity?

Or would that be too much like . . . like *enjoying* my imprisonment?

The green woman appears in the glass behind me, eyes round and shining, antennae vibrating with interest. She touches the velvet skirt, tugs at a loose, billowing sleeve, and chortles, a delighted sound. "So you *do* like it?" I say, smiling slightly. Then I pull the laces at the front of the gown and slide it off, standing in my linen shift. "Here, Ellie," I say, holding the gold dress up to her naked body. "Let's see how it looks on you."

The green woman's eyes somehow manage to widen to impossibly huge disks in her little green face. Her sharp teeth flash, but the expression is eager, excited. It takes some doing to get her long limbs into the sleeves, for she's not used to clothing of any kind. Even when the garment finally hangs on her rod-like figure and I've done up the front laces, it doesn't fit right, having been sized specifically for me.

But Ellie stands in front of the mirror, turning this way and that, watching how the golden velvet shimmers from different angles. She preens and prattles and bats her eyes, flirting with her own reflection with outrageous vanity.

I watch, chuckling quietly. "You look quite the lady. If you like, I can make you—"

With no warning whatsoever, the green woman tears the dress off over her head and tosses it to one side. Then she turns to me, gesturing largely, pointing to her stomach and her mouth.

"Yes, fine." I gather the discarded gown off the floor. One seam ripped along the bodice, but otherwise it seems none the worse for Ellie's rough treatment. "I could eat, I suppose."

I drape the gold gown over the footboard of the bed, don my old work dress again, and allow the green woman to lead me from the room and out to the courtyard. The table is set and ready for me. Suddenly exhausted after spending my day in concentrated work, I sit heavily in my seat and watch with idle interest as platters appear, seeming to run on their own out from the colonnade to spring up onto the table. Only then can I spy the goblin men carrying them balanced on their heads and the tips of their huge ears. The little men set the platters down around me and perform elaborate leaping bows.

I lift the lids, hardly batting an eye when several times I uncover yet another goblin eating the remains of whatever had been inside. Enough of the dishes remain untouched that I eat quite well. Shockingly well, really. My appetite is enormous, and for once I'm able to indulge it. So unlike back home.

This thought brings sudden tears. I fight them back, determined not to dwell on thoughts of Brielle. I won't wonder what my sister is eating tonight, how she's getting by without me to watch over her. Brielle is tough, smart, and capable. She'll be fine. She must be fine.

The goblins, as though noticing my sudden shift in mood, spring up onto the table again. As I watch, they begin tumbling and rolling about, their ears flapping, their bare bottoms flashing, their knobbly feet kicking in the air. They pile on top of one another, forming elaborate pyramids, higher and higher, until the men on the bottom struggle and strain to hold up the others. At last, they collapse in a pile of thrashing limbs, shrieking with laughter and rage by turns. It's a simultaneously ridiculous and impressive display of acrobatics. Unexpected laughter bursts from me as I watch, my voice ringing along the colonnades.

"Thank you, my friends," I say as I finish my meal and stand. "That was charming."

The little men elbow and grin at each other before offering final bows and scattering. They dive off the table, roll, and vanish into the shadows, leaving behind a ringing sort of stillness that's a bit unnerving following all the noise.

I look up, noting how the sky purples with twilight. Another day has come and gone. Another small fraction of my prison sentence has passed.

I return to my room, taking care not to look at the violent images in the corridor windows as I pass. The gold dress lies where I left it on the bed, and I touch it thoughtfully, fingering the velvet and checking the ripped seam under the sleeve. I can't quite bring myself to pick it up and mend it. Instead, I simply sit in my seat by the fireplace, waiting for the night to darken. When the room gets too gloomy, I call the blue fire into being. My eyes grow heavy, and I think I might let them rest, just for a moment . . .

My head drops, jolting my neck, startling me awake. Have I been asleep? For seconds or hours? I can't tell. I sit up, stretching my arms, rolling my neck and shoulders. The room is quite dark. The fire has burned down to a pale blue glimmer on the hearth. I must have nodded off for a while then.

The door opens.

I tense in my seat. I almost look toward the door but stop myself and force my gaze to focus on the low fire instead.

"Good evening, m'lady," my bridegroom says.

12

The shadowy figure crosses the room and takes his seat on the chair opposite me. He says nothing beyond his initial greeting. I hold my tongue as well for as long as I can bear. But as the moments drag out, my discomfort grows.

Finally, I sit up a little straighter and, turning in my chair, face the shadow. "Have you figured out a way for me to communicate with my sister?" I demand, my voice too loud in that stillness.

The shadow does not answer at first. Then he leans across the space between us and sets something down on the floor. I turn, but not quite fast enough to catch a glimpse of his hand before he's retracted it. I see only a delicate crystal vial on the floor. The blue firelight glints off its cut edges and makes the liquid inside sparkle like diamonds.

The dark voice speaks, a low rumble like distant thunder. "That is water taken from the Starglass Mirror. I had thought to keep a little by in case . . . but no. After much consideration, I have decided your need is more important. I want you to have it."

I slowly lift my gaze to the shadow in the chair. "What . . . what does it do, exactly?"

"It is scrying water. I used the waters of the Starglass to discover you. To see your face and learn of your whereabouts. This small amount is not so powerful, but as you already know your sister's face, it should not be difficult to find her, to see her, and to let her have a glimpse of you as well."

"I . . ." I press my lips into a line, my brow furrowing. "I don't know how to use magic. I wouldn't know how to do it."

"I will help you."

"Now?"

"If you like."

My heart jumps with a sudden burst of hope. Will it work? Will I really be able to see Brielle? "Yes. Please," I say, breathless with eagerness.

The shadow rises. I turn in my seat, trying to watch him, to see what he does. It's impossible to discern much of anything beyond the short range of the hearthfire's glow, but I see his indistinct bulk approach my tall mirror. There's a creak, a groan, and then he returns to the fireplace and lays the mirror on the floor, facing up. He pushes it so that one end falls within the circle of light, reflecting the ceiling overhead.

"Take the water," he says. "Pour it on the glass."

I spring from my chair and hurry to do as instructed. I unstopper the vial and kneel beside the mirror, peering down at my own face, oddly distorted from this angle. "Is there . . . Do I need to do anything special?" I ask.

"Simply pour it out. Slowly."

Nodding, I tilt the bottle and let the stream of shining water fall. It splashes and pools across the mirror's surface but does not run to the edges and away. Instead, it forms a puddle, perfectly round, like a second mirror lying atop the first.

"Close your eyes," the shadow says.

I obey. I hear him kneel across from me, hear his voice murmuring deep and low. An incantation? What would happen if I opened my eyes and stole a peek at him? Would the firelight reveal his face to me? And what kind of face would it be? The fae were said to be dangerously beautiful, far beyond the beauty of humanity. Would my so-called husband prove the legends true?

But he was clear about the rules of our marriage—I am not to see him. Not even a glimpse. I don't know why, nor what will happen if I do, but . . . I can't risk it. Not if it might compromise my chance of getting home again.

The shadow finishes speaking, and I hear him rise and step back. "Now," he says, "look into the Starglass."

I open my eyes and lean over the mirror until my face appears in the puddle. My own dark eyes ringed with dark circles look up at me, strange and otherworldly in the glow of the blue moonfire.

I hardly recognize myself.

"Speak your sister's name. The magic I have called into being should summon her. It may take a few moments, but wait. And don't blink, or the connection will sever."

I nod, my cheek tensing. "Brielle," I whisper. "Brielle, where are you?"

At first, there's nothing. Only my own eyes, staring and huge, my own face, pale and pinched.

Then the water shimmers, clouds. I almost blink, only just remembering to keep my eyes open. "Brielle?" I say again. "Brielle, can you hear me?"

"She cannot hear you," the shadow says. "But she can feel you."

My brow tightens. "If she cannot hear me then— Oh!" I lean closer, my breath catching with eager surprise. "Brielle!"

She's there, as clear as day in the water mirror. Behind her I can just see an impression of trees. She seems to be in a wooded glade, crouched over her reflection in the same position I'm in now. Is she looking into a pool? Oh, seven gods! Is she in Whispering Wood?

"Brielle! It's me!" I wave one hand and watch my sister's eyes widen.

Her mouth forms an "O" of surprise, then her lips seem to say, *Vali?*

"Yes! Yes, it's me!" My smile grows and tears sting my eyes. I only just stop myself from blinking them away. "Yes, I can see you! I can see you!"

Brielle leans in closer, so close I can count the green flecks in her hazel eyes. Am I wrong, or does she look older? Is her face a little paler, narrower, her features sharper?

Brows drawing together in a firm knot, Brielle starts to speak again. No words come through, but I can almost hear her fierce voice declaring, *I'm going to save you! Tell me where you are!*

I shake my head quickly. "No, Brielle, don't do that." My mind whirls. I have to do something! Convince my sister that I'm happy, safe. I smile hugely and speak with care, enunciating words so that my lips are easy to read. "I'm fine! Really, I am! And I'll come home again soon."

Brielle's jaw hardens, making her look even older still. Her lip curls in a snarl. *I'm going to find you,* she mouths again, and reaches out a hand. *Vali—*

Perhaps she touched the surface of the pool, for suddenly her face breaks apart in a series of ripples. The pool of water rolls away, spilling from the edges of the mirror onto the floor. I stare down into my own face reflected in glass. "Brielle? *Brielle?* Oh, she's gone, she's gone!"

"I'm sorry," the shadow says softly. "There was very little magic remaining. I couldn't sustain it longer."

I sit back, blinking hard as my dry eyes readjust to the darkness around me. Two tears escape, and I hastily dash them away. "I . . . I don't think it worked." I lean back against the leg of the chair. I don't have the energy to get up from the floor, not yet. "She didn't hear me; she didn't . . . believe me. She probably thinks I'm enchanted. That I've been ensorcelled into thinking I'm happy when I'm not."

The figure in the darkness moves. I think he crouches on the floor opposite me, just on the other side of the glass, but I can't say for sure. "I'm sorry," he says. "I can send my people again, carry her any message you wish."

"It won't make a difference." I sniff loudly. "She'll still try to find me. No matter what."

"Then I will send someone to watch over her. To make certain she doesn't come to harm."

I look up. "You can do that?"

"Yes."

"Then, yes. Please. Do it. I would feel . . . much more at ease."

"It shall be done."

Dropping my head again, I look into the mirror, which now reflects nothing but the ceiling. For the first time since coming here, the tightly coiled fear in my gut seems to relax, to shrink. It isn't that I feel safer. Then again, I've not felt safe in a long, long time. Not since Mother died. Not since Father drowned himself in his own grief and rage.

But I don't need to feel safe. What matters is Brielle. Always Brielle.

My mouth opens. A "thank you" starts to form on my tongue, but I stop myself quickly, closing my teeth and pinching my lips tightly together. I won't thank this man, won't even allow a momentary flash of gratitude. He doesn't deserve it. He's my kidnapper. I owe him no thanks.

"Good night," I say instead. It sounds very loud and abrupt after the long stillness.

The shadow is silent. Then he stands slowly. I glance up, able to discern an impression of a huge form looming over me.

"Good night, m'lady," he says.

Then he's gone, shutting the door behind him.

13

There now." I use my shears to snip a final thread, then turn a shining orange satin garment around, checking for leftover pins. Holding up the finished product with both hands, I turn toward my watching audience and smile. "What do you think, Birgabog?" I display the tiny pair of trousers proudly. "You'll look quite a dandy in these!"

A goblin stands on my hearth, fists planted on his hips, legs widespread. His huge, froggy eyes narrow, and one ear twitches, considering. "Birgabogabogabog!" he proclaims at last in a voice somehow both piping and guttural. His wide mouth cracks open, displaying huge block teeth in a yellow smile.

I slip down from my chair, kneel on the hearth, and offer the trousers. The little man leans forward, his long nose twitching, his huge nostrils flaring as he sniffs the garment all over. Then two nimble hands dart out and snatch the trousers. With a few quick springs, he scales the fireplace to the mantel. Chattering and muttering, he puts the trousers on his head, stuffing one of his huge ears into each pantleg, all the while kicking his bare feet over the edge of the mantel with no regard whatsoever for modesty.

I sigh and rise from the hearth, brushing off my skirts although moonfire never leaves ash behind. I eye the goblin. "Something tells me you know *perfectly* well that's not where those belong."

He stands up and waggles his ears, making the ends of the trouser legs wave like satin flags. "Birgabogabogabog!" he cries, twirls on one hairy toe, and ends in a bow. With that, he crouches, knees up past his shoulders on either side of his head, then springs, soaring in a clean arc right over my head and landing on the floor close to the open door. I try to watch him go, but he's much too fast for my eye to follow. His tiny voice echoes down the corridor and away beyond range of hearing: "Gogagogagogagog . . ."

"You're welcome," I mutter and turn to my little table. A week ago it was covered in glittering jewels; those are now stashed in the bottom of the clothing chest. In their place lie shears, threads of many colors, pins, needles, chalks, and trimmings. More of the same litters the floor all around, some gathered in baskets that I convinced the goblins to fetch for me. The left arm of my upholstered chair has been turned into a pin cushion, spiky with silver needles hastily shoved in place while I dealt with a particularly difficult gather.

I pick up a tiny bunch of pins and satin the same color as the goblin's new trouser-hat. I'd begun to make him a vest, but what's the point? He might try to wear it as underpants. Though if he did, I wouldn't discourage him! I have become oddly inured to the sight of miniature naked men running about the place, their manhood unashamedly displayed. Yet a little decorum would go a long way.

Puffing a breath through my lips, I toss the bit of satin onto the worktable and rub my eyes with a callused finger and thumb. I've spent too long today over those tiny stitches. Time for a break.

Only . . . a break means facing the tumultuous thoughts in my head.

I let my hand drop to my lap and stare into the empty fireplace. Behind me I hear Ellie's voice in the bathing chamber, singing some odd, lilting, watery song as she scrubs the huge pool. By the accompanying rustle of fabric, I gather that she's wearing the newest gown I made for her—a stunning creation of green brocade, fitted to accentuate the most graceful elements of the green woman's long, oddly jointed figure. No mortal woman could pull off such a garment, but on Ellie it's fit for any royal ball.

It's not fit for scrubbing soap scum from tiles, however.

I frown moodily, casting a short glance back over my shoulder. I'd offered to help, of course, but the green woman shooed me from the room with one webbed hand. The people of Orican House are determined to treat their master's human wife like a fine lady, regardless of my wishes in the matter. Between Ellie and the goblins, they cook, clean, fetch, carry, scold, pinch, cajole, and wheedle by turns, until I feel quite exhausted with being so gods-blighted *cared* for.

But now that my initial fears have faded, I can't deny that it's been a restful week. I've eaten and slept and bathed and created, with never a worry about where my next meal will come from or when the next blow will fall. It would be all too easy to relax and accept this new reality, to enjoy the luxuries provided.

Jaw firming, I sit bolt upright in my chair. After a quick drum of fingers on my arm rests, I stand abruptly. "I'm going for a walk, Ellie," I call over my shoulder toward the bathing chamber. "I'll be back for supper."

Some weird trilling chirrup echoes against the tiles. Smiling, I step from my room into the windowed passage. Funny, how quickly I've grown used to communicating with a being whose language is so entirely different from my own.

My smile vanishes as I take the left turn down the hall and set out with a quick stride. It isn't funny. Not really. Sure, I may be growing accustomed to the strangeness of my new surroundings, to the oddities of the folk with whom I share this enormous house. But *funny* isn't the right word.

It's now been ten days since I stepped across my father's threshold into this new life. Seven days since I last spoke to my so-called bridegroom. Since that night over the scrying water, I've taken care to keep my fire burning bright until well after I fall asleep. He hasn't visited, and I haven't caught so much as a glimpse of a flitting shadow.

Stepping through the patches of colored light cast through the windows, I clench my hands in the folds of my skirt. At first I took comfort from Lord Dymaris's promise to send someone to watch over Brielle. But as the days wore on, worry crept in. I know my sister. I know Brielle won't be able to leave well enough alone. Fear for me will drive her deeper and deeper into Whispering Wood as she seeks to find ways through to Faerieland.

I've got to stop her. I've got to return to her before she gets herself into trouble so deep she can never escape. Lord Dymaris has been clear about the year-and-a-day limit to our marriage, but . . .

Again and again, I've pondered his words. Considered all that he told me from as many angles as I can. There's little enough to go on, but I think I've reached a conclusion. At least, I hope so.

The passage ends. I blink and shade my eyes as I gaze into the magnificent garden stretched out before me. Several times now I've ventured out to explore its many paths and groves, breathing deep of the gently perfumed air and resting my eyes from too much concentrated needlework. I already have a favorite spot, a winding path along the banks of a lily pond, shaded by pink flowering fruit trees. There's a stone bench nestled among the roots of the largest, most gnarled of the fruit trees, and I sit there for hours at a time, watching bright-colored water birds bathe in the shallows of the pool while enormous flame-colored fish idle away the days just beneath the glassy surface.

I make my way there now, stepping from full sunlight into the shadows of the trees. I trail my fingers through the low-hanging boughs, relishing the softness of their pink flower petals. Softer than velvet, softer than silk. What would it be like to make a gown out of these? A foolish fancy, but the air of this world sometimes makes the most foolish fancies seem possible.

Turning a corner, I come in sight of the bench. I stop short. A frown puckers my brow as I peer into the shadow cast by that huge old tree. Was the bench empty, or . . . no. No, the air is slightly darker there, forming a silhouette I recognize.

I swallow hard. Has he seen me, too? It's almost impossible to tell. But yes, he seems to be turned my way. Has he observed my comings and goings over the last week and realized this has become a favorite haunt? Perhaps I should turn on my heel and hurry back the way I came.

But I can't avoid him forever. And if I want to get home to Brielle sooner rather than later . . .

I gather the folds of my work gown in both hands and, setting my jaw, approach the bench. I perch carefully at the far end, leaving as much space between the shadow and me as I can.

"M'lord," I say politely.

Though he doesn't answer aloud, I can almost imagine that dark, bone-chilling voice responding in kind: *M'lady.*

For a while we sit in silence. I watch the play of sunlight through the blossoms, the contrast of pink petals against dark branches and bright sky. A bird with a bright yellow belly and a white crest sings cheerfully at the edge of the pond as it flutters its wings, spraying droplets every which way. I close my eyes, drinking in the sweet-perfumed air.

"I've been thinking," I say, opening my eyes again slowly. "About our . . . situation. This marriage, as you insist upon calling it."

The shadow is so still that I cast a quick glance its way, again wondering if I imagined seeing something there. It's almost invisible. But when I tilt my head to one side, it clarifies somewhat. He is there. I know it.

Drawing a steadying breath, I continue: "For one thing, I don't think you want it any more than I do. The marriage, I mean. You said yourself that you'd not expected to see a human when you looked into the scrying water. I'm not what you had in mind for a wife. Not a real wife, anyway. You claimed me because, as you have taken pains to tell me on several occasions now, you *needed* me. I've been considering what that could mean. And I think . . ."

I hesitate. Now that I'm about to say the words aloud, they seem foolish. But I've come this far; I might as well finish what I've started.

"I think perhaps you are cursed."

The shadow offers no discernible reaction. Am I mistaken in thinking I feel a quickening of interest in the air?

"Don't worry," I add. "I've gathered already that part of your curse includes an inability to discuss it with me. I suppose I'm meant to break it somehow, but I cannot break it if I'm not told what it is and what I'm meant to do. And the year and a day you have set until the end of our marriage, that must be the deadline of the curse."

Still nothing, no response. No indication that he's heard me beyond a vague prickling on the edge of my awareness. I pinch my lips together and once more look up at the sky between the shading branches overhead.

"I've thought about what you said—about how this house is *folded* into a different reality. I don't pretend to understand it exactly but, well, if I were to venture a guess, I'd say that you and all your people here in the house with you are exiled. Hiding. From what or from whom, I don't know. But if I can break this curse, then you will be able to return to your proper home."

I duck my head, twisting my fingers before folding them tightly. "I know how it feels. Wanting to go home," I say softly. "I know what it's like to be parted from those I care about. I know . . . that is, I suspect if I were in your shoes, I would probably do much the same as you." I glance sidelong at the shadow. "I don't know exactly what your curse is or how it is to be broken," I continue, "but you have been . . ."

Here I falter. Could I say he'd been *kind?* Certainly not! How can I attribute kindness to my kidnapper?

". . . courteous," I finish lamely. That much is true at least. While I might justly protest being stolen away from home, I've been treated with great consideration and care ever since. "If I can break your curse, I will. But . . . but only if . . ."

A hot flush creeps up my cheek. I turn away from the shadow, determined not to let him see it. The idea of a curse occurred to me three days ago, and the more I ponder it, the more convinced I am that I'm on the right track. But it was only last night, while staring into the brilliant moonfire flames on my hearth, that I realized what the solution might entail.

My shadowy bridegroom needs a wife. He's said as much several times over.

A bride. A willing bride. Willing to take a husband she cannot see. And before the year and a day is over . . .

I duck my head, squeezing my hands tightly together. If *that* is what's required, I can't do it. Not even on the chance I'll be able to return to Brielle sooner. I've never been foolish enough to indulge in dreams of romance, but I know that necessity will drive me into the arms of some suitor eventually. After all, what other option do I have for getting both Brielle and me out from under Father's fist?

Men have smiled my way upon occasion. In the last year alone, three brave fellows dared ask my father about me. He turned them all away with coarse words and threats . . . much to my secret relief. Someday, sooner rather than later, however, I'll have to take one of them. I know it. I'm not a fool. And when that time comes, I know what will be expected of me. The duties of a wife to her husband.

Until then . . .

I straighten my shoulders and lift my chin. "I'll do what I can," I say. "Only that. Nothing more."

For a little while longer we sit there, the shadow and I. Silent. I breathe in the perfumed air, watch the dance of the golden fish beneath the floating lilies and try not to look at my companion. What is he thinking? Maybe I'm entirely off in my guesses. Maybe he's secretly laughing at me.

Or maybe . . . maybe I'm not imagining that sense of gratitude. Like a hum in the atmosphere. Not quite felt yet *understood* somehow.

I stand abruptly, looking back the way I came. Without turning, I toss the words over my shoulder: "If you would like to join me after dinner, I . . . I will look forward to your company."

With this, I set off quickly, ducking under the sweeping flowered boughs and hurrying back to the house.

The goblins perform for my benefit again at dinner. They wear the little clothes I've made for them, not one of them correctly or with any sense of modesty, enthusiastically sticking them on whatever limbs or features strike their fancy at the moment. While I eat, they arrange themselves in increasingly complex acrobatic configurations, culminating in a pyramid fifteen goblins high, with the last, tiniest goblin balancing on the tip of the enormous nose of the goblin beneath him.

Then, one of the goblins at the base sneezes. I burst out laughing as the whole structure topples down and the little men roll, scramble, hop, and fly out of sight.

Ellie arrives at the end of the performance, her expression disapproving. She still wears the green gown I made for her, which looks limp and the worse for wear following her cleaning of the bathing chamber. She clears the plates and platters away, chirping derogatory comments and kicking or swiping at any goblin men who happen to come within her view.

"You don't have to clean up after me, you know," I say, rising and trying to take a plate from the green woman. "You can show me where everything goes, and I'll do it myself. I'm quite used to looking after my own needs."

Ellie gives me one of her blankest, most uncomprehending stares. Then she firmly pulls the plate from my grip and marches away through the colonnade, disappearing into some part of the house I have yet to explore. With a sigh, I turn to the corridor leading back to my own room.

My stomach flutters; nervous excitement mingled with the never fully banished fear.

Will Lord Dymaris accept my invitation to join me tonight?

"Seven gods, what were you thinking?" I mutter, hurrying from the courtyard. I made the invitation on pure impulse, but what will I do if he actually shows up?

Talk to him. Of course. It's that simple, really. I'm going to talk to him. I won't overtly question him about the curse—if curse there truly is. But in conversation, I might be able to pick up clues and hints, more pieces of this puzzle. If I can put it together sooner rather than later, break the curse in a few days, then perhaps I can go home long before the year-and-a-day term is up.

I hasten down the passage alight with the last bits of sunlight shining through the colored panes of glass. I pause, looking up at one of the windows, the image of the pale queen and the dark man locked in a passionate embrace beneath three suns and three moons. Something about that scene strikes me as odd, but for the moment, I can't say what or why.

Three suns. Three moons.

Do they symbolize the passing of three days and three nights? Or . . .

One hand creeps up to my face, lightly touching first one cheek, then the other. I remember the startling sensation of lips pressed against my skin, and flush warmly.

Three kisses, my so-called bridegroom had said. Part of a traditional Eledrian wedding night.

"And then I must wait until you ask me to kiss you a fourth time."

A little shiver runs down my spine. I turn away from the window and hurry on to my room. It's already getting dark, so I quickly speak the fire to life before heading to the bathing chamber to wash my face and hands. The touch of water soothes me, and I return to the bedroom in a quieter frame of mind. After all, Lord Dymaris has visited me several times now without once bringing up the matter of the fourth kiss. Even if it is the means to breaking the curse, I don't think he'll push it.

Not yet, anyway.

I sit in my usual chair. Not liking to let my thoughts run wild, I take up a bit of sewing and concentrate on the seams until my eyes grow too tired to focus. Then I lean back in my chair, idly watching the moonfire flames as they dance across but never consume the white stones. Their light slowly dims.

The door opens.

My heart gives a painful thud. A thrill races through my veins. I pick up the little silk jacket I was working on and pretend to study it, though it's far too dark to see anything properly. "Good evening, m'lord," I say without lifting my face.

"Good evening, m'lady."

He takes his usual seat across from me and is silent. I continue to fiddle with the tiny jacket, hoping my shaking hands aren't too obvious by the low firelight. My mind spins, trying to think of something to say, some sort of conversation that would be both safe and revelatory.

"I suppose you must—" I begin.

In the same moment, he says, "I fear there is—"

We both stop. Then I blurt an, "I'm sorry," over the top of his, "I beg your pardon." Another silence follows until I whisper, "Do continue, please."

He clears his throat. "I was only going to remark that I fear there is little use in making clothes for the goblins. They are notoriously averse to clothing. There was a time, you see, when they were kept as pets by the fae. Dressed up as dolls and made to perform tableaus for the entertainment of great lords and ladies. Since those days, goblins refuse to wear clothing. They view it as a form of enslavement."

My mouth drops open. I look down at the tiny garment in my

hands, then hastily set it aside. "I had no idea. I thought . . . well . . ."

"You thought I did not provide for the care of my own servants?"

"No. Well, yes. Well . . ." I swallow and frown. "Have I offended them?"

"Not that I have noticed," my shadow companion replies. "They do like gifts, and they get jealous easily. When they saw you making garments for Ylylyly, they were much enraged at first. They came to me with loud complaints, and though I reminded them of their own stance on clothing, they were determined to be unreasonable. But then your gifts began to arrive, and they cheered immediately." He leans forward in his seat as though to press a point home. "Your generosity was well thought of and well received. I merely meant to advise you not to worry overmuch if they don't value the garments themselves or wear them correctly."

"Ah." I pick at the tiny sleeve I'd been painstakingly fitting into an armhole. "Well, perhaps I'll think of something else they would like better." I shoot a quick glance across to him. "What about Ellie? Have I offended her?"

"Ellie?" There's a momentary puzzled silence. Then, "You mean Ylylyly? No, you could not have pleased her better if you'd tried. Though I would not expect her to begin wearing clothing on a regular basis."

"No." I shake my head and chuckle softly. "No, I've come to accept that already. She is a . . . a free spirit."

"That is one way of putting it, yes."

"Has she been with you long?"

"She has served the Dymaris family for six hundred years."

"Six hundred . . ." I stop and bite my lips. Of course, the fae live and experience time very differently from humans. "And how long have you known her?"

"Two hundred and five years as of this summer. She was my . . . I'm not certain how you would put it. Nursemaid, perhaps?"

"Your nursemaid? Two hundred and five years ago?" I nod slowly, pondering this revelation. "You're old."

A great bark of a laugh erupts from the shadows across from me. I jump and grip the arms of my chair again, every hair on my head rising.

"Pardon me!" the shadow says hastily. "I did not mean to frighten you. I am not used to interacting with your kind. Humans, I mean. I must indeed seem quite ancient to you. I almost fear to ask your age."

A lilt at the end of his last statement implies a question even though he does not overtly ask it. I clear my throat. "I was eighteen last autumn. I suppose from your perspective that must make me something of an infant."

"Indeed," comes the dry reply. "A toddling babe, still very much in need of Ylylyly's care."

Is he teasing me? It doesn't seem possible that a voice that deep and dark could speak so lightheartedly. I bite back a smile. "Is that why you assigned her to me? Because you think I'm a child?"

"Certainly not." The shadow chuckles again. "I may know little of humans, but I have sense enough about me. I can see that you are young, yes, but a woman grown, both in age and experience."

Not much experience, I think grimly but don't say it aloud. Instead, I say, "Regardless, I'm glad to have Ellie. She has been kind to me. Very patient."

"She speaks highly of you as well."

My eyebrows rise slightly. "You . . . she . . . you discuss me?"

"Yes. She reports to me each night. Her primary duty is to see to your comfort." Another silence follows this statement. After several breaths, he speaks again. "You have been comfortable, I trust?"

"Yes." I purse my lips and look down at my hands again.

"My people have treated you well, accommodated your needs and wants?"

I nod. What's the point in reiterating the hard truth that it doesn't matter how attentive his servants are, it doesn't matter how many comforts they offer, how I have only to speak a wish to have it granted with alacrity? I'm still a prisoner. A favored pet in a gilded cage.

The fire on the hearth jumps and dances, the low flames playing along the glowing white stones. A silver filigree screen shields the blaze, prevents any trailing skirt from singeing. The light shining through it casts intricate, lacy patterns on the hearth. I watch the effect, idly wondering what it would be like to pick such a shadow off the ground and sew it to the edge of a garment.

I shake my head and close my eyes. What am I doing? If I'm going to sit here in company with this . . . this person, I need to make use of the time. Can I mention the curse again? I spoke of it overtly in the garden, but he was nothing more than a phantom impression then. It might not even have been him at all . . . though the fact that he's visiting me now after a week-long absence implies that it *was* Lord Dymaris's shadow I spoke my invitation to this afternoon.

But how to bring up the topic of the curse without directly addressing it? If I'm correct in believing he can't talk about it for fear of repercussions, then it's up to me to find ways to work the conversation back around to it, to subtly gather information. Heroines in legends and tales of Faerieland always find clever means to gain the clues they need to solve their predicaments.

I chew the inside of my cheek and frown. I'm not clever. I never have been. I've never had the time to be clever! I work hard, I survive, and I care for my sister. That requires no cleverness, just grim determination day after day after day. Brielle is the clever one. She always rushed to the town square when wandering bards passed through town, soaking in the stories and songs. She returned home in the evenings to fill my ear with garbled versions of what she heard, and I tried to patiently listen with half an ear. But my mind was always much more focused on the needs of the moment, leaving me little patience for faerie tales.

If only I'd paid better attention.

"Why do you not make garments for yourself?"

I start upright in my seat and glance across at the shadow. I'd been so taken up with my own thoughts, I'd not realized how long the silence lasted between us. "I beg your pardon?"

"I cannot help but notice that you have yet to try on the various gowns provided for you," he says. "At first I feared you did not like them, and I thought to find other choices that would please you better. But then you began creating new garments for Ylylyly and the goblins. I gather that the pleasure of refashioning the gowns pleases you more than the gowns themselves. And yet, you make nothing for yourself, only for others."

I think of the gold velvet dress, which I stuffed into the bottom of the clothing chest along with the unwanted assortment of jewels. Several times during the last week I considered changing into it following one of my luxurious scented baths. Every time, something inside me had balked. It's too great a temptation. If I give in, if I allow myself the enjoyment of such a gown, how quickly will my other defenses break down? How long until I forget the truth that I am a prisoner, held against my will? That I should be fighting with everything I have for my freedom?

I glance at the shadowy darkness where I think his face might be. "I . . . um." I moisten my dry lips and continue in a carefully steady voice. "I am simply not used to sewing for myself. Back ho— Back before, I worked in a dressmaker's shop."

"Ah." He seems to contemplate this for some moments. "Yes, I remember glimpsing something of that fact. It was mostly shadows to my vision, but I thought perhaps I saw you working your magic."

"My magic?" I snort, only just stopping myself from laughing outright. "I am no magic user."

A short silence follows this. Then, "Are you sure?"

"Quite sure, yes. I'm merely a stitch-girl in Mistress Petren's shop. She occasionally calls me up front to deal with a difficult fitting, and I've a knack for drape and an eye for a flattering silhouette. But there's nothing magical about that. If it's a magician you need, I fear your scrying glass has sorely misled you."

I flush and turn away, looking into the darkness on the far side of the fire. Seven gods, I hadn't meant to say that last part out loud! The words ring in the silence of the chamber, sounding sharper than they had when falling from my lips.

Then again, why should I try to hide my anger? Even if there is a curse, even if Lord Dymaris is desperate for someone to rescue him, does that give him the right to steal me away from my world, my family? Besides, I still don't *know* if there is a curse at all. This whole conversation might merely be another layer of fae game-playing. A way for him to toy with his prey.

"The Starglass is never wrong."

His voice rumbles softly, almost inaudible above the crackle of the fire.

I shiver and pick at the bright threads embroidering the arm of my chair. Why, oh, why did I invite him to visit me this evening? I should have left well enough alone. I'm ill-prepared to match wits with a being nearly two hundred years my senior, brimming with magic and menace and knowledge far beyond my understanding.

For a long while, we simply sit. I eventually turn back to the fire and watch again the play of light and shadow through the filigree screen. I feel his gaze on the side of my face and take care not to let my expression betray emotion. Another few moments, and I will ask him to leave. Not too soon, though, or I might come across as frightened. That, I cannot bear.

"Are you familiar with the origins of your name?"

I blink, once more glancing sideways at his inscrutable bulk. "Yes," I say slowly. "Yes, my mother named both of us for heroines of old. My sister is called after a famous huntress who was said to run wild with wolves on winter nights and could hit the crescent moon with arrows of silver. As for me . . ." I laugh softly. "I was named for a barbarian queen who . . . who . . ."

"Who took up an iron sword and drove the fae from your land in ancient days long before the Pledge."

Another rush of heat floods my cheeks. I duck my face, letting locks of hair fall like a veil, shielding me from his scrutiny. Queen Valera of yore is always depicted in stone or paint with the severed head of an elven king under her foot. She's quite the grim heroine but well-loved throughout the kingdom in all her gory glory.

"My sister's name suits her well," I say with a half-smile. "Mine, not at all. I am no warrior queen."

He doesn't answer. I feel something in the air, in the darkness. As though he's thinking a thought so strong in response to what I've said that it almost makes itself understood despite his determined silence. In the end, however, I can no more guess at his thoughts than I can read the mind of a statue.

"What of your name?" I ask after a little. I let my lips shape the word softly, "Erolas."

"I am named for a wind—a soft, gentle breeze."

My eyebrow rises slightly. His name sounds even less suited to him than *Valera* is to me.

"My mother told me," he continues, "that while the hurricane brings destruction, the *erolas* carries healing to the stricken land."

Until that moment, I wouldn't have thought it possible for a dark, dangerous voice like his to sound so gentle. "Are you a bearer of healing, m'lord?" I ask with only the faintest trace of irony.

"Not thus far in my life. But it is a goal toward which I strive." He stops, and I hear his robes rustling as he shifts in his seat. "I am still young, after all. Perhaps there will be time."

Young? I frown. Comparatively speaking, how old would two hundred five years be considered to human age? The question springs to my tongue, but I bite it back. Instead, I ask, "Is your mother still living?"

"No. She was killed when I was a child."

The gentleness is gone. His voice holds the stone-hard tone that sends shivers straight to my core. I wince, wishing I'd held my tongue. There's a story here, but I don't pry. Not yet. Maybe later.

I say quietly, "My mother died as well. When I was a young girl and my sister a new baby."

"I am sorry."

"Yes. Me too." I draw a long breath. "My father is still living."

"You are blessed then."

I restrain a snort. "What of yours?"

"I have no memory of my father."

"Oh? Did he . . ." I hesitate, uncertain how much information I dare press for. Then again, what can hurt? "Did he die before you knew him?"

"No."

At first, I don't think anything more will be forthcoming. The silence is long and painful, giving me time enough to wish I could take back such a thoughtless question. I open my mouth, hoping to offer an apology.

But suddenly he's speaking again, his words flowing in a great rush as though afraid they'll be stolen away before he can get them out: "I gave up all memory of my father for a chance to look in the Starglass. The price of such visions is steep. And I was desperate."

I gape into the dark space where he sits. Before I can think of a response, he continues: "He is dead, though. I know that much. Along with my elder brother, my three uncles, my grandfather, and his brothers. All the men of my line."

This is it.

My heart lurches to my throat, beating fast.

I can't say how I know, but I do.

This is the clue I've been searching for tonight. There is something in what he said, something I ought to understand. All the men of his line . . . dead? The fae do not die easily. Something had happened to wipe out his family, to leave him the only surviving male of his name.

Is this why he needs a bride? To continue the family line? No, that can't be right. He promised not to touch me, to return me to my father's house in a year, so I can't be intended for childbearing.

Something else then. But what?

Suddenly the figure on the seat rises. I recoil into my chair. A powerful awareness of his size comes over me. I feel terribly small, frail.

"You are tired," he says. "I will leave you now."

"I . . . yes. Yes." I sit up a little straighter, lift my head, and nod slightly. "Th-thank you for the pleasure of your company this evening."

The words are simple enough, a polite sentiment spoken unthinkingly. But I feel shock in the atmosphere, hear his sharp intake of breath. I blink hard and drop my gaze. I shouldn't have said that! Why can't I be more careful? His presence far too easily unnerves me, puts me at a disadvantage.

"The pleasure was all mine." The shadow moves, and I glance up in time to catch what I believe to be a deep, graceful bow. "M'lady."

"M'lord," I respond softly.

He turns and crosses the room. The door opens in response to some unspoken command, and for a moment I see his silhouette framed in the doorway. Gods above, but he is enormous! His head very nearly touches the lintel. And are those . . . *horns?* Or is my mind playing tricks on me?

The door shuts.

I nestle back into the chair and watch the moonfire burn lower and lower, waiting for my heartbeat to steady. I mull over what he said, trying to see it from different angles.

His mother—killed.

The men of his line—all dead.

It must be important. It must connect to my situation.

But how?

At last, I rise and move to the bed. I remove my outer dress and climb into the soft blankets, lying on top of them, for the room is pleasantly warm and there's no need for a covering. I lay staring up at the ceiling overhead. My fingers play idly with the front laces of my shift.

Is it really all quite simple? If I invite Lord Dymaris into my bed, would a single night be enough? Might I wake the next morning, the curse broken, free to return to my old life? To Brielle?

For a few dangerous moments, I dare let my imagination lead me. I see myself bathed in moonfire light, rising from my chair by the hearth, approaching the featureless figure seated across from me. Reaching out to him, finding his hand in the dark. Drawing him up from his place and leading him away from the fire, deeper into the shadows.

I imagine unlacing my gown, pulling the fabric back from my shoulders. Letting the garment slide down over my hips until it pools on the floor around my feet. It wouldn't be so dreadful. The darkness is so deep, I'd hardly feel naked at all.

Would he hesitate to reach out to me? To close the small space between us, to draw me into his arms? I close my eyes, remembering the three kisses on my wedding night. The gentle pressure of his lips against my forehead and both of my cheeks. At the time, I'd been shocked, terrified.

Now I seem to feel that sensation again. His lips were full, soft. Not at all what one might expect from a monster bridegroom. How would they feel pressed against my mouth? And his hands—those huge hands that enfolded mine when he knelt before me and gave me his name. His touch was cold, so cold, and I vividly remember the chilling sensation of long, sharp nails just grazing my skin. What would it be like for those hands to explore my trembling body, freezing my flesh with their touch?

I shudder and roll onto my side, curling my knees up to my chest. It's too much, too terrifying. I can try all I like to convince myself . . . but I'm simply not brave enough.

There must be another way. There must be some other means of breaking this curse.

I lie awake for a long time.

15

The following morning, before I've even touched the breakfast of fruits and tiny, dainty eggs in pink shells that the goblins bring into my room, Ellie steps through the door with a bundle of lace in her arms. Tying my hair back with a bit of ribbon, I look around, surprised. "What is that?"

Ellie trills something and sets the bundle down on the bed. I move to touch it, realizing as I do so that although the lace is pretty, delicate stuff, snowy white and soft, it's merely a wrapping. Something else lies inside.

Curiously, I pull back the folds. A gasp of delight escapes my lips.

Contained within the bundle is yard after yard of the most exquisite fabric. Pink and white and softer than silk, it's almost too beautiful to touch, too beautiful to look at. I put out a tentative, trembling finger and just barely run it along one fold. Then, working up my nerve, I lift the fabric, drawing it close to my face to study the weave. But I can't see how the threads have been woven together. It's like no other fabric I've ever seen, and yet it looks and feels . . . familiar.

"Petals!" I look up, meeting Ellie's blinking gaze and curiously waving antennae. "It's made of flower petals!"

It's true. The cloth is made of the same flowers that bloom from the trees along my favorite walk in the garden. Only the day before, I ran my fingers through the bounteous blossoms, daydreaming what it would be like to make a dress out of something so soft and lovely.

Had . . . had *he* read my mind?

I blink, frown, and drop the fabric abruptly into the lace. "What is this, Ellie?" I ask, turning to the green woman. "A gift?"

A bribe?

Ellie burbles and trills, stroking the cloth with one many-jointed hand. She picks up a corner fold and holds it up to my face, nodding admiringly. I smile despite myself. "This is much too fine for someone like me!" I push Ellie's hand gently away. "This is fit for a princess. A queen! But . . . it is lovely."

I drape the fabric over the end of the bed, where I can look at it while I eat my morning meal. I peel and pop the tiny eggs into my mouth and nibble the exotic fruits, all without tasting them. My mind is full, studying the way the soft petal folds drape, how the light catches and plays with the colors. Images appear in my head, intriguing silhouettes. If I were to gather a little here, tuck a little there . . . if I didn't fight the natural inclinations of the cloth but worked with it, allowing the drape to fall just so . . .

Setting aside the tray and my half-eaten breakfast, I wipe my hands and pick up the cloth, running it gently through my fingers. It's so incredibly delicate! By rights it should fall to pieces, the fibers fraying at the first application of needle and thread. But when I make a few experimental stitches with one of my silver needles, the weave proves much sturdier than I expected. Magic, perhaps.

For some while I simply sit in my chair, holding the fabric, turning it this way and that. I lose all track of time as my mind wanders down different paths of possibility, envisioning gown after gown, adjusting the mental images, reimagining.

At last, I call Ellie to me and convince the green woman to stand with her arms out as I drape the fabric across her willowy body, pinning it here and there and standing back to study the effect. Ellie bears this patiently for a quarter of an hour before her antennae begin to vibrate with irritation.

"You're right," I say, plucking out the pins that hold the fabric in a gather at the green woman's right hip and left shoulder. I let the soft folds fall back into my arms, and the naked nymph steps free, shaking her head and stretching her arms as though liberated from chains. "It's not right on you," I admit. "It's . . . it's . . ."

It's meant for me.

I stand frowning down at the mounds of gently perfumed softness in my arms. Resistance still burns in my heart, but it fades in the light of the hotter, more urgent burn of inspiration.

At last, as though succumbing to temptation, I shake my head and call out, "Birgabog!"

A tremendous clatter like a whole set of kitchen utensils tumbling downstairs rattles in the chimney. Then a little naked figure somersaults out onto the hearth, springs upright, and waves trouser-clad ears at me. I gulp back a laugh, for the goblin gazes up at me with dignity, and I don't want to offend him.

"Birgabog," I say, "I need something. A dress mold. A proper one, like what I had back in my shop." I narrow my eyes at him. Does he understand what I'm saying? It's impossible to tell. "Can you get one for me?"

"Birgabogagogagog!" the little man cries, raising one finger high in the air, as though declaiming a great truth. Then he bows, twirls, and darts away up the chimney. Gods only know where he's going or what he'll fetch back when he returns!

Well, it's out of my hands now. I shrug, carefully draping the miraculous cloth over the end of my bed, select one of my chalks, and begin sketching concepts on the wall. The ideas seem to pour from my fingers, faster than I can keep up with, and I scarcely notice Ellie's disapproving tuts and fussings behind me.

A few hours slip past. I come out of a chalky daze of creativity to find a dress mold in the room behind me. It looks very much like the one I often used at Mistress Petren's, and when I inspect it closely I discover that it is indeed the same. There's the chip on the stand where a pair of dropped shears gouged the wood. I would recognize it anywhere.

I smile with delight. "Thank you, Birgabog!" I call to the empty air. Mistress Petren will be baffled, no doubt, at the sudden disappearance of one of her molds. But she has others. She'll get by.

Moving to pick up the lovely fabric, I pause abruptly and look down at my chalky fingers. "This won't do." I hasten to the bathing chamber to wash my hands, and by the time I reemerge, Ellie's there, moving pins and shears to make room on the table for the platter of food she's brought.

"Oh no, I don't have time to eat!" I exclaim.

The nymph shoots me a look that could curdle cream. I shut my mouth and obediently sit where she indicates.

While Ellie presses breads, cheeses, and cold meats into my hands, I chew and swallow absently. My gaze travels between the chalk drawings on the wall to the fabric on the bed. I scarcely taste anything, and as soon as Ellie steps back and gives me room, I spring up and rush to the wall, making corrections on several of the sketches, crossing out several others with aggressive, determined strokes. Only then do I pull the mold closer to the window, take up the fabric, and begin a few experimental drapes.

I smile.

The day passes. Sunlight travels in colored patches across my floor and up the wall. Just as the light is beginning to fade, I make the first few tentative cuts with my shears. It's spine-chillingly terrifying to see the blades pass through that cloth. But I think . . . I hope . . . I *believe* I have it right. Finally.

Exhausted, I set the shears aside and rub a hand down my

tired face. The mold stands with fabric draped and pinned. To the untrained eye it might look haphazard, ungainly. But the vision is begun.

Ellie approaches and stands behind me, tilting her head from one side to the other as she studies my work. "What do you think?" I ask, rising from the floor and stretching my lower back.

She burbles something and swings an arm around the room at the drawings, then points at her own green frock and chirrups. I guess at her meaning.

"I knew exactly what I was doing with that gown and the others," I say. "I've used those fabrics before, or fabrics much like them. That's why they didn't take as long. But this is all new for me, and I . . . I want to get it right." I shrug and roll my stiff neck. "It's not as though there's any rush."

The moment the words are out of my mouth, I regret them. A weight falls on my heart. The smile on my face melts away. I allow Ellie to take my hand, to lead me from the room, down the passage to the courtyard where a meal is laid out for me. The goblin men serve me and dance for my entertainment, but I scarcely notice them. I eat, but the food tastes like dust in my mouth, and I struggle to swallow.

What am I doing? *What am I doing?* The whole day passed, and I never thought about home. Not once. I never thought of Brielle, never stopped to wonder if my sister is even now plunging into Whispering Wood without a care for her own safety. I let my mind go wherever it wished, pursuing airy visions as they presented themselves to my imagination, becoming lost in my own little world.

Anger burns in my breast. I return to my room and stand looking at the dress form and the lovely fabric for several long minutes, my pulse thudding in my ears. I ought to take up those shears, tear into the cloth, rip it to shreds and toss it from the room in tatters. My fingers twitch toward the table, and my mind urges me, *Do it! Do it! Do it!*

But my heart constricts painfully. My fingers curl tight, their nails driving into my palms.

Then I grab the dress mold and drag it over to the wall, close to the window. I drape the heavy curtain over form and cloth, covering them completely, hiding them from view. This done, I go to my chair, adjust its angle until I can't see the bulge in the curtains, and sit, my spine very straight, my hands folded on my knees.

I call the moonfire to light, but only a tiny blaze. It soon burns down to a low glow, and the shadows in the room lengthen, deepen.

The door opens. Lord Dymaris steps inside and approaches the fireplace.

"M'lady."

I don't respond. With a wave of one hand I indicate the chair opposite mine, then fold both hands tight in my lap. My shadowy bridegroom hesitates for the count of three breaths. Then he sits. I feel his gaze on the side of my face, but he doesn't break the silence.

My lips are dry. I moisten them quickly then turn and face the shadow. "I am going to ask you a question. And I want you to answer me truthfully."

"I will." He pauses, then adds, "If I can."

A muscle in my jaw tenses. I draw a long breath through my nostrils. "Erolas," I say.

A frisson in the air between us—a spark moving from me to him and back again at the sound of his name. It's an odd sensation, so unlike anything else in my range of experience. But unmistakable, undeniable.

"Erolas," I say, "why did you send me that cloth?"

"Do you not like it?"

"Answer my question."

Silence fills the space between us. Silence . . . and that connection. That tension in the air. I brace myself, then lean into that sense. How I know to do so, I can't explain. But I do. I feel like a baby, newly discovering my own hands, learning how to flex my fingers, to grip, to hold.

The shadow speaks again at last. "I . . . wanted to give you something you would enjoy." The words are carefully, almost reluctantly spoken. "The other gifts I provided were . . . not well chosen. The jewels, which I had hand-selected from my mother's extensive collection, Ylylyly tells me now reside in the bottom of your chest. The gowns, which I am told are fine examples of human fashions, have not been worn and are instead cut up to make new garments for nymphs and goblins. At first I thought perhaps you were destroying them to spite me, but . . ." He stops a moment as though gathering his thoughts. "I realize now that it is the creation of beautiful things that pleases you, not the beautiful things themselves. Your joy is in your magic. So I thought to give you something of extraordinary beauty from which you might make something more extraordinary still."

My heart beats a little faster than before. There's something else, something he isn't saying. I take hold of that connection between us and pull. "Go on, Erolas."

He clears his throat. "The fabric I gave you—the silk woven of ornthalas petals—is of fae make. Humans have yet to discover the secret of spinning flowers into thread. I thought . . . perhaps it was foolish of me. But I thought if I could give you something you loved but which you could not have in your own world, then maybe you would take some joy in your time here. Here in Orican, I mean."

I stare at that shadowy form. His words ring in my ears. I feel the truth of what he says, dragged from his lips by the force of his name. Frowning, I duck my head. Resentment burns inside me because . . .

Because it worked. His little game. I spent the day in a creative frenzy, my passion for my work totally swallowing up all other thoughts and feelings. Never in my life have I experienced the joy of my craft as I did today. Satisfaction, yes. Interest and pleasure at seeing my ideas come together, certainly.

But today there was so much more. I was consumed with excitement, with the possibilities suddenly at my fingertip. And intoxicated by the luxury of time in which to pursue those possibilities. Every thought was caught up in new ideas for shape and drape, in touching and experimenting with that incredible, impossible cloth. In stretching my own limited understanding to encompass whole new ranges of inspiration. I hardly stopped even to eat or drink and resented the moments that dragged me away from the sheer joy of invention.

If I'm honest with myself . . . if I'm brutally, painfully honest . . . I can scarcely wait for tomorrow to come. For the sun to rise so that I might once more pull the mold out from behind the curtain and continue seeing where the possibilities take me.

Back home, there was no time for such feelings.

Tears fill my eyes. How can I let myself think this way? Brielle is home. Yes, life is hard, the struggle of day-to-day existence enough to beat me black and blue. But Brielle is there, so that's where I ought to be as well.

"You tricked me," I say.

"That wasn't my—"

"You tricked me into being *happy*." I clench my hands together, squeezing as hard as I can. "I won't fall for it. I won't."

"Please, Valera."

And there it is—that simmering power, that sensation like heat in the air. I gasp and lift my chin again, staring into the shadows across from me. I'd forgotten the connection goes both ways.

"Please believe me, I did not intend the gift as a form of manipulation. I am . . . I know this situation is difficult for you."

He shifts in his seat, and by the low glow of the firelight, I think I see him bow, resting his head in his hands, his elbows propped on his knees. When he speaks again, his voice is deeper than before, thickened with some emotion I cannot name.

"I was so caught up in my own needs, I failed to consider how it would feel to you. To be plucked from your father's doorstep, like a wildflower falling to the hand of a thoughtless child. I thought I understood how humans worked. A gift or two, pretty gems, pretty gowns, a handful of gold for your trouble . . ." He draws a breath and releases it slowly. "Everything I thought I knew about humans is wrong. At least where you are concerned."

I don't speak. I look down at my hands, pale in the light of the blue fire. My pulse thuds in my temples, but I try to calm myself, to consider his words in the spirit in which they are intended. They're truthful, at least. I can feel how the bindings of his name prevent him from lying to me.

A choice lies before me. A choice that makes my stomach knot. I can choose to see the gift as manipulation, an attempt to appease me, to make me docile and compliant. Or I can see it as an attempt to make my difficult situation a little less terrible. To shed a drop of light in the darkness.

I open my mouth. Pause. Almost swallow back the words. But what is the point of hiding?

"If you want to make me happy, you will let me go."

"I know."

"Yet you keep me here."

"I must. But only for—"

"A year and a day," I finish for him. Closing my eyes, I breathe in and out in a quiet, careful rhythm, counting to ten. "The fabric is lovely," I say at last.

The connection between us, that invisible something for which I have no name, quickens. "You like it?"

"Yes. Very much."

"I am glad."

And he is. I feel his gladness like a glow pulsing from the darkness surrounding him. My pleasure gives him pleasure in a way I hadn't realized was possible.

It's terrifying.

Hastily, I draw back from the connection, from the power of his name. I can't even say how I do it. It's magic of some sort, and I am no magic user. One moment I feel that burning cord stretched across the space between us; the next moment, the sensation is gone. Though I know the cord itself still exists. It always will now that I possess his name.

That doesn't mean I have to feel it.

I swallow, my throat thick and tight. "Good night, m'lord," I say abruptly.

He rises at once, as though in response to a command. I hear a little sound as he starts to say something but stops himself. "Good night, m'lady," he says instead.

He slips from the room without another word.

16

For two days, I work on the gown. I stitch and adjust and pin and drape, and slowly, slowly, the ideas in my head begin to manifest in reality.

When fear freezes my hand, I pull one of the gowns from the chest, chop it to pieces, and use large swaths of cloth to make mock-ups, to see if the ideas leading me wildly down the road of inspiration are even feasible. But these mock-ups taunt me, for even when they work, they are only creations of ordinary silk or satin, nothing like the petal-blossom fabric. I can't know for certain how it will turn out unless I am brave, unless I take risks.

Then, one evening, it all comes crashing down.

I've been hours at work, pleating along the waistline of the pink gown—tiny, painstaking pleats, dozens of them, held together with silver pins. I'm so close to my work, and the vision in my head is so clear, so perfect, that I don't think to step back and check my progress until I've gone around the entire circumference of the waist. Only then, blinking and sore-shouldered, do I scoot back on my knees.

I frown.

I scoot a little farther. Stand. Turn my head to one side.

Oh, great gods above. It's all wrong. It's *all wrong*.

That night, I can't eat. Ellie tries to drag me out to the banquet table for supper, but I send her away with a growl and a wave of my hand. Instead, I kneel on the seat of my upholstered chair, my arms folded along the headrest, my chin resting on my elbows, and stare at the dress. The hideous, horrible abomination with its awful pleats and its terrible silhouette, and its . . . its . . . Oh, how I *hate it.*

I bury my face in my arms, then slowly melt down into the chair, curling my knees up to my chest. Exhaustion aches through my limbs, throbs in my temples. I've spent too much time on this project over the last three days. It can't possibly be healthy. But how can I bear to leave it? It's meant to be something so wonderful, so exquisite! I can feel it, I can feel the shape just at my fingertips.

Only I've gone and ruined the whole thing with those wretched, wretched pleats.

I sink into a doze, not quite sleep, not quite wakefulness. Merely a numb space of self-loathing and frustration unlike anything I've ever felt before. The closest I've ever come to this feeling was two years ago when Mistress Petren gave me a chance to drape a lady's ballgown according to the latest trend for large, voluminous sleeves. During my work I had a sudden burst of inspiration for a new silhouette that would go so well with the gown's basic lines, with the soft, shimmering fabric, with the lovely silver trim. How I longed to pursue that image so tantalizing and clear in my head!

But I had my orders. The lady wanted voluminous sleeves, so voluminous sleeves she must have. I repressed that image, smothered it almost to death, and forced myself to do the work I was told to do. Ingenuity has no place in the work of a stitch-girl in Mistress Petren's shop.

This feeling was much like that . . . that horrible sick, helpless frustration. Only it was worse, ten times—no, a hundred times worse! For this time, the constraint doesn't stem from Mistress Petren's rules or the current strictures of fashion or a client's wishes. The only limitation to achieving my true vision now is . . . *me*.

The door opens.

I start at the sound but don't sit up straight. Gods above, I'd not realized how dark the room had grown! Now I listen to the familiar sound of heavy robes dragging on the floor as my unseen bridegroom enters. He shuts the door softly and approaches me.

"M'lady," he says.

I grunt and wave a hand dismissively. My head is still pressed into the top of my knees, but I turn it to one side, gazing into the moonfire light. "M'lord," I mutter.

He pauses. I can feel his gaze on me, can almost feel the concern simmering in an unspoken question on his lips. I hear him take a breath and start a few times to speak before finally settling on a safe, "How has your work fared today?"

I growl. The sound is so raw and animal, it surprises me. I sound almost like my father in one of his rages. The thought makes me grimace, but my tongue speaks before I can stop it. "It's hopeless! Hopeless and stupid, and I hate it, and I'm giving up!"

The words echo in Lord Dymaris's silence. Oh, I must sound like a petulant child! This is certainly no way for a lady to behave. I give my head a shake, squeezing my eyes tight, and try to summon the will to sit properly, to drop my knees, lower my feet to the floor, straighten my skirts, fold my hands in my lap, and offer an apology for my unseemly words.

But why bother? My jaw hardens. It's not as though I care what my kidnapper thinks of me. Do I? Of course not. I tighten my arms around my knees while my heart beats against my ribcage.

Fabric rustles again. I listen to Lord Dymaris move behind my chair, cross my room. He's going to look at the dress on its form. Oh, gods on high, why didn't I tear the whole thing to bits before he got here? But it was so much work to get it this far, and even though the work is all wrong and I loathe the sight of it, the idea of pulling it all to pieces . . . no. No, I can't bear it.

I wait in painful suspense. He's going to venture an opinion. I know he is. Maybe it's not as bad as I think? I mean, I know it is, but maybe . . . maybe it isn't?

Lord Dymaris clears his throat. "I think it looks rather nice."

Something inside me bursts.

I pop up straight, shifting my knees beneath me so I can stare over the back of the chair into the darkness in that corner of the room. I can just discern the silhouette of my so-called bridegroom standing there, and I hurl my words straight at him like knives. "*That's* the whole *problem*. It's *rather nice*. But that fabric is not meant to be turned into something *rather nice*. It's supposed to be *exquisite*. The most exquisite, most perfect gown ever *dreamed*. A feast for the eyes, a joy to look upon, a delight to every sense. Instead, it's just . . . just *that*." I gesture furiously with one arm. "*Rather nice*. I'd rather it were utterly and abhorrently offensive! At least then it would have a reason for being."

He turns toward me. I can't see him, of course, but I once more feel the intensity of his stare on my face. The heat of anger roaring in my veins turns into a hot flush burning my cheeks. I've never in my life given way to such a fit of passion! Not even during my initial fear and rage the night of my kidnapping. All this . . . over a dress?

What a fool he must think me!

I duck back behind the chair, sitting heavily with my feet out in front of me. I hear him coming and hasten to smooth the folds of my skirt. I even run my fingers through my loose, wild hair, though it does no good. The flush in my cheeks burns brighter. I've let myself come undone, revealed a side of myself that even I hardly knew existed. It feels so vulnerable. Like I'm exposed, somehow.

I swallow hard and try to inhale slowly, to still my racing heart.

But I can't.

He returns to his seat just beyond the edge of moonfire light. I shoot quick glances his way, my gaze not quite comfortable resting on his shadowy form. I hear him sit, hear him heave a very faint sigh.

Then his voice rumbles again in the darkness. "Perhaps I can help you. What do you need in order to make the gown exquisite?"

Though I'd just resolved to compose myself, that resolution crumbles under the weight of his question. I groan and cover my face with my hands, pulling at the skin under my eyes. "I don't know," I moan. "I don't know, I don't *know*. That's the whole problem, isn't it? And . . . and worse still, it's not even true!" The words pour out as if a dam in my soul has broken and nothing is left to hold them back. "It's like . . . it's like I *do* know. I *do*. It's in there in my head, the knowledge of what this gown needs, but it's . . ." My hands grip the hair at my temples, pulling hard. "I can't *reach* it. There's an image, there's a knowing . . . but it's *just* beyond my grasp."

How must I sound in his ears? Like a madwoman, no doubt. But I don't know how better to explain this frustration, this pain. This ache.

"It's going to drive me mad," I finish in a whisper.

Slumping deep into my chair, I abandon all concern for posture and poise. A pincushion that fell into the seat corner jabs uncomfortably into my hip. I fish it out and fling it into the moonfire. It rolls right up to the white stones but doesn't catch fire. The pale blue flames lick around it harmlessly, glinting on the little silver pins.

"I wish I'd never set eyes on that gods-blighted cloth," I mutter.

Only after the words leave my lips do I realize how loud they are in the stillness. A swift dart of shame pricks my conscience. After all, the cloth was his gift to me. And a truly magnificent gift at that. A gift so perfectly selected to bring me delight that it . . . it almost frightens me. Anyone with sense would be pleased by the richness of that gift, but few indeed would know the true worth of it as I do.

And here I've gone and thrown it all back in his face with my petulance and ingratitude.

My lips part. Am I going to apologize? Anything I might say sounds so insipid in my head that I can't quite bear to speak it out loud. I shut my mouth again, pulling my lips into a tight line.

Suddenly I'm aware of . . . of something. A tension in the air that wasn't there a moment before. It feels like . . . I look up sharply and glare across my worktable at the shadow-filled chair beyond the firelight.

"Are you *laughing* at me?"

"I would never!" His voice chokes slightly, then goes rough and low but with an edge to it that betrays his mirth. "I see that you feel it most keenly. I wouldn't dream of mocking such pain."

"Uh huh." I roll my eyes and toss up my hands helplessly. "Fine, I know I sound ridiculous. It's just a dress, after all! But . . . but you don't know how excruciating it is to be *so close* to something so perfect, so beautiful. To *feel* it almost there, almost within my grasp, and yet . . ."

I quickly clench my jaw before an expletive escapes. I've disgraced myself enough for one night; I won't add unladylike language to my heap of shame. Instead, I clench a fist and pound it on the arm of my chair. "I can't explain it," I finish with a sigh. "I just . . . I just can't."

"It's beautiful."

The laughter is gone. Instead, his voice holds a low humming rumble like the deepest note of a bass stringed instrument. It simmers with power, vibrating in my gut so strangely that it momentarily shocks me.

But I give my head a quick shake and cast him a baleful stare. "Don't try to take back your words. *Rather nice.* That's what you said. *Rather nice* is not the same as *beautiful.* And I won't be placated!"

He chuckles again, but that musical, rumbling hum underscores the sound. It sends a shiver straight down my spine, but the sensation is not unpleasant. Quite the opposite, in fact. I press back into my chair, wishing the wingback would fold in around me and hide me from his invisible gaze. I hear the shift of his weight in his chair and sense that he's leaning toward me.

"That's not what I meant," he says. "The dress . . . I am not one to judge such things. I lack the ability to tell the difference between nice and exquisite. But I know a great deal about magic and—if you'll excuse the word—about *passion.*"

I blink at that word. Should I say something? But what? "I . . . um . . ."

He continues relentlessly: "I sense such passion in your spirit! It's unlike anything I've seen before. The fae, as you may know, are neither artisans nor crafters. Our only creations are illusions. Even our most magnificent palaces, edifices of glory throughout the ages, were built by others. We can boast only laying claim to them and holding them as our own.

"The passion of a true creator, now that is a sight worth seeing! The passion radiating from your spirit, bright as the *quinsatra* itself, surrounds you like a halo. An aura of pure power. It is . . . You are . . . dazzling."

Dazzling?

My mouth hangs open. I'm dumbstruck, stupid.

Dazzling?

I've never in my life been anything of the kind, and well I know it. I rarely go out in company, and the few times I did go, I was the quintessential wallflower, clinging to the shadows while other, brighter girls called attention their way. I have no conversation, for my life and experiences have been too narrow to allow me any developed interests or opinions. I am so far from dazzling . . . It must be a joke.

I sit up straighter and pointlessly shove one hand through my hair. "Now you're making fun."

"Indeed, I am not!" The words burst from the shadows, almost pained in their intensity. All the laughter is gone from his voice. I stare across at him. Am I seeing things, or did he just reach one hand out to me but think again and retract it from the moonfire light?

"Valera," he says.

My heart quickens at the sound of my name from his lips. I'll never get used to the sensation, that pulling of the cord connecting us. My breath catches.

"Valera, if you had the freedom to pursue this passion of yours—if there were no fetters, no encumbrances—what would you do?"

No one has ever asked me such a thing. What does it matter what I *would* do? I do what I *can,* nothing more, nothing less. And I have no time to ponder dreams or fancies.

I set my chin and narrow my eyes. "I would return to Brielle." Though my words are firm, they sound hollow. Empty, even. But that can't be right! All I want, all I truly want, is to be reunited with my sister. Right?

Lord Dymaris shakes his head, the heavy shadow moving slowly. "That's not what I asked."

I feel the weight of his question, his true question. A question that has prodded the edge of my heart for many years, but I've always shoved it away, refusing to face it.

What would I do in a world without the responsibilities I bear? A world in which I could choose my own path, pursue my own passions. A world where I was truly free.

"I would . . ." I stop, afraid of the answer trying to work its way up my throat to the tip of my tongue. Instead, I give an answer that sounds good but reveals little. "I would take an apprenticeship, become a proper seamstress. Then I would open a shop."

"And this would . . ." He hesitates as though carefully choosing the right word. "This would satisfy you?"

I shrug. "It would fulfill our needs."

He breathes out a word I don't understand. I do, however, understand the exasperation in his tone that makes goosebumps rise across my flesh. "But what would *satisfy* you?" he urges. "What do you truly desire, Valera?"

There it is. He's gone and used my name again, gone and pulled unfairly on that cord between us. Drawing me toward him, drawing my heart, my soul.

Why must he do this? Why must he try so hard to . . . to *know* me? Surely it can't matter! He needs a bride, and he needs her for a year and a day. Anyone would do, anyone willing to sit out her time and fulfill the parameters he's set. Surely there's no reason for him to push for more than that.

There's no reason for him to peel back the layer upon layer of protections I've gathered around me throughout the years.

But when he speaks my name, I . . . I can't help it. I feel my defenses weakening. I feel the depths of my own vulnerability. It frightens me. And yet . . .

And yet I can't deny the pleasure of the sensation.

"If . . ." I stop and swallow, wetting my dry throat. "If there were a world in which I could make such decisions for myself . . . if it were possible . . . then I would spend my days exploring the possibilities I've begun to explore with this gown. I would . . . in this imaginary world . . . I would have endless supplies of beautiful fabrics and trimmings, and endless time to do with them as I willed. I would create works of art for all manner of people: lovely, plain, even ugly. As long as my clients trust my eye and taste, I would dress them all magnificently, discovering that which will reveal their true beauty."

This is dangerous. I should never give my thoughts such freedom. They'll run away with me, and where will they ultimately lead? Only to dissatisfaction. Disappointment. Even despair.

But now I've started, I can't seem to stop.

"If I had the freedom, I would discover possibilities others have not yet begun to search for. To see where the modes of the present and the ideas of the past may meet and become something new, something . . . extraordinary. And I would never allow a pattern or a fashion plate to determine the truth, but only the individual garment itself. I would let it show me what it is meant to be, and then I would make it so."

I can see it now—all those airy visions that have danced along the edges of my imagination for years, only to be dashed by the crushing realities of day-to-day existence. Oh, I should know better than to indulge like this!

Suddenly, movement draws my eye. The moonfire has sunk low on the hearth, casting a dull glow. Lord Dymaris, taking advantage of the darkness, reaches across the space between us. I feel his outstretched hand, though I cannot see it. It hovers in the air before me, and I stare into the space where I know it must be.

"Valera," he says.

I try to breathe but can't seem to remember how.

"Valera, if I could have one wish granted in this moment, I should wish to fulfill this dream of yours. If I were free—no fetters, no encumbrances—I should like to see your magic unleashed. To witness it in its full glory. For truly, I do not think there could be a more beautiful sight."

My heart strains, pulling inside my chest. It wants to answer the call it hears when he speaks my name. It wants to reach out through this darkness, to search along that cord of connection . . . to find out what might happen if that connection is truly realized.

I want to take his hand.

No. No, this can't be real. I can't really be thinking this way.

But I am. The urge is there, so strong. I can't ignore it. I want to take his hand, to feel what his fingers are like interlaced with mine.

I scarcely know him. This faceless fae, my kidnapper. My prison keeper.

This man who has in so short a time discovered more of me— the true me, the *real* me—than I even knew existed. This man who has seen me at my worst—furious and rude and despairing and petulant, everything a lady should always suppress, always hide from the public eye. He's seen *me*, unadorned and unmasked.

And he finds me . . . beautiful?

It's not real. It can't be. It must be a trick.

Why can't I believe it's a trick?

Why am I so tempted to let my hand glide across that empty space between us, to rest in his?

It would be too easy to give in . . .

I push back into the seat, firmly tucking my hands under my arms. With a wrench, I pull my gaze away from the shadows where he sits and stare into the remnants of the fire. My unburned pincushion seems to taunt me where it sits, all the little pinheads flashing like so many accusing eyes.

Lord Dymaris withdraws as well, sitting back in his chair. The quickness in the air between us lessens, and that tightness around my heart gives way as the cord relaxes.

Suddenly, I utter a little gasp.

"What's wrong?" Lord Dymaris asks.

"I . . . nothing. It's just . . ." I lick my dry lips and huff a little smile. "I think I've figured it out. What's wrong with the gown, I mean. I think I've . . ." I sit forward in my chair, twisting to look back into the dark corner where the dress mold stands. It's too dark in the room to see it, and I won't be able to work on it properly until morning. But a weight in my soul lifts, slowly at first, then more swiftly as the new idea clarifies. Inspiration begins to flow unhindered once more.

"I'm glad." My bridegroom's voice draws my attention back his way. He sounds sincere yet again. He always does. Which is what makes him so frightening. "Magic like yours cannot be dammed up for long."

I shake my head, facing his shadow-self again. "I've told you already, I don't have magic."

"So you say."

He stands then, and I hear the movement of his robes as he offers me a deep bow. "I will leave you now. You must desire to contemplate these new ideas in peace. Good night, m'lady."

I stand. Though I feel foolish to bother with such formality after the unladylike behavior I've just exhibited, I bob a quick curtsy. "Thank you, m'lord. Goodnight."

When he's gone, I sit back down in my chair. I'm tired, so very tired. I'd not realized how exhausting frustration could be until now that the frustration seems to be lifting! I want to think about my gown and mull over this new plan I have to fix it. But instead . . .

Instead, I find myself thinking about that voice. That deep, rumbling hum. That powerful timbre that sets my heart racing and my skin tingling with sensations I scarcely dare name.

You are . . . dazzling.

I open my eyes wide and stare into the darkness right in front of me. It seems as though I can just perceive the outline of a great outstretched hand.

What would have happened if I'd been brave enough to take it?

17

I spend the next several days working on the new dress. Several times I almost despair of bringing the ideas in my head to life. Several times, as I pick seams apart, I fear the fabric will be ruined and believe I've spoiled it all. Several times I come close to tossing the dress mold through my glass window in a rage.

But these emotions—deeply felt and horrible though they are—are all part of the ultimate joy. And joy there is aplenty, joy the like of which I've felt only the barest glimmerings before now.

As the days slip by, I learn to open my heart to that feeling. To not fear it.

Lord Dymaris persists in his nightly visits. He asks after my day, inquires about my work. After our last encounter, I am reluctant to answer. He can't truly be interested in the complications of bindings and linings and fell-stitching and drape, all vitally important to me but painfully dull listening for anyone not in my trade! But when my answers are short, he presses for details, for further explanation. Bit by bit, he draws out my words until several times I lose myself entirely and become caught up in the thrill of explaining my work in detail far beyond anything he can possibly enjoy. Until I realize what I'm doing, flush, and hastily bring my wordiness to a halt.

Then he says, "Go on. What about this-and-such?"

And I'm off again, carried away with enthusiasm for my craft.

Sometimes I've stopped to wonder: Why does he listen so attentively? Why does he return night after night for more of what surely must, from his perspective, be mind-numbing conversation? I'm not exciting, I know that well enough. I could never be a success at Lady Leocan's dinner parties. I'm too shy. And much too obsessed with my own small world of needle and thread. And yet, Lord Dymaris's attention never flags or fails.

If I didn't know better, I would almost describe him as . . . *captivated*.

But no. In the dead of night, after he has come and gone, I lie alone in my bed, rubbing my callused fingers together and forcing my thoughts back into proper order. He is *not* captivated. Far from it! He has need of me, and that need is best served if I am happy and compliant. This is the truth, and I must not forget it. Even if . . . even if I want to . . .

I heave a sigh and roll over, tucking into my pillow. I won't think about Lord Dymaris. I won't. I force myself to think about home.

Home with Brielle. Home in that cold house we can't possibly afford to keep up while we slowly freeze and starve. Home, where every day we must dread encountering our father on a back stair or in a doorway. Home, where my life is made up of a stitch-girl's drudgery, and desperation, fear, and loneliness.

When I return to my proper life—when my imprisonment ends and I'm back where I belong—all this inspiration, all this joy that I now give free rein will have to be dragged back under control. Whipped and beaten into submission. The real world is much too hard a place for dreams. For joy.

But it's a world with Brielle in it. Which matters more in the long run.

Eventually sleep claims me and, despite these somber reflections, I rise at daybreak reinvigorated for the tasks before me. I can't help myself. Perhaps this is a temporary joy, but it may be all the joy I'll ever know in life. I aim to indulge. So, I measure, pin, hem, tuck, line, and trim, and slowly the gown blooms before my gaze like a rose unfurling its petals.

One day, it's complete.

The end comes upon me quite suddenly. I'm applying neat little stitches to the neckline one moment. The next, I'm snipping the end of my thread, taking a step back, and realizing . . . there's nothing more to do. The dress, while far from perfect, while not exactly as I'd seen it in my mind, has become what it was always meant to be.

It's breathtaking.

I can't even smile as I circle the dress form, my gaze lovingly surveying my work. This is not a moment for smiling. This feeling is too big, this satisfaction too great. I come around to the front of the gown, fold my arms over my chest, and nod once, decisively. "Job well done," I whisper, allowing myself that much self-praise.

Now if only . . .

I bite down on my lips as though I can bite back the thought. But it's there, insistent, prodding at my brain.

If only I might see it on a living person. Not a mold. If only . . .

If only I dared try it on.

That evening, I eat more than I have in I don't know how long. Now that the frenzy of creation has passed, I'm both tired and ravenous. The goblin men keep heaping my plate, laughing at me as I tuck in and holding their own pot bellies to indicate how fat I'll grow. I roll my eyes and flick grapes at them, which sends them scampering around goblets and ducking behind bowls of fruit before reemerging to shake their tiny fists at me.

Night steals softly upon me. I return to my room and collapse in the upholstered chair by the hearth, my bare feet sticking out in front of me in an attitude of absolute exhaustion. Back home, I always ended my days at Mistress Petren's worn to the bone, my eyes bleary, my head aching, my shoulders cramped. This is a different kind of fatigue. A much more pleasant sensation. I've done good work. Really good work. Entirely born of my own mind and wrought of my own hands, with no help or interference from another soul.

If I could bottle this feeling and hold onto it forever, I would.

"M'lady."

I start in surprise. I hadn't heard the door open, hadn't heard Lord Dymaris enter. "M'lord," I say, trying to sit up properly in my chair. But why bother? He's already caught me in this ungraceful sprawl. It hardly matters now. I wave a hand vaguely into the space behind me and say, "It's finished."

He doesn't take his usual seat. I listen to his footsteps as he approaches the dress mold. Can he see the gown in the near darkness beyond the firelight? Apparently so, for I hear him grunt. It isn't much, but it's definitely an approving sort of sound. I smile, and something warm glows in my breast.

He returns to the fire and assumes his seat just beyond reach of its light. I can just see the shape of his legs sticking out before him, crossed at the ankles. It's the most relaxed I've ever seen him. An oddly comfortable sort of silence fills the space between us, and the blue fire on the hearth seems to dance cheerfully on its white stones.

"Will you wear it?" he asks at length.

I pinch my lips into a hard line. "I . . . don't know." I want to. Oh, how I want to! But some part of my heart still resists. "It's not as though I have anywhere to go."

He's silent for another long moment. Then: "Did you often have opportunity to wear fine gowns? Back in your own world, I mean?"

"What? Me?" I chuckle and shake my head. "No, certainly not. We . . . didn't move in those circles." My voice sounds bitter, and

I don't want that. Not tonight. Not after what I've accomplished today. Hastily, I add, "I'm not one for dancing, anyway. I rarely even made it to the village dances, and then I only watched from the outskirts."

"Glorandal Night is coming."

I blink and cast a glance his way. "Is it?" I hadn't realized how swiftly the time was passing. Glorandal Night had been a month away when I left home. It's a night of celebration throughout the kingdom, throughout the worlds. A night of equal importance to humans and fae, dedicated to the memory of the marriage between Glorafina and Andalius, a union blessed by the Great Goddess herself in ages of old. Glorafina was a fae, and Andalius a mortal man. According to legend, their love brought about the end of the bloody Silver Wars, which had wreaked havoc on the worlds for generations.

It's not uncommon back home to glimpse the fae among the village dancers on the green on Glorandal Night—wild shadows, half unseen in the moonlight, filling the air with their laughter, which intoxicates the senses like wine. Human maids are usually strictly warned against dancing with the fae, but not on Glorandal. On that night alone they may safely join hands without fear or treachery, for not even the most wicked fae will break the sacred trust forged by Glorafina and Andalius.

Last Glorandal Night, Brielle begged me to take her to the village green. Despite my best efforts, she slipped out of my grasp and plunged into one of the dancing circles. When I finally found her again, close to dawn, her eyes were alight with fire, her face flushed, and her bare feet bloodied from too much dancing. She slept the next day and night straight through but woke refreshed and full of vim. When I asked what happened to her, she could offer only the vaguest answers. "It was awfully fun, Vali," she said with a merry, mischievous smile. "Wicked fun!"

I smile a little at the memory even as a sharp pang passes through my heart. Where is Brielle now? Safe at home, tucked into her bed? Or out beneath the spreading trees, searching through thicket and glen, trying to find a way into Faerieland?

Lord Dymaris's dark voice rumbles in the darkness, interrupting my train of thought. "My people always celebrate Glorandal Night on the dancing lawn in the garden."

"Oh? The lawn just beyond the fountain?" I ask. Since I first glimpsed the great circle of lush green grass overlooked by the massive fountain with its heroic figures and monsters wrought in gold, I've thought it would be the perfect setting for a dance.

"There will be music. Orican boasts many fine musicians. And food, and drink."

I blink. "You mean *here?* There's going to be a Glorandal Night party *here?*"

"Not *here,* exactly. But in another fold of *here,* yes. You will see them only as shadows, but by moonlight you may glimpse a little more. And I can arrange it so that the music carries through."

My mind spins, trying to catch up with what he's saying. "Are you inviting me to attend?"

He clears his throat, and I see the indistinct shape of his legs shift as he adjusts his seat. "Only if you like. I will, of course, remain unseen and need not trouble you with my presence. But if you would like to experience a taste of the festivities, I . . . I rather think you would enjoy them." He pauses again, then adds tentatively, "You might wear your new gown."

I lace my fingers together. I suddenly realize just how slouched into the chair I am and push up into a more graceful position, straightening my back and shaking loose locks of hair over my shoulder. "Thank you, m'lord," I say uncertainly. "I will consider it."

He grunts an acknowledgement. A few minutes later, after a few more unrelated comments and stray observations, he rises and makes his exit. Suddenly weary, I undress and collapse into bed, tucking my head deep into the pillow.

But I lie awake much longer than I like to admit, my eyes shut, but my mind full of images of dancing shadows under moonlight.

I'm listless after finishing the gown, having fallen prey to the lethargy and malaise that accompanies the end of a creative fit of passion. My fingers itch to be working, but I can't summon the energy to start any new, less thrilling project.

Eventually, after I spend the morning prowling my rooms, lingering in a scented bath, picking at the food Ellie brings me, and trying not to look at my dress for fear of finding some fault in it—or worse still, picking it apart for no fault at all—I allow Ellie to drive me from the room to take a stroll.

I intend at first to walk in the gardens but change my mind and make my way to the courtyard instead. Lord Dymaris told me my very first night that every door of Orican was open to me. Why not test his word and see a little more of my enormous prison?

Starting from the courtyard, I choose a passage branching off from the colonnade and set off. It proves to be one I walked before, the corridor leading to the open window overlooking the waterfall and the moonlit landscape far below the towering cliffs. Better prepared this time for what I'll see, I approach the window and gaze out on that sweeping vista. It's undeniably beautiful. And terrifying. The bizarre sight of night and day skies pressed up against each other with no twilight between makes my brain hurt. I don't linger over the view.

Instead, I try some of the doors lining the corridor on one side. They all open at my command, and I peer in on a series of impressively beautiful and ornate private suites. Bedrooms with adjoining bathing chambers, much like my own. Many of them are even larger than mine, boasting sitting rooms and massive dressing rooms stuffed full of the most elaborate garments imaginable. Each suite boasts unique touches, testimony to the individuality of each occupant, no doubt. One of the suites exhibits a motif of birds that repeats itself in the wall hangings, curtains, crown moldings, woven rugs, and even many of the gowns. Another of the rooms is decorated entirely in weapons and instruments of the hunt. A third room belongs to a musician—instruments lay every which way, and a massive silver harp dominates the center of the sitting room. It's much too large an instrument for any human to balance and play, and I can only imagine the magnificence of the musician to whom it belongs.

As I wander from room to room, my curiosity grows. These chambers have an oddly lived-in feel to them, yet the house itself is apparently populated by no one other than Ellie, a few other green-skinned nymphs I catch occasional glimpses of, and dozens upon dozens of goblin men. None of these rooms feel right for those beings.

Maybe the people of this house live in a different fold of reality?

As I enter the next room, I catch a flicker of a shadow. Lord Dymaris? No . . . this shadow is too slim and feminine, nothing like the broad, towering apparition I've come to associate with my pseudo-bridegroom. Maybe I really am catching glimpses through the folds and into the reality where Orican House is still inhabited. Not silent and nearly abandoned as it is here.

Can the shadows see me too? Do I appear as a shadow to them?

Disconcerted, I back out of the room and command the door to shut behind me. Without venturing into any more of the rooms along that corridor, I return to the courtyard and pick another passage to explore. This one leads through massive, pillared halls and galleries, open spaces filled with light from skylights overhead. Small clusters of fine furniture break up the floor space, and I can almost imagine the graceful forms of fae men and women strolling among the potted plants at their ease, enjoying conversation or other entertainments of the day before gathering in the courtyard to feast.

Feeling small and mouse-like, I wend my way to another big window at the end of this series of rooms. It's clear glass, so I look out and blink in surprise. A view of the ocean spreads before me, its white-capped waves lashing under a violently stormy sky. It's as unlike the view above the waterfall or the garden walk as it can possibly be.

"Another fold," I whisper, backing away and shivering. How many times has Orican been folded? How many realities does it touch?

A bit disoriented now, I take a turn, thinking it will lead me back to the courtyard, but it brings me to a truly massive hall under a domed ceiling. Ahead of me are two enormous doors. A front entrance?

What sort of world waits just beyond those doors?

Curiosity and trepidation mingle into a single unnamable emotion. I approach the doors, biting my lips and twisting my skirts in both hands. "Open," I say softly, not quite certain I want to be heard.

The doors obey at once, gliding silently outward on their hinges.

A still, solemn forest stands before me.

There is no road or path. Gigantic trees grow right up to the door, gnarled roots pushing up through the stones of the doorstep. They're so huge, and the shade they cast is so deep, I almost think it's night outside. But here and there, patches of sunlight make their way to the forest floor, filling the world with a green-and-gold aura. Solemn stillness holds the air captive without even a trace of distant birdsong to interrupt.

It feels . . . familiar. Is this Whispering Wood? I swallow, my chest tight, my head suddenly spinning. It *feels* like it might be Whispering Wood, as if this part of reality might stand on the edge of my own reality, my own world.

Brielle would know. Brielle spends so much time in Whispering Wood, but I've only ventured beyond the edge of the tree line once in my life, back when I was quite young. Before Mother died. I was so scared that I ran out again almost at once and never wanted to go back.

I take a step. Then another. Then another, until I stand on the edge of the doorway.

What if I were to step outside? Could I run through those trees and leave this world behind? Escape Orican and Faerieland altogether? If I did, would I be able to find my way home . . . or would I wander lost in the massive forest until I succumbed to starvation or fell prey to wild beasts?

Is it worth the risk?

I look down at my feet. One step will take me over the threshold. One step . . .

Suddenly, the shadow is there beside me.

I feel rather than see his arrival. I look to my right and find that tall, broad, but faint outline of a man just beside me. "Have you come to stop me?" I ask. My voice sounds strangely loud, ringing through the stillness of that waiting forest.

He's silent. Of course he is. A shadow cannot speak. I think he moves one hand, but he's too indistinct for me to say for sure.

I sigh and step back. "Close," I command, and the doors swing shut, blocking off my view of the forest. "Don't worry," I say, feeling the weight of the shadow's unseen gaze. "I'm not prepared to brave the wilderness on my own. Not yet, anyway."

I wrap my arms around my middle and turn, intending to go back the way I came. But I'm a bit twisted around in this large open floor plan. Which way did I come from? I'm as lost as I would be in any forest.

The shadow moves to my side, pauses, then continues slowly as though expecting me to follow. I shrug and walk with him, believing he'll take me back to the courtyard. Instead, he leads through a series of arches and magnificent rooms until we reach a set of arched double doors. Here he pauses.

"Can't you open them yourself?" I ask wryly. I speak a word of command, and they part before me.

I blink, surprised. He's brought me to the chapel of the gods.

He glides through the opening, but I linger, peering up at those great figures on their pedestals. I feel suddenly shy, afraid to step into their notice. But the shadow moves to the center of the aisle and stands, waiting for me.

Straightening my shoulders, I hasten to him. We walk down the aisle more slowly than I like, making for the curtained exit at the far end. My skin crawls under the awareness of those stony gazes, and I find myself drawing unconsciously closer to the shadow.

"I saw you here, you know," I say after we've progressed a little way in silence. "On my first day. I followed you into the chapel. That is, I think it was you. I saw someone, a shadow like you, kneeling in prayer before the Great Goddess." I look up at him, studying the indefinite blur of darkness that is his face, wishing I could gain some sense of his expression. There's nothing, but . . . I can't help thinking there's a quickening of interest in the air.

"I wish you could tell me the truth," I continue. "I can't help feeling that my purpose here goes beyond you and your curse. That there's more at stake." I sigh, my brow furrowing. "I wish I knew the whole story. I wish I knew if . . . if I could forgive you for what you've done. For kidnapping me."

The shadow is harder to see here, just a patch of slightly darker space in an already gloomy chamber. Does it exist in another fold of reality? Does it struggle to see me too? Can it hear anything I say? It was able to reach through realities at least once that I recall, the time it gave me Brielle's letter.

"I wish I knew if you are . . . good." My voice is scarcely more than a whisper. "I *want* to believe it, I just . . . It's difficult for me. I don't know if what I'm feeling is true or . . ."

Or am I merely falling for treacherous fae manipulations?

I've always been told they are subtle beyond all reckoning, but I'd never imagined cunning like this. He treats me with such consideration. He worries about me. He seeks to understand what makes me happy, then does what he can to give me happiness. He listens. Then he asks questions and listens some more.

I've never been treated with so much *kindness*. And until now, I'd never realized how starved I was for it. For someone to care about *me*. My interests, my hopes, my passions. My needs.

And what baffles me more is the fact that the more I open up to him, the more I reveal of who I am, the more delighted he seems.

You are . . . dazzling.

I close my eyes, fighting against the memory of that voice, which is still far too clear, far too present inside my head. It frightens me, the way he said those words. And even more so, the way he acts, the way he treats me. I could so easily begin to believe such kindness is real. To trust it. Even to depend on it.

But that . . . no. Kindness is an illusion, a most dangerous illusion. I dare not trust him.

No matter how I want to.

I drop my head to stare down at my feet, at my worn slippers, so drab on that floor of inlaid precious stones. My throat thickens, and I blink, surprised at this sudden upswelling of emotion. Gods above, what am I doing? Quickly I lift my head and firm my jaw, looking at the dark blankness where the shadow's eyes ought to be. For a moment I hesitate, uncertain what to say.

"I know my own way back to my rooms now," I speak at last. "Thank you."

With that, I turn sharply and hasten on to the end of the chapel, fleeing the stony gazes of the gods and the unseen gaze of the shadow who is my husband.

If that was Lord Dymaris who walked with me through the chapel of the gods, he doesn't bring it up when he visits me that night. Nor the next night. Nor the night after that.

His visits are never long. Or rather, if I'm honest, they're not as long as I should like. He enters my room, speaks his usual simple greeting, "M'lady," then sits. He asks me questions about my day, which I answer, sometimes curtly, sometimes with more enthusiasm.

One night I tell him of a recent interaction with the goblins, how I found myself in the ridiculous situation of trying to keep one ugly little man from stealing the trousers off another ugly little man's head. I tell the story with zeal, my hands and arms broadly gesturing, and as I reach the crescendo, he laughs. It's such an unexpectedly warm sound. Bright and spontaneous, like the sun bursting suddenly through heavy winter clouds.

Surprised both by the laugh and the sudden rush of heat flooding my cheeks, I drop my arms and fold my hands in my lap. I look away from the shadow in the chair across from me, gazing instead into the dark space off to the side of my fireplace. Silence falls, but a silence still ringing with the echo of both my own voice, runaway with enthusiasm for my tale, and Lord Dymaris's outburst of mirth. Is he as embarrassed as I? It's impossible to tell. That shadowy formlessness gives nothing away.

Suddenly he speaks: "What is your sister like?"

I look around sharply. "My sister?"

"Yes. I know you love her dearly and worry after her safety. And I gather she is not very like you."

"No, no." A soft chuckle escapes my lips along with a smile. "She is nothing like me. She is . . . very brave. Fearless to the point of recklessness. She hates all that is cruel and rotten in this world and would throw herself in opposition without a thought for her own safety. Many times when Father . . . when he . . ." I stop. One hand moves to my cheek. "I had to protect her, you see. She couldn't protect herself."

He is still. Too still. But something moves in the air between us, and I feel again that strange sense of connection like a cord tied around my heart and stretched taut and invisible through a dimension outside time and space. In that vibration I sense a sudden strong and terrifying anger.

"He beat you." The words come out rough, like a growl.

"He . . . is a broken man," I say. I pick at the threads of embroidery on the arm of my chair. They've become tattered since my arrival. "He loved with all his heart, and then his heart was broken, and he has only pieces left. Pieces that hurt him, cut him from the inside like knives."

"You make excuses."

"No." I shake my head. "No, there is no excuse for what he does. But there are reasons."

A long silence follows this. Then, in a voice even darker than before: "You love him. Despite all he has done to you."

I lift my chin, glancing at the shadow. "Yes." The word comes out softly.

"Why?"

"If I don't, who will?"

"Maybe he doesn't deserve love."

"He doesn't." I shrug. Then I repeat simply, "He doesn't."

What more can I say? I can't explain myself. It isn't something I can put into words.

"Have you heard anything of my sister?" I ask after some moments of silence. "You said you would send someone to watch over her."

"She is well," comes the swift answer. "Just as you predicted, she tries to pass through Wanfriel. That is Whispering Wood, as you know it. But I have sent my servant to deflect her. She can pass only so far into the forest before her path inevitably turns her around and leads her home again. She is . . ." He pauses as though trying to find the right word. ". . . frustrated," he finishes at last.

I smile and sigh mirthlessly. "No doubt she is. Poor girl. Poor foolish girl."

The moonfire light dances and flickers, casting its bright lacy pattern through the filigree screen. I watch it dance, wondering if perhaps it's time to call an end to this evening.

Instead, on impulse, I say, "What was your brother like?"

"My brother?" he blurts, sounding startled.

"Yes. It's only fair. If I must talk of my sister, you must tell me something of your brother. Were you close?"

"As close as two brothers can be. Inseparable, you might say."

I hear layers in his voice. So many layers—sadness, joy, anger, and more. More than I can possibly discern.

"I'm sorry," I say. "I didn't mean to pry."

"No, no." I think I see the shadowy shape of a hand raise in a gesture of compliance. "No, it is good to speak of him. It has been . . . a long time. A very long time." He sighs heavily, then says, "We called him Taerel. That wasn't his true name, you understand, but the name he was known by. In our language it means *terror*. And it was well earned, though only in the best sense, you must understand. He was a maker of mischief, but there wasn't a drop of cruelty in his veins. He loved animals, the more deadly and dangerous the better. When we were still boys, he snared and brought home a lamia cub and convinced our mother he could tame it, make a pet of it. But it was insatiably ravenous, and though it grew fat on the fine meats and fruits and other delicacies Taerel fed it, it was never enough. Finally, one day, in a bid to supplement its ravenous appetite, it tried to eat me."

He tells the tale as if it were a fine lark. My eyes widen with horror. "What happened to you?"

"My mother plucked me from the monster's jaws, stunned it with a blow of her hand, and ordered Taerel to haul it back where he'd found it. I was scarcely thirty years old at the time, but I remember like it was yesterday."

I smile and snort. "Thirty. Such a baby."

"Indeed."

We truly do come from different worlds.

"Your mother sounds very brave."

"I never thought to meet a woman her equal."

The words hang in the darkness, so bright with pain and with love, I can almost see them suspended like little jewels strung on silver threads. I feel a question bubbling up in my throat, and on impulse I let it escape from my lips:

"How did they die?"

A long silence follows. In that silence, the cord of connection between us tightens, a sensation so strong it's almost physical. And painful. My hand creeps to my own heart as though I can touch that cord, grab it, pull on the tension to make it relax somewhat. And still the silence extends. Have I offended him?

"I shouldn't have asked that," I say. "I'm sorry."

"Don't apologize." His voice is sharp, but there is no harshness in it. Is he in pain? I peer across at him but can see only the usual indistinct massive shape in the chair. "I'm . . . trying to think of a way to answer," he says at last. "But I cannot."

So. Their deaths were part of this curse. Part of the secrets that hold Orican captive and keep its master in the dark. This is, in itself, a revelation.

"I see," I whisper. I will have to ponder how this connects to the other few bits and pieces I've managed to pick up. "I see," I say again, my voice trailing off.

Soon, Lord Dymaris rises. "I will bid you goodnight now, m'lady," he says.

I nod and murmur, "M'lord."

He crosses the room to the door, which opens at a silent command. There he pauses. Briefly I see the silhouette of his body and an unnerving impression of horns.

"Tomorrow night is Glorandal," he says. His voice is tentative. Even a little . . . shy? "I will be down at the dancing lawn until sunrise. You are welcome to join me. If you like."

I perch on the edge of my seat, gripping my knees with both hands. "Thank you, m'lord." It's neither an acceptance nor a refusal. Merely an acknowledgement.

"Sleep well, m'lady," he says.

Then he is gone.

I'm oddly agitated the next day. I can't explain it. The few times I force myself to sit in my chair and try to unsnarl this tangle of emotions, I'm immediately unsettled by a complexity of thought foreign to my experience. I jump up at once and resume pacing the room, trying to force my brain to settle, to fix on something, anything other than . . .

Other than *him*.

Though I'd promised myself I wouldn't, I fiddle with the gown. Adjust the trim along the neckline, only to change my mind and put it back the way it was. Play with the length of the hem, pinning up layers to see how they fall, then shaking my head and removing the pins, hoping I haven't damaged the delicate fabric.

Finally, Ellie drags me away from the dress mold and out of the room entirely, burbling firmly and waving her antennae so severely, I haven't the nerve to protest. I take a walk through the upper reaches of the garden, keeping well away from the reflecting pool, the fountain, and the dancing lawn. Instead, I stroll through a waist-high maze of flowering shrubs, pretending as I go that my eye isn't darting after any flickering shadow, searching for a phantom apparition that isn't there. Birds sing sweetly from the trees, and a brightly plumed thing with a long, needle-like beak sits on the head of a statue in the center of the maze like an elaborate, living hat. It watches me warily, its expression faintly accusing.

"What?" I demand of it, planting my fists on my hips. "It's not my fault! I didn't *ask* to be kidnapped. I didn't *ask* to be made some sort of savior-bride. I'm doing the best I can!"

It turns its head, blinks one beady yellow eye. Then, with a flutter of wings and spread of an enormous, multicolored fan tail, it flies off to some distant corner of the garden, out of sight.

I watch it go. And I feel suddenly . . . alone.

A long bath fills the afternoon. I sink deep into sweet-smelling suds, kicking idly at the little glowing baubles as they bump against my toes. Ellie drags me out of the water before I go completely wrinkled and rubs creams into my skin and oils into my hair. I refuse to let her style my hair, however. Instead, I call a moonfire to life on the hearth even though the room isn't yet dark, and I sit beside it. Its mild heat dries my hair gently as I comb it, leaving it smooth and shining with health.

Finally, the sun finishes its slow journey across the sky and begins to sink. The colored patches of light from my window travel up the wall all the way to the ceiling, and I'm obliged to ask the moonfire to burn brighter before the room is totally lost in gloom. Ellie bustles in, carrying food from the courtyard feast. She burbles a great deal, but no amount of bullying or scolding can convince me to eat more than a few mouthfuls. I pick at a pastry, pulling it to pieces with my fingers.

My eyes keep trying to drag my face around to the dress on its mold.

But no. I won't look at it. And I won't think about it either. After all, I'm not going down to the garden tonight. Am I? No, of course not. That would be ridiculous. I'm a prisoner, a captive. Lord Dymaris, for all his courteous speeches—for all his demonstrations of admiration and kindness—for all the endearing timidity with which he extended his invitation—is a fae. He's tricked me into this marriage, stolen me away from the only life I've ever known, and . . . and . . .

"And I'm not going," I growl, turning the comb in my hands. "I'm not."

I sit a few moments longer, gazing into the fire.

The moon will be out tonight. There's always a full moon on Glorandal Night.

Would the moonlight allow me to catch more than a glimpse of my shadow husband? Would such a sight go against the parameters of the curse?

Not that it matters. Because I'm not going.

I get up, set the comb down on the table with a bang, then cross the room to my bed, tear off my gown and toss it carelessly to the floor. I'm halfway into bed before I pause.

My traitorous eyes turn against my will and look at the dress.

It wouldn't hurt just to try it on . . . would it?

19

The fabric gathers gently on my right hip and flares away in layer after layer of shimmering softness. It's exactly what it's meant to be. No pleats, gods help me! Merely a gentle gather and a natural fall of shimmering soft pink.

I've added neither structuring frames nor lace petticoats to create volume. The layers themselves provide more than enough sweeping fullness, and they fall naturally, fluttering gently at the slightest movement.

The bodice is slight and simple: a seam up the middle that stops between my breasts, then two panels that come to points at my shoulders. No sleeves other than the most delicate trailing of petals. The back drapes open far below my shoulder blades. It's a daring cut, nothing like the styles currently in mode back in my own world. And yet each element is so graceful, so light. The overall affect is one of pure sweetness, like a spring flower newly budding.

I give a twirl in front of the mirror. It's a silly girlish gesture, one I've seen the ladies in Mistress Petren's shop perform more times than I can count. I've never before had opportunity to do it myself, and I laugh at my own absurd enjoyment. My hair is loose down my back, and though I like the effect with the gown, such a style is not considered ladylike back home.

"You might not be back home," I mutter, using my hands to gather silky locks at the back of my head, "but that doesn't mean you can't behave with proper decorum."

I glance around the room, searching for a means to hold up my hair. I have a few ribbons I've been using to tie the end of my braid, but those aren't right. No, a gown like this deserves something better, something a little more . . .

My gaze lands on the chest by the wall.

I purse my lips, conflicted. Then, letting my hair fall, I pick up my skirts, cross the room, and kneel to toss back the lid. A quick rummage inside, and I find what I seek—a pair of simple silver combs edged in delicate white gems like tiny glinting stars.

I turn the combs in my fingers, my lips pinched between my teeth. I promised myself I wouldn't touch any of the jewels. But these would suit the dress so well.

"And it's not like I'm going to *keep* them," I whisper, returning to the mirror. "I'm just borrowing them for the night. That's all."

Using the combs, I hastily twist and pin my hair half-up. I can't gather all of it, not with only two combs, but the result is presentable if perhaps a little simple. Lady Leocan wouldn't be caught dead out in public with a hairstyle like this. But Lady Leocan isn't here.

Twisting, turning, I admire the dress and the combs from as many angles as I can manage. Then I stand and face myself straight on, looking into my reflected eyes. They seem odd in the moonfire light. Dangerous somehow. As though the girl with those eyes might take rash chances.

She's a girl who would dance in the moonlight with a fae.

I smile a quick, furtive sort of smile. "I don't have to dance," I say firmly, as though trying to convince myself. "I'll simply stroll down, see the dancing lawn, speak to Lord Dymaris, and return."

A tiny flutter of guilt stirs in my heart—guilt that I should feel so much anticipation at the prospect. I quash the feeling. After all, I'm not intending to have *fun*. Not really. It's just a little walk. To satisfy my curiosity. Nothing more.

Skirts gathered in both hands, I step to the door. It opens at my command, and I pass into the corridor. A shiver runs down my spine. This is the first time I've stepped outside my room at night since arriving at Orican. I feel . . . reckless. And just the tiniest bit wild.

Which is nonsense, of course.

Shaking my head and taking care to settle my features into severe, dispassionate lines, I hasten down the left-hand corridor. Before I've reached the end where it opens out onto the garden, music reaches my ears—a distant melody of pipes and drums. It's very like the music played on the village green back home. Very like, and yet utterly unlike.

I reach the opening at the end of the corridor and stand at the top of the garden. My breath catches in my throat. The formal landscape lies before me, transformed under the silver light of the full moon. The blooming flowers seem to simmer with new life, an energy that pulses from their cores in radiating auras my eyes cannot quite see but my spirit feels with an intensity far beyond sight. The tall trees and dense shrubs cast shadows darker than night itself and stretch long across the paths and lawns, yet the darkness serves only to make the stars shine so much brighter. The reflecting pool catches and holds the moon in a perfect reflection.

A delicate wind whispers through the garden, dances across the pool, and hastens up the stone steps of the tiers to tickle my face, bringing with it a delicious bouquet of perfumes. All together it is intoxicating. I couldn't resist if I wanted to.

And I don't really want to.

Bunching up handfuls of skirts, I step out of the corridor and into the moonlight. I've taken the steps leading down the tiers to the reflecting pool many times by now, but tonight it feels all new. My senses are alive and tingling. Glorandal Night is a magical night, after all. Even back home, though I never danced, never joined the merrymakers in the village square, I always felt the magic brimming in my blood. Here that feeling is so much stronger, as though barriers I never realized existed have been torn down.

I walk alongside the reflecting pool, my bare feet silent on the white marble stones that line its edge. The massive fountain standing at the end of the pool is alive with flowing streams of moonlit water, which gurgle sweetly in rhythm with the music playing. And beyond the fountain in the wide circular dancing lawn . . . are those men and women dancing in many concentric rings?

My eyes widen in a futile effort to force my vision to see more clearly. Moonlight gleams on flashes of flowing gowns, wafting locks of hair, glittering jewels, lithe and graceful figures. But the glimpses are only momentary, perhaps nothing more than a trick of my moon-drunk mind.

Resting my hand on the fountain's basin, I pause in its shadow, hesitant to step out into full view. The phantom figures on the lawn pay me no heed. They raise their arms above their heads, long sleeves and cloaks and capelets trailing like wings, then clap and whirl away. Circles blend into circles, forming patterns of such complexity, one would have to be a bird in the air above to fully appreciate the sight. Even from this less exalted perspective, it's a wonder to behold.

For a while I simply stand where I am, drinking in the sights, the sounds, the scents of the night. Slowly, however, I become aware of the golden figures of the fountain towering above me. I've looked at them many times before by daylight. They seem to be an artist's interpretation of some fae legend: winged heroes and heroines of old, locked in endless battle with horned and fork-tongued demons with long, claw-tipped fingers.

I don't know the story, but several times while exploring the garden I've lingered over the fountain, circling the basin to see the fantastical figures from different angles. And at some time during my studies, a subtle change crept over my perspective. Those horned beings, though very strange, are somehow more beautiful than their foes. Their faces reveal nobility that is lacking in the stern brows and ferocious glares of the elegantly winged men and women with which they battle.

I've even dared to wonder if the horned ones might be the true heroes of the tale.

Observing the fountain now, I frown. Though moonlight gleams on the topmost figures, those closer to the basin are cast in deep shadow. Am I mistaken . . . or is there an extra horned head among the statues?

My dry throat constricts. I swallow with some difficulty.

"Good evening, m'lord," I say softly.

For a moment, I fear my voice won't carry above the lilting pipes and the deep rumble of the drums.

Then he answers, "Good evening, m'lady." There's a pause before his voice sounds again, deeper than the beat of the drums. "You came."

The shadowy figure moves slightly, the tips of its horns just catching a glint of moonlight. Unnerved, I draw back a step. It's like seeing the fountain statues coming to life. But Lord Dymaris does not step out of the shadows.

"The dress," he says. "It is . . . You look lovely."

I flush and duck my head. "Thank you, m'lord."

We are both silent then for a little while. I tear my gaze from the fountain and focus on the lawn. But I cannot concentrate on those flitting, mostly unseen figures. My awareness spikes at the nearness of his shadowy form.

The song comes to an end. The phantom dancers raise their hands in a last clap so perfectly simultaneous that it rings out across the garden, rolling away in a series of joyous echoes. Then they bow deeply or sweep graceful curtsies, which is like a dance in itself, before pairing off in couples and drifting off the lawn, their insubstantial images vanishing the moment they step from the circle.

"Who are these people?" I ask, my voice soft in the following stillness.

"They are the folk of Orican," Lord Dymaris's answer rumbles from the shadows. "People under my care."

"Can they see us?"

"We appear to them only as shadows, much as they appear to us. They are near, however. Only one fold of reality removed from us." He pauses before adding, "They are aware of your coming. And they are pleased."

My eyes struggle to make sense of the darkness and the moonlight, trying to catch another glimpse of the dancers. I see only the faintest flicker of movement beyond the edge of the dancing lawn, yet senses for which I have no name buzz with awareness, telling me that a great crowd stands and moves and speaks all around me.

Are they as eager to catch a glimpse of me? Of their lord's human bride? I flush again and almost duck back behind the fountain.

"How do you like the music, m'lady?"

Glancing back up at the fountain, I can't quite determine which horned head belongs to a living being and not a figure of stone. "Very much," I say. "That last song reminded me of a tune they play back home on Glorandal Night, *The Maiden and the . . .*" My voice trails off.

"Go on," he prompts. Does he already know the song of which I speak?

I lift my chin and continue more clearly: "*The Maiden and the Shadow.* It tells the story of a peerless lady whose father despairs because he can find no man fit for her to marry. He sends suitor after suitor to her, but she rejects them all. One day, a suitor comes to her in the garden, and the sun casts his shadow before him on the path. Seeing that shadow, her heart skips a beat, for she believes she has at last seen the man she can truly love."

A thoughtful silence follows. Somewhere in the night, musicians test their instruments, strings and pipes experimenting with soft notes, seemingly at random, like night birds in the trees.

"What happened when she saw the man himself?" Lord Dymaris asks softly.

Oh, seven gods, why couldn't I have held my tongue? Why couldn't I have simply said I liked the song and left it at that? Or better still, why hadn't I maintained my resolve and stayed in my rooms all night?

"She, um." I tuck my chin. "He could not measure up to the idea his shadow inspired in her heart. She wedded him even so but died of sorrow soon after for love of someone who never existed."

I wait, counting my own heartbeats. My eyes try to drag my head around, to look up at the shadow and gauge his reaction. But I won't let them. I stare hard at the empty dancing lawn instead.

"Seems a sad tale to accompany such a lively tune," Lord Dymaris says at last, his tone dry.

"Yes, well. Perhaps it would be too sad altogether if paired with an equally sad melody."

"Perhaps."

The musicians finish tuning and, after a short pause, begin another lively number. Shadowy figures appear on the edges of the dancing lawn, hastening to assume positions. As one, they link arms and begin to spin together, changing partners every few paces, forming another wildly complex and breathtaking pattern beneath the moon and stars. Painfully aware of the blush in my cheeks and grateful for the darkness to hide it, I watch silently. My bare foot taps in time to the beat of the drum.

Suddenly the figures seem to dim and almost vanish altogether. I blink and look up and see a wisp of cloud trailing across the moon, dragging larger, denser clouds in its wake. The music plays on, and I feel the pulse in the ground as the dancers stamp their feet. But I can no longer see them.

"Would you take refreshment, m'lady?"

I start and step abruptly to one side, the soft folds of my skirt rustling. Lord Dymaris stands beside me—tall and indistinct, shrouded in night. I feel the intensity of his eyes looking down at me.

"There is both food and drink," he says.

"I can't see it."

"No, it is in another fold. But I can draw it through."

I remember when I met him in the garden the first time— so long ago it now seems!—when his shadowy self handed me Brielle's letter. "Yes," I say. "All right."

He waves an arm; I can just discern the sweep of a sleeve indicating which way I should walk. I lift the hem of my skirt and proceed with him around the edge of the dancing lawn until we stop beneath a spreading tree. I sniff experimentally. Beneath the heady aromas of the garden drifts the barest hint of sweets and savories and spices. Just enough to make my mouth water.

"Here." The bulk that is Lord Dymaris moves. The next moment, I can just see what looks like a crystal goblet before me. "This is *qeiese*, a traditional Glorandal brew. It should be safe for your consumption if you sip it slowly."

"Should be?" I pause, my fingers already closed around the goblet stem.

"Taken in excess, it might drive you to a deep, dream-filled sleep. Many a mortal maid has lost her head sipping *qeiese* on Glorandal Night. Go slowly."

If I were wise, I'd refuse the drink entirely, but . . . I don't feel wise tonight. I feel reckless.

I lift the cup to my lips and take an experimental sip. A burst of light and lightness and pure summertime fills my mouth so that I half wonder if my whole face is lit up in the darkness. I swallow, and warmth pours down my throat, pools in my gut, and seems to radiate out through every limb. Gods above, if a single sip affects me so profoundly, what would a whole goblet do? I blink, sputter a little, and an irrepressible smile pulls at my mouth.

I raise the goblet, but before I can take another sip, long fingers close around my wrist. "Not too fast, m'lady."

I almost resist. After all, why should he give me the drink at all if I'm not to enjoy it? But no . . . I already feel as though I could spread my arms, sprout wings, and fly. Best not to push my luck.

I relax my fingers, allowing him to take the goblet away. He plies me with food next, delicacies both sweet and savory. Each no more than a single mouthful, so that my tongue is always left wanting more. But the next delicacy comes, replacing the craving for the first, and so on until I'm almost exhausted by the sheer variety.

"Enough, enough!" I cry when I've taken the tenth of these delicious mouthfuls. "I'm thirsty now!"

Lord Dymaris grunts, and the goblet appears before me again. "It should be safe enough for you to have another taste."

Delighted, I gulp a large mouthful this time, closing my eyes as the sunshine and brightness fills me up and pulses through my veins. A little gasp of a laugh escapes my lips, and I flush, press two fingers to my mouth, then shake my head and laugh again.

"That is enough, I think." Lord Dymaris again draws the goblet from my reluctant fingers. "I fear it is too strong for you, m'lady. You are so slight and unused to our fare. Would you care for some water instead?"

"I care for a dance."

The song has ended. Though I cannot see them, I feel the unseen dancers dispersing. The dancing lawn is empty beneath the moon-shrouded sky.

Lord Dymaris stands beside me in the darkness. He is very still. I cannot even hear him breathe.

"Come!" I say, laughing again, a bright golden laugh. "Dance with me!" I gather my skirts and skip lightly from beneath the spreading tree, out into the middle of the empty lawn. There I fling out my arms, toss back my head, and twirl. This is what this lovely gown was made for—movement, free and light and full of untethered joy. No somber prisoner would dare to wear a gown like this.

It is a gown fit for a bride.

So I close my eyes and spin again, breathing in the scents of the night, reveling in the softness of my petal skirts against my legs, the bite of cool wind against my bare arms. As I spin, a single bodhran drum begins to beat a deep throbbing rhythm that captures my feet. My toes skip and dance through the grass in time to that beat. The pipes join in, and delicate strings blend together into a full symphony of sound. I let the music carry me. I've never danced on Glorandal Night before, yet somehow my spirit seems to know the steps.

Suddenly a hand is around my waist. I turn sharply, gaze up into deep, featureless shadow, and my face splits in a smile. My other hand is caught in a long-fingered grip.

Then I'm spun across the dancing lawn, my stomach pitching with delightful sensations at every whirl. The music wraps around us, so bright, so golden, it seems to be made of strands of light, the only truly visible thing in all the darkened garden. I close my eyes and let the song sweep me away. My hair floats in ripples around my shoulders, and my many-layered skirts flutter like blossoms in a sudden breeze.

Wilder and wilder the music swells, and the hand holding mine lets go and grips my waist. I reach up, catching hold of solid, muscled shoulders, and gasp in delight as I'm lifted right off my feet, caught in a heady whirl of darkness and song.

The music comes to an end. Distantly, as though from a world away, I think perhaps I hear a sound like applause, but that may have been nothing more than the murmur of the fountain. My feet are still off the ground as I'm carried around in one final turn.

Then slowly, unhurried, those strong arms lower me until the grass tickles my bare toes. I stumble to catch my balance and fall against the tall figure. For a moment, my cheek presses against bare, warm skin. I feel the thud of a heartbeat.

My eyes flare open. With a little gasp, I step back, but my fingers tighten their grip on the silk-clad shoulders. I stare up at the shape looming over me, trying to see something, anything. But it's too dark. I can discern no more than a faint silhouette and the outline of two great curved horns above me. It's too strange, too frightening, so I close my eyes, tilting my head back. My breath comes in short bursts, my lungs struggling to catch up after that wild exertion.

In the silence left behind by the music, I hear his deep breathing. It rumbles in the pit of my stomach.

"Valera."

His voice reaches out to me along that invisible cord of connection stretched between us. He's not spoken my name in days; I'd almost forgotten how it feels, how my body and soul respond to the sound.

One of the two hands holding my waist lets go. The next moment, something touches my cheek. A rounded knuckle that turns gently as it trails down my face, a light, delicate touch.

"Valera," he says again. "Valera, I . . ."

His fingertip traces the line of my jaw, then under my chin. I catch my breath.

That's when I feel it—the sharp edge of a claw.

I release my hold on his shoulders and step back quickly. The hand on my waist immediately lets go. My cheek burns as though on fire, and that place on my chin throbs as though in pain, though when my trembling fingers touch the spot I feel no blood.

"I'm tired," I say. I back away several more paces, my fingers clenching in the folds of my skirts. "It was . . . I very much . . . Good night, m'lord!"

Whirling on my heel, I lift the front hem of my skirts and all but run across the lawn. The clouds disperse. Moonlight floods the gardens once more, gleaming bright on the horned and winged figures on the fountain. I don't look behind me; I don't try to catch a last glimpse of the dancing figures making their way back onto the green. I don't try to see the lanterns of moonfire or the shimmering flowers with their otherworldly glow.

If I look, the moonlight might reveal the face of my bridegroom. And that goes against the bonds of our marriage.

So I flee along the edge of the long reflecting pool and find the stairs leading up through the garden tiers. I don't stop until I reach the safety of my room and stand with my back pressed against the door, my chest rising and falling as I struggle to reclaim my breath.

One hand moves almost against my will, touching that place on my cheek his knuckle so gently grazed. It still feels warm somehow.

20

The next day passes in a blur. Worn out from the night before, I remain in bed a long while, sleeping and sometimes drifting into a half-wakeful, dozing state.

Several times I open my eyes and look across the room to the dress displayed on its mold. A little smile twitches the corner of my mouth, and I quickly turn and bury my face in my pillow, drifting back to sleep.

Late in the morning, Ellie bullies me out of bed and into the bath. I linger there longer than usual as well, until the bubbles have all reduced to scummy suds, and even the little glowing orbs have lost interest in me and rest at the bottom of the pool. Still I sit, trailing my fingers in the water. I close my eyes and hear again the sweet songs of pipes and the pulse of drums rolling in my gut.

I feel again the sensation of strong hands on my waist, lifting me in the air so high I might have spread my arms and flown away into the dark sky . . .

Ellie's burbling voice brings me round again. Flushing, I look up at that green face and the irritable, bobbing antennae. "Sorry, Ellie," I say, climbing out of the water and allowing the nymph to pat me down with soft towels. "I don't know what's gotten into me today."

I drift between malaise and dreamy euphoria throughout the afternoon, eating little despite Ellie's stern chortles. The goblin men try to entertain me with new acrobatic feats, but I hardly see them and leave the table in the courtyard with scarcely a word of thanks or appreciation. The goblins mutter behind me, but I hurry on my way without bothering to apologize, without trying to explain myself.

Really, what is there to explain?

I make my way back down the corridor of stained-glass windows, bypassing my room and continuing on to the garden. It looks so different by daylight, beautiful but no longer brimming with dangerous enchantment. Though I strain my ears, I can detect not even the faintest echo of the music that so thrilled me last night.

Venturing down the tiers, I proceed along the edge of the reflecting pool, beneath the shade of the flowering trees. Though my eyes dart at each shadow, I catch no glimpse of a phantomlike silhouette.

Probably just as well. I have things to consider, thoughts to mull over. Best not to be distracted.

When I arrive at the fountain, sunlight glints off the golden limbs and heads and horns, the glare too bright, too dazzling for my eyes to rest on for more than momentary glances. The air is uncomfortably warm under that direct heat, but I sit on the edge of the basin and dip my hand in the water, which is deliciously cool.

After a while, I look up. Here on the shadowed side of the fountain, the golden figures aren't too bright for my eye, and I peer at them closely. Particularly those horned devils with their forked tongues and clawed hands.

The little thrill that had nestled in my gut all morning turns to a coil of dread.

Ducking my head, I bend over the basin, cupping cool water to my mouth. I pause with my hand still upraised, touching my lips with damp fingers.

"I must give you my name before I may kiss you thrice. And then I must wait until you ask me to kiss you a fourth time."

Can I do it?

Last night, I'd almost believed I could.

No. No, that wasn't true.

Last night I'd *wanted* to. The temptation was intense, intensified still more by the delicious flow of *qeiese* in my veins. I'd wanted to ask right then and there, while the moon's face was hidden by the clouds and the echoes of the dancing music still swelled in the air around us.

But it wouldn't be just one kiss. I'm not a fool. If I ask for the fourth kiss, I'm asking for . . . everything. Asking for the marriage to be made true. Asking for my bridegroom to take me as his bride.

My gaze flicks up to the horned men on the fountain and away again.

It would break the curse. I'm almost sure of it.

And when it's over . . . when the fourth kiss and all the kisses that follow come to an end . . . what then? Having gotten what he wants from me, will he do as he promised and deliver me to my father's doorstep?

Is that what I want?

"Of course it is." I give my head a fierce shake and stand abruptly, backing away from the fountain and wiping my wet hand on my skirts. "Of course you want to go home. That's all you want. And the sooner you do, the better. The better for Brielle. The better for him. The better for . . . for you . . ."

My brow furrowed, I turn away from the fountain and its golden figures, making my way back through the garden and into the safety of my rooms. Ellie is there, straightening and tidying, but takes one look at my face and, with a polite trill of burbles, bows out. Feeling a little too hot and sweaty after my walk, I sit in my chair before the empty fireplace, glaring at nothing in particular.

Then I blink and sit up a little straighter.

My gaze has been unconsciously fixed on the empty seat across from mine. The seat where, every night, a dark, featureless shadow takes his ease.

Twilight comes at last, dimming the world. I don't venture out for dinner, and Ellie does not come to fetch me. Eventually I rise and return to the bathing room, taking my time over a second bath to wash away the heat and sweat from the garden. When I climb out of the water, I don't immediately don my regular work gown but sit a little while wrapped in a towel, combing my hair.

Then, my jaw set, I return to the bedchamber, march to the clothing chest, and throw back the lid. My fingers rummage down inside until they touch something at the bottom. With a tug, I pull out the seamless white garment that had been left for me on my very first night in Orican. Even after several weeks crushed at the bottom of the chest, it is unwrinkled and lovely.

My heart beating fast, I drop my towel and slide my arms into the garment. It has no laces or buckles or buttons. It simply wraps in the front, crossing in a deep V over my breast, and ties on the opposite hip. It's deliciously soft and delicate.

When I take a step, the front splits, exposing much of my leg.

I stop short, heat rising in my face. I pull in both lips, biting down hard.

Then, straightening my shoulders and taking smaller steps, I return to my chair by the fire and perch on its edge, taking care that the silky dress doesn't open or expose too much. After all, I've made no decision. Not yet.

The room darkens. Twilight gives way to night. I call up the moonfire on my hearth, but only a little blaze. Just enough to glow on the whiteness of my gown.

I feel very . . . visible. The moment he steps through the door, he can't help but see me, see what I wear.

Maybe I ought to get up and change. Now, before it's too late.

I turn in my seat, looking back across the room. My work dress lies atop the chest. But what if he enters the room while I'm still slipping out of this garment? No, better to hold very still. Make no promises or decisions.

After all, it was just a dance. That's all. And I was more than a little tipsy, and the music had gone to my head, and the moonlight had dazzled my brain, and when all those elements are removed, what's left? Little enough. A dance, nothing more.

The fire burns down on the hearth. My eyes grow heavy. I adjust slightly, leaning back in my seat, and watch the fire flicker. My ears prick for the sound of the door opening. My fingers run along the soft folds of the white gown, and I idly wonder if I could learn the trick of creating a garment without seams. Maybe it's magic . . . maybe it's . . . maybe . . .

With a gasp, I open my eyes and sit upright. The fire is out. Pale sunlight pours through my stained-glass window, casting colored shapes on the floor. I blink blearily and rub my sore neck, then press a hand to the small of my aching back. Seven gods, did I fall asleep in the chair?

Then I look down and catch my breath. Gods above, what am I *wearing?*

Oh. That's right.

Heat flushes in my cheeks. My gaze flicks to the empty seat

across from me. Still empty.

But that's just as well. Isn't it? I wasn't fully myself last night. Maybe the *qeiese* was still working its way through my system, making me reckless. So yes, it's just as well that he didn't come last night, didn't find me in this revealing garment. Just as well I'd not faced the moment of choice that I'm totally unprepared to make.

Just as well.

Yes.

I stand, rolling my stiff neck and shoulders. Time to get out of this white gown and hide it back in the chest before Ellie finds me in it. She reports to her master every night. I can't have her reporting things that simply aren't worth mentioning.

I take one step toward the chest where my work gown waits, then pause. Frowning slightly, I turn to the little table covered with odds and ends from my sewing projects, thread and thimbles and needles and trimmings, all the regular detritus of a seamstress's trade. In its center sits something that wasn't there before. Something I didn't put there. A black box. Unadorned save for a simple gold latch.

How did it get here? Did Ellie slip in while I slept? Or had . . . had . . . No, it couldn't have been Lord Dymaris. Surely I'd have noticed if he entered my room. Something in the air would have awakened me.

Or maybe he came, saw me in this white gown. And left again. Without a word.

My lips pressed into a hard line, I pluck the box from the table and almost rebelliously undo the latch and toss back the lid. Inside, on a plush red cushion, lies a necklace. A gold necklace hung with seven oval charms.

"What in the worlds?" I set the box down and lift the necklace free, holding the charms close to my face. An image is etched into the surface of each one: sun, moon, stars. Those I recognize well enough. Another looks like drops of rain, another a tongue of flame. Another just seems to be whirling lines. A wind, perhaps?

The charm in the center has no mark. Its surface is perfectly smooth.

Is this another gift? But . . . why? Lord Dymaris knows how little I care for jewelry. Or had he caught sight of the silver combs in my hair on Glorandal Night and believed I'd had a change of heart? Even so, this is an odd, simple piece compared to the glittering gems in elaborate settings now stashed inside my chest.

The light from the window catches on the charms. I tilt my head, noticing something I'd not seen at first glance. Each of the charms has what looks like a seam running around its circumference. Are they lockets?

A little fumbling, and I manage to get the first one—the one with the whirling decorative lines—to spring open. Instantly, something bursts in my face and whirls around my head. With a cry of surprise, I leap back, dropping the locket as my hair is dragged straight up in a long coil. The something rises until it hits the ceiling, then darts across the room, bouncing off the mirror, making it rock on its stand. It spins around the pink gown to the dress mold, and the skirt flares and flutters.

Hardly thinking what I'm doing, I lunge across the room and grab at invisible nothing. My hand closes around something solid, graspable. For a moment I stand in dumb shock, my mouth hanging open.

"Wind." The word whispers from my lips. "I-I'm holding onto *wind!*"

It's as soft as newly carded flax and so fine my eye can scarcely discern it. Though it seemed large and gusting before, it's now a mere flickering breath that wafts and moves as though not entirely inclined to escape but wanting to put on a show of rebellion, nonetheless.

Fabric woven of wind.

Impossible.

And so incredibly beautiful.

A smile breaks across my face, driving out all my embarrassment, all the inexplicable unhappiness I felt upon waking in this empty room. My mind churns with new thoughts, new ideas. When has a mortal seamstress ever had opportunity to hold such a wonder?

Somehow—I can't even begin to describe how—I *fold* the wind, making it smaller and smaller. It yields to my touch until I've got it small enough to fit neatly back inside the locket. The gold clasp shuts with a satisfying click.

I stare at it. Then at the six other lockets. Do they also contain fabrics? Threads spun of starlight and moonlight and flames, woven together into the finest, most incredible textiles?

Can I, a human armed only with needle and thread, actually

make something of them?

My smile grows. I feel it, foolish and unstoppable, covering my whole face. Maybe I'm wrong to indulge in such delight. Maybe I'm wrong to succumb so easily to fae enticements. I can't help it.

In a small, bitter, far back corner of my heart, a part I hardly dare admit even exists, I acknowledge the truth: I don't want to go home. Not yet. Just . . . not yet.

21

After donning my work gown—and stashing the white garment back in the bottom of my chest like a dirty secret—I spend the morning opening each locket by turn and examining its contents. The only one I shy away from is the locket with the flame emblem. That one I might save until I have a bit more experience with magical fabrics.

The others are delightful, however. Cloth of twinkling starlight, more brilliant than diamonds. Cloth of sunshine more dazzling than gold. The water droplet locket proves to hold a cloth of fine mist that settles around me, damp and close, obscuring the walls of my room entirely from view. It leaves dew drops behind on everything even after I've folded and stashed it away.

The final locket, the one with no marking emblem, is the most interesting of all. When I first peer inside it seems . . . empty. Then I happen to spy an extra shadow lying on the floor beside mine, a shapeless lump like a pile of rumpled cloth fallen unheeded.

"Shadow," I whisper, reaching and picking it up. It's a little rough against my fingertips, the warp and weft quite dense. Interesting. I drape it around my shoulders, and my eyes widen with surprise.

Curious, I get up from my seat, approach the mirror . . . and give a startled cry. Only my disembodied head is visible in the glass. I shrug out of the cloth and am obliged to wait for my heart to stop racing before I have the courage to pick it up and stuff it back into its locket.

The rest of the day I spend with chalk in hand, sketching ideas on the wall of my room. Ellie enters several times, bearing food and scolding when I eat only a few mouthfuls. But she seems to recognize that her human charge is once more lost to the enthrallment of creative inspiration. After a few futile burbles, she gives up and leaves me be.

By dusk, I collapse in my seat by the fire, my fingers white with chalk, my head spinning. Designing a dress for the pink petal fabric was simplicity itself in comparison to this task. Nothing in my training or experience has prepared me to work with fabrics of this kind. How does one make a garment out of wind? And what sort of garment would be suited to wind anyway?

Darkness closes in. Night falls.

Eventually the storm in my brain fades, replaced by that strange, fever-like heat beneath my skin that plagued me last night. Lord

Dymaris will come soon. Surely he will. I look down at my work gown, then cast a glance across the room to the chest.

No. No, I won't change into the white gown. Not tonight.

Shaking my head, I settle back into my chair, gripping the arms hard. I won't give in to the wildness brought on by Glorandal Night. I will simply talk to my bridegroom. Thank him for his handsome gifts. Maybe ask him a few questions, learn what manner of garments the fae usually make out of wind and mist and starlight. Keep the conversation easy and natural with no reference to that dance, no reference to that moment when the music stopped, when I stumbled, when my cheek pressed against his chest.

When I felt his heartbeat surging.

There's no need to talk about such things.

I wait until the fire burns down to nothing. Then I wait a while longer.

At last I remove my outer gown and climb alone into my enormous bed. I lie in the darkness a long while, my eyes open, while visions of shadows seem to dance in my head.

"When will Lord Dymaris return?"

I sit in my usual place by the empty hearth, my work paused in my lap. Even while resting, my fingers must keep a tight grip on the wind fabric, which pulls and struggles, taking every opportunity to escape. I've managed to bind it with a bit of silver thread, my stitches a bit more erratic than my professional pride likes. Getting used to sewing a wind will take some practice.

I look up from my stitching to where Ellie stands in the bathroom doorway, her arms full of empty bottles and discarded towels. The green woman's antennae waft, and her large black eyes blink slowly at me.

"Lord Dymaris," I repeat. "Your master? Does he often go away like this?"

It's been more than a week now. More than a week since that heady dance in the gardens on Glorandal Night. And not once has the shadowy figure of my bridegroom paid me a call. I've almost stopped looking for him. I can recall only one other time that he left for this long, soon after my arrival in Orican. Otherwise, he has been faithful in his nightly visits.

It's not as though I truly *miss* him, of course. Now that I've had time to let the enchantment of Glorandal fade from my blood, I know better than to give such feelings any credit. They stem from nothing more than a temporary madness.

Still, it does seem rather . . . odd. Odd that he would simply disappear like this. With no word of explanation, with no hint of when I might expect to see him again.

Ellie tilts her head, blinks again, then babbles something in her lilting language. Her antennae wave in such a way as to imply a shrug, and she saunters from the room, still burbling. It sounds like a string of complaints, but beyond that I have no guesses. Maybe she doesn't care for her master's mysterious doings either.

My mouth pursing in an irritable frown, I turn back to my sewing. The wind struggles, and several of my stitches loosen, the seam threatening to tear apart. "Wretched thing," I mutter, glad to have an outlet for my frustration. "Hold still, why don't you? It's not as though it hurts! I've almost got a—"

I stop.

My head slowly rises, my work dropping into my lap.

What is that sound?

The wind gives a gusting burst, reclaiming my attention. Hastily, I lay the bundle, needle and all, on my side table and pin it under a heavy polished weight that Birgabog brought me specifically for this purpose. Then I stand, my head tilted, listening closely.

There it is again. Distant. More like a feeling than a sound. A rumbling in the floor, through the walls.

"Ellie?" I call out. "Ellie, do you hear that?"

No answering burble comes. Just a long silence.

Then once again. A vibration. An echo.

It feels strangely familiar.

I hurry to my door and peer out into the corridor of windows. All is still, the colored glass bright with sunlight streaming through. Frowning, I hasten down the corridor out to the courtyard. There I feel the vibration again, stronger this time. And accompanied by a faint but distinct sound.

Boom. Boom. Boom.

Three times, sharp and crisp. Then another pause.

Then three times again, the same sound.

Boom. Boom. Boom.

"Is . . . someone knocking on the front door?" I turn in place, looking up and down the courtyard for some sign of goblins or nymphs. "Does anyone hear that?" My voice echoes along the colonnades and up to the empty windows above.

No one answers.

Boom. Boom. Boom.

I haven't ventured to that huge entrance hall since I found it, the day after finishing the petal gown. But my feet seem to remember the way, and I dart swiftly across the courtyard, through the series of spacious, elegant rooms, and finally come within sight of those huge double doors. For a moment I stand looking at them, my brow puckered with uncertainty.

Boom. Boom. Boom.

Yes. Someone—something—is out there. Knocking.

I swallow. It can't be wise to open the door. Who can say what stands on the other side? Some monster crawled from the hidden depths of Whispering Wood, no doubt. I should turn right around, return to my room, shut the door, and wait for whoever or whatever it is to go about their business.

Then again, what if it's someone lost in the wood? Someone seeking shelter from the terrors and shadows, who, spying a break in the trees, spying a house ahead, came rushing to this doorstep hoping for aid?

What if it's . . .

"Brielle?" I whisper.

Now the idea has entered my head, I can't dislodge it.

This doesn't mean I'm going to be stupid, however. I set my jaw, curl my hands tightly in the folds of my skirts, and march to the door. Standing with my ear against it, I strain to discern something about whatever or whoever stands on the far side.

Boom. Boom. Boom.

I stagger back. That knock seemed to land directly where my ear rested. Drawing a steadying breath, I call, "Who's there?"

After a pause: "I am not in the habit of giving my name to any who ask. I stand on the threshold of my friends. They should know me within."

The voice speaking is a woman's, yet cold and deep. Utterly imperious. The sound reverberates into my very bones, making me quake with my own unworthiness. Such a voice is not meant to be questioned; such a voice is meant to be obeyed.

I glimpse my hand reaching for the door latch. With an effort of will, I drag it back and clasp both hands tightly behind my back. "What do you want?" I inquire, hoping my voice doesn't sound as thin and nervous through the door as it does in my own ears.

Another pause lasts a little longer than the first. Something about that silence distinctly emanates indignation. Finally, the voice says, "Who are you to question me thus? My Family"—the word is spoken as though it is in itself a name—"has never been barred access by the Lords of Orican!"

I step back, my brow furrowing. Something about that voice is not right, something I can't name. It feels as though it's trying to get inside my head. Do the words hold magic? Insidious, ensorcelling magic?

"I'm sorry." I speak clearly, though my voice trembles despite my best efforts. "The master of the house is not home at present. I mean no offense, but I cannot open his door to just anyone."

This time, the silence on the other side feels strangely contemplative. Then the voice speaks again: "And are you Lord Dymaris's new young bride?"

I catch a quick, startled breath. But why should I be surprised? While my experiences since passing through Whispering Wood have been limited to Orican, Lord Dymaris must have a life and connections reaching far beyond the boundaries of this house. Word of his marriage was bound to get about eventually.

I suddenly feel . . . small. Very small. And trapped. Recently the boundaries of this strange new world have seemed less confining. In fact, I've enjoyed a measure of liberty since coming here that would have been impossible to imagine while living under Father's roof.

But the truth remains: I'm a prisoner. Held against my will by my so-called husband.

I stare at the door, which is richly paneled with ornate gold moldings in the shape of blooming lilies and birds. My mind spins, but I can't think of anything to say.

"Your silence is answer enough," the voice on the far side muses. "I heard rumors of you. I thought perhaps you might be lonely out here by yourself, so I came to pay my respects and wish you well.

Do open the door and let me in! We can sit a while and get to know one another."

I still don't answer. My hand seems to move of its own volition toward the huge door latch.

Wait! No, this is not what I want to do. Imperious voice notwithstanding, the person on the other side of that door could be anyone or anything! I'm no fool. I step back and put my hands behind my back, clasping them tight.

"Perhaps you have questions about your lordly husband." Even through the door, it's a rich voice, deep as a red wine. "I have known dear Dymaris for many a long age now. I could tell you such tales! Please, my dear, allow me to shed some light on your curiosity."

Once more, I find myself strongly inclined to open the door. I squeeze my hands tighter, refusing to surrender to the impulse. My mouth opens, but every word that springs to my lips seems suddenly perilous, as though the mere speaking of them will doom me. As though I'll give away something I can't take back.

"You aren't the first, you know," the voice continues. "Gods above, how many of his brides I have visited over the cycle turnings!"

"What?" The question escapes my lips in a whisper, surely too faint to hear. But I clap a hand over my mouth, my eyes widening.

"Oh yes, Dymaris likes his mortal playthings. A pretty face, a lusty form . . . he has his fill of them, believe me!" The voice ceases to pretend at pleasantry now, having acquired a knifelike edge. "Three kisses he gives, and they try to resist, but never once has he failed to break down their defenses. When at last they beg him for their fourth kiss, then . . . ah! Then! One hears such tales, you know."

I try to lick my dry lips, but my tongue has gone wooden and heavy.

"I take it you have not yet requested your fourth kiss," the voice continues relentlessly. "A stalwart maid to the last! I've never known him to exercise such patience. That's right, little bride! Hold onto that maidenly virtue of yours while you can! For when you succumb, then you shall learn the truth of your bridegroom. The dark truth so few dare know."

I stare at the door. In the center of the panel is a molding of flowers, but it seems to shift, morph, transform into a weird, warped, mask-like visage, with narrow, cunning eyes and a cruel mouth. And the voice on the other side of the door flows through that image.

"He likes soft flesh. Soft, mortal flesh. His kind, they are neither giving nor gentle lovers. They are predators, taking what they will, savage and brutal. But!" The voice rises to a bright laugh that sends shudders coursing down my spine. "But perhaps the gifts he has promised you make it all worthwhile! What is a little pain and a little shame in exchange for such bright, sparkling trinkets?"

I take one step back, then another. That laugh rings in my ears, brilliant and false and cold as diamonds of ice. My heart beats wildly, and when the knocking on the door resumes, I half fear it will burst open, that the ugly mask of molding will be replaced by a still more terrifying, living face.

"Go away," I say. My mouth silently shapes the words, but I

cannot hear myself above the ringing of that laughter. Then I fling myself at the door, pound it hard with both fists, and scream as loud as I can, "Go AWAY!"

The laughter stops. So suddenly, so completely, it jars my senses. I reel as though I've been struck and sink to my knees, one shoulder pressed against the door. My eyes stare and my mouth gapes open as I struggle to draw a full breath.

Slowly my whirling head clears. Did I imagine it? That voice, those poisonous words? Was it a dream conjured by my own not so deeply suppressed fears?

The anxieties I feel at the prospect of a wedding night with a bridegroom who may be a monster . . .

I pull away from the door and look up. That molding in the center is a flower, a gracious lily with unfurled petals and feathery stamens, wrought in plaster and covered in brilliant gold leaf. Now that I look at it again, I'm not sure how I ever thought it was a face.

Rising and rubbing my arms, I back away from the double doors. Even though the voice on the other side has vanished, even though the knocking has ceased, I don't like turning my back to it. I cross the expanse of the hall backwards until I finally can slip sideways into another room.

Then I turn and run.

22

My feet slapping on the marbled floor, I flee through the gracious rooms with their pillared arches and silk-upholstered loungers. I take a turn, stop, and turn another way. How do I get back to the courtyard? I should stop. I should get my bearings . . . but the instinct for flight takes over, and I run again.

I sense movement all around me.

Flickers of shadows.

The faint echo of voices.

I turn my head sharply. Are those figures I see fleeing across the great room? Is that . . . is that a woman cradling a small child to her breast, a man with his arms protectively around her? The image is brief, almost instantaneous, but in that instant I could swear their heads are crowned with tall, spiraling horns.

They're gone in a single flash of my eyelashes. A shadow flits across the floor and away.

I turn, redouble my speed, and charge into another set of rooms. These are a little less spacious, a little less fine. Sunlight pours through tall windows, but a thick cloud passes overhead, casting the world into deep gloom.

More shadows crowd the edges of my vision, just beyond the line of perception yet terribly present. A snarl of racing legs, thrashing arms, and widespread beating wings. More screams echo in the silence inside my head. I press my hands over my ears, but still the echoes resound—men, women, and children screaming, underscored by inhuman roars. And the hideous, gut-wrenching sound of weapons hacking into flesh.

I stop, turning in place. My eyes swivel, trying to see what I cannot see. No matter how quickly I turn, I cannot catch a direct view. Nothing more than flashes. I'm screaming. I realize it and stuff my hands hard against my mouth, trying to stifle the sound.

Ducking my head, I run again, taking the first turn I come to. The courtyard appears before me, and for a moment my heart lifts with relief.

The next moment it jolts with fresh terror. Shadows fill the whole of that open space. Wild, manic shadows in attitudes of desperation and despair. Revulsion and heartbreak roll over me in waves.

Gathering my skirts, I run through the shadows, trying to reach the corridor on the far side leading back to my rooms. Darkness swarms in around me, closer and closer. I feel the pressure of bodies, feel the stink of fear.

My vision tunnels, and I scream again, the breath crushed from my lungs: *"Erolas!"*

I wake with a gasp.

I'm lying in my bed. Staring up at the rafters of the ceiling.

My heart thuds wildly in my breast, but I draw a long breath and let it out slowly, closing my eyes again for a moment. It was a dream. Just a dream—

"Vali! Are you awake?"

I sit up, my weight sagging deep into the mattress of my loose rope-frame bed. Where am I? Where . . .? There's my little tallow candle in its clay stand, burned down to a waxy stub. There's my wooden comb where I left it on my side table. There's my work gown, my cap, my shoes, waiting for the day's service.

Am I . . . is this . . .?

Home.

"Vali! Hurry! We'll be late!"

I open my mouth, try to speak. *I'm coming, Brielle!* The words form on my tongue but won't emerge no matter how I struggle.

Frowning, I push back my covers and slide my legs out over the edge of the bed. Wait . . . wait, what is this? What am I wearing? This isn't my simple muslin shift. My body is draped in robes of elaborate silk sewn with twinkling jewels. Bracelets of gold, dense with gems, encase my arms from wrist to elbow, and my neck is heavy with the weight of necklaces. I reach up to tug at them, to try to get them off, but they tighten at my touch.

"Vali! Vali, where are you? Vali, I need you! Please, Vali!"

I'm here! I'm here! Brielle! I try again to cry out the words, but the necklaces have me in a stranglehold, choking away my breath, my life. I collapse back on my pillows, struggling to pull them free. *Brielle! I'm here!*

My vision goes dark.

But in the darkness . . . warmth.

A scent like spices and blooming night jasmine fills my nostrils. A sense of strength, of power encircling me. Holding me. Caring for me. I lean into that sense, my hand unconsciously reaching up to catch hold and cling. My striving, terrified soul relaxes, and the fear eases away.

"Erolas," I whisper.

"I'm here, Valera. I'm here."

I open my eyes.

A blue glow suffuses the room, gleaming off the white fur of my coverlet, glinting on the shining specks in the marbled stone of my bed. I turn my head slightly and see the dress mold in the corner, still draped in the lovely pink gown from Glorandal Night.

I turn my head the other way. An indistinct figure sits in the chair just beyond the edge of the moonfire light. His back is to me.

I blink. My mind feels dull, foggy. What happened? My memories are confused, full of shadows. Did he find me lost in the labyrinthine halls and rooms of Orican? Did I faint?

Did he carry me here?

I look down, suddenly uneasy. I'm lying on top of the furs, still wearing my worn old work dress. No elaborate silks or twinkling jewels, no bracelets like manacles clutching my forearms. For a moment I close my eyes and hear Brielle's voice desperately calling for me. It seemed so real. And so close. Just on the other side of my door.

But it was only a dream.

Drawing a deep breath, I sit up and look across the room. The shadow by the hearth has shifted, and I think perhaps he's looking back at me, though I can't say for sure. I bite my dry lips, trying to moisten them, then slide out of the bed. My bare feet land on the floor with a soft thud. My arms wrap around my middle, and I stand for a few breaths, uncertain what to do.

Then I cross the space and take my seat in my usual chair across from my bridegroom.

"M'lord," I say softly.

"M'lady," he replies.

It's the first time I've heard his voice since Glorandal. My heart gives a traitorous shiver.

We sit a little while in silence. Finally, I pull myself up straighter and look across at him. "I didn't let anyone through the door while you were gone." I don't know why it's important, but somehow I know it is.

"I know. And I thank you."

Memories of those fleeing shadows play before my mind's eye. "Are . . . are your people all right?"

"For the present."

"You went away to help them?"

"Yes."

"What happened to them?"

He doesn't answer. Of course not. The curse prevents him.

Grimacing, I look down at my hands in my lap. Suddenly all the speculations I've toyed with seem so foolish. Knowing a curse exists is one thing. Realizing how near and dangerous it is . . . that's entirely different.

And I'm meant to break it? To save him and those terrified people I'd sort of glimpsed in a half-dreaming state of panic? It's too much. Too much to ask of me. I'm not brave. I'm not a barbarian queen, skilled with a sword, ready to throw myself into the thickest fray. I'm no heroine of legend, quick-witted and cunning. I'm a seamstress—no, less than a seamstress. A stitch-girl. My fingers are callused from many pricks of the needle, and I know how to drape fabric to flattering advantage. How can I possibly help?

But Lord Dymaris hasn't said he needs a warrior or a heroine. He needs a wife.

Slowly I lift my gaze and peer into the darkness across from me.

Trying to see what cannot be seen. I feel his eyes study me as I study him. I ought to say something. What, though? My mind is muddled.

But my body is on fire.

A certainty grows inside me. But beneath that certainty lurks fear.

"Hold onto that virtue of yours while you can. For when you succumb, then you will learn the truth of your bridegroom, the dark truth so few dare know."

Can I believe the strange woman's warnings or not? How can I know for sure? How can I put my trust in this man or even in my own feelings? He kidnapped me. All the rest—the kindness, the courtesy, the attempts to please and delight me—what do they matter in the face of such a terrible act? He claims he has reasons, claims he has needs, but can I believe any of it? It might all be part of his game, his ploy to get me willingly into his bed.

For all I know, he really is the monster the stranger claimed.

And yet . . .

I stand suddenly. My knees tremble, and my gut roils with a sensation I cannot name. A terrifying and utterly intoxicating sensation.

Am I really going to do this? Do I have the courage?

"Erolas," I say quietly.

I feel him looking at me, feel the intensity of his focused gaze.

"Valera," he responds.

His voice is deep, rough, but I detect the faintest tremble. That invisible line of connection between us seems to spark until I can almost see it, bright as a burning filament.

"May I . . ." I duck my head, my fingers curling into fists. Somehow I must summon the courage to speak, must find the way to force the words across my lips. "May I touch you?"

He doesn't answer for such a long time, I fear I will fall into the silence and drown. The moonfire snaps on the hearth, its flames burning low. The shadows around us seem to deepen, darken, until I am all but blind.

Finally, he says, "Yes."

I move my feet, one after the other, approaching his chair. I can see no more than a dim outline of his form. He's tall even when seated, his head level with my shoulder. I think he sits with his hands gripping the arms of his chair, his face upturned to me. By that dim light, I can just discern the faint outline of horns.

I reach for those first. Best to know at once, best to acknowledge the reality of who and what my bridegroom is. Shivering, I stretch out my hand until my fingers brush a cool, coiled surface, then trail up a curve to a wickedly sharp point, sharp enough to make me flinch away.

He holds perfectly still. Did I hear his breath hitch? It's difficult to tell through the throb of my own pulse in my ears.

Setting my jaw, I extend my hand again. This time I touch the top of his head and feel soft, thick hair. When I run my fingers through it, I find it very long, even longer than my hair, smooth as silk and faintly oiled and scented. Here then is the source of that delicious, spicy perfume I've unconsciously associated with him.

I let my fingers trail down, running gently across a broad

forehead, a stern browbone. Is he frowning? Or is his brow naturally puckered like this? Impossible to say.

I lift my other hand to join the first in exploration, touching the planes of his face, the sharp cheekbones, the smooth cheeks. I find his ears and feel how they taper to points.

His breath catches—a short, shuddering gasp.

I withdraw my hands. My touch has excited something in him. The invisible connection between us seems to tense, to twist, as though drawing me nearer. But I'm not ready for that yet.

Neither am I ready to back down, however. Now that I'm here in this moment, I'm not eager to retreat. Without a word, I reach for his face again, feeling along the line of his jaw. Hard muscles flex under my fingertips, and my senses quicken with the increasingly rapid inhale and exhale of his breath.

My hands move downward along his throat, feel him swallow beneath my touch. I come to his shoulders. Here I find fabric— light and loose, edged with some sort of gold braid. But it isn't fastened across the front, and I easily slip my fingers beneath to the smooth skin of his shoulders. Very wide shoulders, their muscles tight with tension.

I rest my hands there for a few moments, standing before him, gazing into the shadow where his face must be, searching for some glint of eyes. But there is only impenetrable shadow.

Blood humming in my veins, I move my hands along his shoulders, pushing back the fabric of his garment. My palms slide down a broad, muscled chest. For an instant, I can feel a heartbeat throbbing under my touch.

A growl rumbles in the darkness.

The next moment he's standing, looming over me with barely an inch of space between us. I start and would leap back, but huge, long-fingered hands grip my wrists tightly.

"Seven gods, Valera!" his voice rasps, his unseen face so close to mine that his breath tickles my ear. "I'm not made of stone!"

I stand rigid, every sense, every nerve in my body sparking with fire. Heat rushes and roars through my veins, making my head light and my knees tremble, ready to buckle and fall against him. Fall into his eager, hungry embrace.

"Please." The word is soft but edged with need so intense it sends a shiver to my core. "May I kiss you?"

My lips part. An answer hovers on the edge of my tongue, just waiting to be spoken.

But those insidious words whisper in the back of my head: *"Then you shall learn the truth of your bridegroom, the dark truth so few dare know."*

I tug lightly at my right hand. He immediately lets go, and I reach for his face. His breath comes hard and fast against my fingertips as I rest them softly against his mouth. I feel full, sensual lips. Lips I have thrice felt against my skin, feather-light and yet burning with promise. Lips I long to press my own against, to claim forever.

Then I search with one finger . . . and brush the edge of a sharp, pointed tooth.

With a gasp, I retract my hand, my whole body jolting with a sudden rush of fear. My heart races, surging with desire and terror in equal measures. I can still hear his ragged breathing in the darkness, can feel his eyes watching me, ravenous with need, with hope.

But I can't do it. I can't.

I want to. Oh, gods forgive me, how I want to! My body aches with need akin to his, and my heart pulls at that connecting thread, longing to draw him close to me, to let our souls and bodies join. It would be so easy to give in.

And then what?

Will I let my mortal flesh be devoured by this beast? This unseen monster, my kidnapper and prison-keeper? Will he tear into me with tooth and claw, sating his appetite on my maidenhood?

And when he has what he wants—when the curse is broken, or his desires fulfilled—will he leave me spent and broken on my father's doorstep? Returned to my own world but never fully able to return. A shade of my former self, forever changed by the darkness lurking beyond the edge of Whispering Wood.

I don't want to believe it. I don't want to think such thoughts about him.

Yet how can I afford not to? The only power I have here is the power to say no. I must hold onto that power while I can.

I step back. For a moment—only a moment—he maintains his grip on my left wrist, his fingers tightening. But at the least tug, he relents, and I retreat several paces away from him, back into the pool of moonfire light. Wrapping my arms around my middle, I lower my head and stare down at my bare feet.

"Goodnight, m'lord," I say, my voice soft but clear in that painful silence.

At first he does not answer. Though I don't look up, I feel the bulk of his body shift, hear the rustle of robes as though he's taking a step toward me. But he stops himself.

The next moment he withdraws deeper into the shadows, away from the firelight. I wait for him to speak his usual "Goodnight, m'lady." My whole soul cries out, longing for him to give me that small grace, an indication that I have not irrevocably damaged the tentative bridges we've been building between us.

But he is silent as he turns to the door. I hear nothing, not even a breath, only the sound of his robes dragging behind him. Then he speaks a word, and the door opens. I drink in the sight of his silhouette, discernible by the faint light streaming through the stained-glass windows in the passage beyond.

"I have a confession," he says.

I blink in surprise. It's not what I expected him to say. My chest tightens, my heart constricting painfully in my breast in fear of . . . I know not what. "A confession?" I echo softly.

He turns. I see his two great horns clearly above the murky nothing of his face.

"It's about your sister."

The whole room pitches around me. I grab hold of the back of my chair. My mouth opens, desperate to speak, desperate to demand what he means. But my throat has closed too tight to let even a breath through.

"My servant returned to me after . . . after the events that took place in Orican earlier today. Something has happened. He couldn't say what, only that the girl—Brielle—threw him off her track. She's gone deeper into Wanfriel, down paths he does not know. He could not follow her."

Brielle.

My mind whirls in a storm bursting with such force, such pain, I cannot remain on my feet. My knees buckle, and though I try to sink into the chair, I miss and instead fall heavily to the floor. Darkness closes in at the edges of my vision, blocking out the moonfire light.

Suddenly he's there. Kneeling in front of me. His long fingers close around my shoulders, holding me upright. "Valera!" His voice is husky, rough with worry. "Valera, can you hear me?"

I shake my head. I don't know if I fainted or, if I did, for how long, but my senses are returning now. I push his arms away, shuddering at his touch, and lift my face to where his should be.

"You promised me," I whisper.

I can't see or feel anything. I can only hear his ragged breathing. "I promised to do everything within my power—"

"You promised me you'd keep her safe!"

"I swear, Valera, I would do anything to fulfill that promise. But she has grown crafty, and my servant has many times reported that she—"

"She is a *child!*" This time the words burst from my lips in a scream, harsh and grating. I want to hurt him. I want to lash out, to turn my own blunt nails into talons and rip his face open. "She is a child, a mere child! How could she possibly . . .? How could she . . .?" I can't even finish the thought. The violence erupting in me is so shocking, so horrifying.

And deep inside my head, a tiny voice whispers, *Is this how Father feels? Is this the depth to which heartbreak will drive a peaceful soul? Has this truly been inside me all along?*

I bury my face in my hands, shaking my head as though I can shake those thoughts away. Then something hard and cold knots in my breast. I drop my hands and look up at him again, at the shadow, the nothing that is my bridegroom.

"You would have kissed me. Knowing what you know." How ugly my voice sounds in my ears. Good. I pour on the venom. "You would have . . . you would have kissed me, taken me. Undressed and unmade me. Knowing all along that you've broken your promise."

"No, Valera!" He sounds desperate. He sounds weak. "I could never use you so! Can you not believe me?"

In that moment, I hate him.

"Then why did you not tell me?" I snarl. "Right away, before . . . before . . . You should have told me!"

"I know." There's a shifting in the shadows, a heavy sense in the air. He still kneels before me, and I think he's bowed his head. "Please, Valera. I would tell you all if I could . . . if the . . . if the terms of . . . I would tell you everything. I would tell you how many lives depend on . . . I would tell you what's at stake. I would tell you what is in my heart, if only—"

"Gods damn your heart!" The words burst from my lips, so much harsher even than I mean for them to be. Part of me, a larger part than I like to admit, regrets them at once, desperately wishes I could take them back. But I'm lost to my own rage, my own hurt, the agonizing spike of betrayal.

"Get out. Get out of my room, Erolas. Get away from me."

He hesitates. I fear—I hope—that he will resist. That he will try to offer an explanation I can't help but believe. I don't know what I want more in that moment: to be given a reason to renew my trust in him . . . or simply to hate him. To hate him as part of me has always believed I should hate him. The wicked fae lord, the otherworldly creature. My kidnapper.

He stands. He pulls the shadows around him, deeper than ever, an impenetrable cloak of night.

"Goodnight, m'lady," he says. His voice is stricken. Broken.

Then he's gone. Slipped through the door, which opens and shuts silently in his wake. And I'm left kneeling on the floor, unable to move, unable to think. Unable to do anything but breathe. Draw air through my nostrils. Hold it. Let it out again slowly. Waiting for my heartbeat to calm.

Then with a ragged, "Oh!" I sink my head into the seat of the chair. The warmth of moonfire light warms my back as I surrender to the flood of despair.

23

Three days later, I wake in the pinking dimness just before dawn and stare at the domed ceiling overhead.

Another day stretches before me—a day of solitude save for Ellie's burbling chatter and the antics of the goblin men. I cannot look forward to the evening, for I already know Lord Dymaris will not visit me.

Nor should he. I don't want to see him. Never again.

Or so I try to convince myself.

Heat crawls up into my face, and I press a hand to my cheek, my brow puckering. Conflicting thoughts and desires war inside my head. Has he gone away forever? Should I hope he has? Was I too harsh with him, unwilling to hear him as he tried to explain himself?

But there's nothing to explain. He broke his promise. Brielle got through into the deeps of Whispering Wood, taking a path not even his servant could follow. A child, a mere child, and she managed to give his servant the slip . . . unless that was a lie. But why would he lie about such a thing, knowing how I must react to the knowledge?

Part of me tries to reason that Lord Dymaris could simply have withheld the information from me. He could have let me continue believing that Brielle was safe and guarded. And in that belief, he may yet have broken down my guard and gotten what he wanted from me, his stubborn, difficult wife.

Instead, he'd risked everything by telling me the truth.

I shake my head viciously. Am I making excuses for him? Am I trying to justify his failure so that I can . . . what? Justify my own longings?

With an angry growl I sit up in bed, grab one of the many soft pillows, and pound it for all I'm worth. It gives gently beneath my fists, an unsatisfactory victim of my rage. But at least it's something. After I've smashed it into an odd, lumpy shape, I sit quietly, breathing in and out.

Maybe he's gone away forever. Maybe he's given up on wooing and winning me. What will that mean for the rest of my time here in Orican? Must I face the rest of my year-and-a-day term alone?

If so, good. I'm glad he's given up, glad he's accepted the truth that this marriage is no marriage at all. That no matter the requirements of his curse, no matter the images flashed before his eyes in the scrying pool, a wife cannot be *captured* and forced to comply to his will.

Not that he's ever forced anything.

"I'm not made of stone!"

I close my eyes. Once more I hear that impassioned voice rumbling in my memory. Something stirs in my gut, a faint reminder of the powerful sensations that had so nearly made me lose my head three nights ago.

"No." Tossing my abused pillow across the room, I push back my coverlet and swing my legs over the edge of the bed. For a moment I sit there gripping the blankets and mattress with white-knuckled fingers. I won't let my mind venture down those dangerous paths, won't let my imagination carry me back into that intoxicating darkness.

Lord Dymaris is gone. Possibly for good. Definitely for the better. And meanwhile Brielle is . . . Brielle might be . . .

I rise, dress, and move listlessly to my workstation, my chair and table near the fireplace. Over the last few days, I've been too distracted by nameless, formless fears for my sister to put much effort into my struggle with the cloth made of wind. Its edges waft gently around the weight anchoring it to the table. I can see the little seams of tiny, somewhat erratic stitches binding the various pieces of it together.

My lip curls as I look at it, my disinterest in the project almost painful. But, gods above! I can't bear to spend another day with my head in my hands, imagining how all the horrors of the fae wood might even now assault my little sister. No. Idle hands lead to idle thoughts, and I cannot bear to think *anything* right now.

With a growl in my throat, I push the heavy weight aside and capture the wind cloth before it flies away. Then I set to work with needle and thread, my fingers flashing in quick precision. After many false starts, I ultimately decided to make a simple garment of long straight seams with buttons up the front. Large flaps of drifting wind drape beneath the arms, forming sails of a sort. It's odd, I know—sails are meant to *catch* wind, not *be* wind. But it makes sense somehow in a non-rational but wholly inspirational part of my brain, so I follow the inspiration, and the resulting garment slowly takes shape in my hands.

Ellie enters with a breakfast tray and warbles something at me while I work. It sounds scolding, but I don't try to discern what's bothering the green nymph. It has something to do with Lord Dymaris, I'm sure. But my dealings with my husband—my captor—are none of her business.

She bustles around to no purpose for a while before finally leaving. I don't touch the breakfast tray. I simply have no appetite.

At last, after hours of stitching, adjusting, pinning, and more stitching, I pluck up my shears and snip a final thread. I hold up the garment to study the results of my labors.

It's difficult to see. The wind itself is invisible, but whatever binding magic transformed it into fabric glints faintly blue and pink and silver, revealing the warp and weft of the woven threads. Otherwise, only a row of silver buttons, which I pillaged from one of the ornate gowns in my collection, and my own stitches are visible.

It's an impossible garment. Yet somehow it holds together.

A small smile pulls at the corner of my mouth. I'm not happy, exactly. But I'm pleased. Pleased that the strange concept in my brain seems to have translated into reality. Pleased that I could make my mortal mind conceive and construct something so far beyond ordinary mortal comprehension.

If I must spend this portion of my life in isolated captivity, this is certainly an interesting way to fill the time.

Now, looking at the finished garment, I'm faced with a new set of questions: Will it work? And, of possibly greater importance: Is it safe to try?

"You've got nothing better to do," I mutter, rising from my workspace. The garment tries to escape, fluttering in my hands like a captured bird. I bundle it up tightly and tuck it under one arm, then duck from my room and down the corridor, out to the courtyard. There I stand a moment, off to the side of the huge banquet table, looking up. The surrounding buildings loom three stories high, in places higher still. But open sky arches overhead.

It beckons me. Enticingly.

Is it worth the risk? Maybe . . . but a girl can always take precautions.

"Birgabog?" I call.

Immediately, a long-nosed, bat-eared little figure wearing a pair of bright orange trousers around his neck like a scarf somersaults into view at my feet. The goblin pops upright, sweeps a bow, and places a gnarled hand against his protruding breastbone. "Birgabogagog!" he proclaims.

"Can you fetch me a length of rope? Something sturdy."

The goblin tilts his head to one side, giving me a narrow look, his sharp eyes swiveling from my face to the wind vest under my arm. Then he shrugs and bounds away.

While I wait, I walk the length of the table, studying both it and the pillars of the colonnades. By the time Birgabog returns with about fifteen feet of strong cord woven from some fibers I don't recognize, I've chosen my spot: the end of the table where the largest stone chair stands waiting for the presiding lord of the house to take his place. The chair must weigh at least four times as much as I do, and its elegantly arched arms provide a secure place to tie a rope. It will do.

Birgabog must have gossiped as he went about his errand. I become aware of many goblin eyes peering out at me from among the colonnades as I secure the cord first to the chair and then to a loop at the back of the vest, laced there for this purpose. Their scrutiny makes me nervous, and I almost snap and tell them to scatter. Then again, what I'm about to do is undoubtedly risky and probably foolish . . . so it might be wisest to have witnesses in case something goes wrong.

I shake out the vest and crane my neck to look up at the sky. It's only fifteen feet of rope. And I shouldn't even get that high. But something about that great expanse unnerves me, and I almost fold up the wispy garment and call off the whole experiment.

But what is the point of a vest made of wind if one doesn't actually intend to use it?

Donning the vest, I take care to fasten the row of silver buttons up the front from navel to collarbone. Then I loop the wrist flaps in place but fasten the belt strap tight around my waist, keeping the sails safely bunched under my arms. Any other cloth would be bulky if bundled and folded like that along my sides. But the wind cloth seems to simply . . . disappear. Indeed, when I look down at myself, I can see the buttons and my stitches at the arm and front panel seams. Otherwise, I seem to be wearing nothing but my regular old work dress.

Well, I've come this far. I might as well complete the experiment.

I climb onto the seat of the chair, aware of all those watching goblin eyes. I sneak a glance around just quick enough to see the tips of long ears vanish behind pillars. With a wry grimace, I peer up at the sky. This is it. After a last tug to make certain my rope is properly secured, I reach for the belt.

My hands freeze, not quite ready, not quite willing to do this dangerous, impossible thing.

"Come on, Valera," I whisper. "What do you have to lose?"

Setting my jaw, firming my stance, I pull the belt free and raise my arms. The sail flaps unfold on either side of me in a rush of wind, swelling, gathering, tossing my hair wildly around my face. I feel the power of it grow, and my heart shivers. But I've come too far to back down now.

I leap from the chair.

And I land hard, jarring the bones in my ankles, then stagger to my knees.

The wind around me drops to little more than a faint breeze, tickling at my skin. I close my eyes tight, growling in my throat, then stare down at my hands flattened on the stone pavement. Warring sensations of frustration and relief waft over me, neither quite able to outweigh the other.

But I'm not finished.

I get up and try to dust myself off—a reflex that proves almost comically futile in this instance. Then I study the courtyard, my eyes narrowing. I need a higher starting point. The tabletop is higher than the chair seat, but not by much. Still, if I jump and it doesn't work, I won't risk more than another bone-jarring.

But will playing it safe produce the results I want?

My gaze travels a little higher. To the roof of the colonnade on my left. A good ten feet high, at least. High enough? I felt the swelling wind around me, felt the power and force contained within my stitches. I'm sure—almost sure—it has the power to lift me if I can just get it to . . . to activate, somehow.

A jump from that rooftop wouldn't kill me. I might break a leg or two. But it wouldn't kill me.

"Birgabog!"

The goblin appears on the table, standing between two tall candlesticks. "Gogagog?" He raises his arm in a smart salute.

"Can you and your fellows get me"—I point to the colonnade

roof—"up there?"

The goblin swivels his head almost all the way around on his scrawny little neck. Then he whips his face forward again, a huge grin mounding the wrinkles beneath his eyes. "Birgabogagog!" he says with conviction.

The task involves a good twenty goblin men pushing and pulling, not to mention a certain amount of indignity. But soon enough, with a few squeaks and gasps along the way, I find myself scrambling up onto the top of the colonnade roof. It's only slightly slanted, but the tiles are rough under my hands and bare feet, and I must step with care to avoid the sharp edges.

I turn and face out over the courtyard. And am immediately struck with a wave of vertigo. Seven gods! The prospect of broken limbs seems much worse now that I'm up here! Maybe I've miscalculated. This seems an awful lot higher than ten feet. More like twenty, or twenty-four, or . . .

Hastily, I turn my head skyward. "You don't have to jump," I whisper. "You're experimenting. That's all. You don't have to jump."

I toss a quick glance over my shoulder at the goblin men, who've lined up along the rooftop behind me, grinning expectantly. "Would you gentlemen kindly hold the end of my rope?" I ask.

They leap to oblige. They feel strong, clutching the end of my tether. Their diminutive size is not an accurate indicator of their strength. Birgabog might be strong enough on his own to serve as my anchor.

I gaze out over the courtyard again. My stomach turns over, and

I quickly close my eyes. Then I tilt my chin upward and slowly peel open my eyelids.

A blue expanse dotted with drifting clouds beckons.

Now that I've come this far, how can I possibly back down?

I open my arms. The sail fabric spreads on either side of me, the wind gathering, swelling, growing. I close my eyes again and feel the power of it around me, neither fully tamed nor fully wild. I've never been sensitive to magic, but not even I can deny the enchantment flowing through the weave that binds strands of wind into cloth. And my own stitches hold it all in the shape I have determined. I feel . . .

I feel the pull of open air.

"One," I whisper. The word slips out and is lost in the rush of wind. "Two." My hair tosses in snarls around my face, but I shake it back, open my eyes, and stare up into the sky. "Three!"

I leap.

There's a moment—a pure, perfect, beautiful moment. A moment of weightlessness, of perfect suspension upon a mere thread of hope.

Followed by a moment of crushing, terrible weight dragging me down.

24

My hope switches from soaring to shattered in the eternity of a single half-instant. I'm falling, tumbling, bound to break into a thousand pieces. But then, with a gusting roar and a tumult of energy that steals the breath from my lungs, my body surges skyward, as though I've suddenly lost all mass and become light as a drifting dream. I tumble higher, utterly out of control, until the snap of the cord at my back jolts the breath out of me.

I twist, looking back down to the goblin men all piled on the end of the cord, holding fast.

And I see how far up I've toppled.

"Seven gods!" I cry, my arms jerking.

The sails flap on either side of my body, and the force of

wind around me shifts, lessens. I'm sinking again and sinking fast. Instinct alone makes me spread my arms wide as though to catch myself. The wind increases. The feeling of weightlessness returns. I manage to achieve a sort of balance, upright, legs kicking, arms stiff but stable at my sides. My heart pounds so fast, I fear it will burst.

But I'm doing it. I'm . . . *flying.*

A cheer rises from below, only just audible over the rush of wind. I look down and see the goblin men whooping, their ugly faces split with triumphant smiles. I breathe a nervous laugh and offer a little wave. My body tilts unnervingly at even this slight movement, but the goblins redouble their cheers. They raise their fists in the air, spin and holler, grab each other, and grin up at me.

While one by one, they drop the rope.

"Wait, *no!*" I cry.

I think I see Birgabog, foremost of the crew, look up. His orange scarf-trousers waft in the wind, and his eyes widen. He lunges for the rope as it rises . . . too late. He makes a tremendous leap, but his gnarled fingers bat uselessly at the end of the rope as it floats beyond his grasp.

I scream. But the wind steals my voice as I'm carried higher, arms and legs flailing, hair and skirts snapping about like flags in a hurricane. The windows of the buildings around me flash before my tumultuous vision, passing much too quickly.

The open sky looms hungrily above, waiting to devour me.

Just before I'm lost to crazed terror, a jolt of desperate reason passes through my brain. I have just enough wherewithal to pull my arms closer to my body. At once I feel the effect—the wind reduces. I'm still rising but not quite so rapidly.

I pull my arms closer and begin to fall. But when I open them again, just slightly, I level out. Heart pounding, head spinning, gut churning, I shake hair out of my face and dare to look around. I immediately wish I hadn't. My stomach plunges, and for a moment I fear my sanity will break from sheer fright.

I have floated as high as the tallest of Orican's many towers. Bobbing gently in the air, I would guess nearly two hundred feet above the courtyard, I can see the many levels of rooftops, walkways, walls, and yards spread out below me like a doll's landscape.

"Seven gods preserve me," I breathe. Though by this time, they've got to be wondering what's the point of trying!

Carefully, every limb trembling violently, I angle my arms and shoulders, adjusting my mid-air stance. It's not altogether unlike being in the water. I'm not much of a swimmer, but both Brielle and I liked to slip away to the lake from time to time, where a hidden bend behind a veil of willow trees offered a little privacy if a girl wanted to shed a few layers and take a cool plunge on a hot summer day. I know how to keep my body afloat for short periods of time.

This is similar. Also easier. I need my muscles to balance and angle myself, but the wind-garment does all the hard work of buoyancy. And now that I'm past the initial terror of thinking I'm about to fly all the way to the highest heavens where the sheer glory of the gods will blast me to oblivion . . . I draw several deep breaths, pushing such thoughts away. I'm all right. I can handle this.

Moving my arms gently, I turn my body slowly around. My gaze scans Orican, both the familiar parts I have walked many times and various courtyards and walkways I've not yet bothered to explore. From this height I can also see the landscape beyond the palace. Not the many different folds of reality glimpsed through windows and from over balcony rails. No, this is the land in which this part of Orican really stands.

Forest. As far as the eye can see.

Orican and its walled gardens provide the only break in the density of green treetops spreading like a vast ocean in every direction.

My chest tightens, my heart seeming to pull deeper inside of me as I take in this reality. I knew already, of course. Or I suspected. My one glimpse through the front doors all but convinced me that the fold of reality in which I currently reside is nestled deep in Whispering Wood. Now I know for sure.

I also know that if I ever work up the nerve to step through those doors, I'll never find my way home.

My heart feels like lead in my breast, so heavy that the wind-vest sags. I sink slightly in the air but quickly spread my arms, palms down, and catch a precarious balance.

Hearing a shout below, I look down between my feet to see the green figure of Ellie far below, making large gestures. She seems to be kicking goblin men and beckoning me by turns.

Her voice sounds faint to me up here, but I can hear the frantic worry clearly enough.

I cup my hands around my mouth. "Coming, Ellie!" I shouldn't frighten her, at least no more than I already have. She puts up with so much from me as it is.

Turning in the air, I try to angle my body downward while simultaneously drawing my arms closer to my body, reducing the amount of wind. It's too much, too fast, and I plunge with a sickening lurch. Reflex makes me open my arms wide again, and back upward I surge. I catch my balance and struggle to catch my breath as well. This is going to be much trickier than I anticipated.

I roll my shoulders carefully and prepare to try again, but just then, distant movement catches my eye. It should be too far away to notice, yet somehow it draws my gaze. I lift my chin to peer out beyond the rooftops of Orican into the forest.

In a small break in the trees—very small, hardly enough to notice—a figure stands. Tiny, distant. Much too far away to see with any clarity.

And yet, somehow, I know her at once.

"Brielle!"

25

I stand in the great entrance hall beneath the huge domed ceiling. Before me looms the double doors, which I have opened only once before.

Behind me, Ellie and the goblin men, having followed me in from the courtyard, watch me closely. The green nymph burbles a string of worried scolding, and the goblin men mutter and grumble among themselves.

I ignore them. I grip my skirts with both hands, staring at the door. Getting safely down onto solid ground again had required several attempts, but the sudden urgency surging through my veins drove me almost to the point of carelessness. My body is bruised all over from a rough landing. I don't care. My wind vest is crammed back inside the golden locket now hanging around my neck. That glorious, terrifying flight already feels like a distant memory.

My heart pounds in my throat.

Brielle.

Brielle is out there.

Or did I imagine seeing her? Did my brain, dizzy with both the success of my creation and the shock of flying to that great height, conjure the image of my sister? Brielle. Clear as day. Standing out there in that open space, staring up at me with her hand shading her eyes.

No. It couldn't have been real. Only in a dream could I have seen across such a distance with such clarity. Perhaps rising above the protective walls of Orican exposed me to the magic of Whispering Wood? Maybe it was all some dangerous enchantment.

Or, possibly, my sister is truly out there. Just on the other side of that door.

I take a step. My gaze drops to the sculpted flower in the center panel of one door, searching for some sign of the hideous face I'd thought I glimpsed the day when the stranger pounded at the door, demanding entrance. But it's just an ornately gilded flower made of plaster. That sense of dread, the undeniable presence I'd felt through the door that day, is absent.

All is still. Very still.

Ellie's voice trills behind me. I pause, hand on the latch, and look back. The nymph stands on the other side of the hall, hands clasped against her bare bosom. Several dozen goblins surround her feet, all watching me with enormous, moon-wide eyes. Ellie shakes her head slightly, her antennae moving and twitching over her head.

But they won't stop me. Perhaps they can't. I am Lord Dymaris's wife. The Lady of Orican. I am free to come and go as I will.

Free to make a fatal mistake if I so desire.

I try to swallow, but my throat is too dry. I face the door again, straining my ears for some sound on the far side. Maybe I can open it a mere crack and peek out, just a glimpse. Surely nothing could get through if I'm quick.

And . . . and I have to know. Drawing a deep breath, I turn the latch. The door is heavy, but it swings easily on its hinges, pushing outward. I keep hold of the latch and, holding my breath, peer out.

"Vali!"

My heart stops.

Someone stands on the threshold, just three steps down. A young woman clad in green, with tall brown boots up to her knees. Her hair is tied back in a knot, but strands escape and frame her face in brilliant red. Wide hazel eyes gaze out from beneath stern, straight brows, and freckles dust her nose.

"No." The word whispers through my lips, a faint gasp.

It can't be her.

It can't be Brielle.

Denial pulses through my veins. This must be some monster wearing a glamour! A wicked trick, a disguise to trick me. Brielle is a child! A bony little girl not even twelve years old.

She isn't a strong, sturdy woman with hunger-sharpened cheekbones and dangerously flashing eyes.

"Vali!" The young woman steps onto the porch, her boot coming down hard. "It's me!"

I tense, my grip on the latch firming, ready to drag the door shut fast. But my gaze shifts from those wide hazel eyes to a spot on her cheek. A tiny brown spot, larger than a freckle but not by much. Shaped vaguely like a tiny heart. Brielle's faerie kiss.

No illusion could have mimicked that birthmark so exactly.

"Brielle?" Her name whispers through my numb lips. "Brielle, are you . . . are you real?"

"Yes!" The young woman steps back again, her eyes widening still more as she looks at my hand on the latch. "Don't shut the door. Please. If you shut the door, the whole house will vanish again. I've come upon it three times before, but just when I think I've got it for sure, just when I think I'll get through, it escapes me, slithering away sideways into this cursed wood, and I'm left where I started, back on the borders."

Her words ring in my ears like the toll of distant bells, heard but unheeded. My heart double-times, galloping in my breast. "No." I shake my head. "No, it can't be. It can't . . . you're . . . you're not . . ."

Brielle nods, dipping her head as though looking down at her own body, twig-thin yet distinctly womanly in shape. "I grew up, Vali," she says quietly. "You've been gone eight years now."

"Eight years?" My heart jumps, ready to choke me with shock, with horror. "No. That can't be right! I've been here a few weeks at most."

But this woman—this woman wearing my sister's face, this woman gazing at me with my sister's eyes—shakes her head sadly. "Maybe it's felt that way to you. But it's been so much longer. And I've been hunting for you all this time. Ever since I caught that glimpse of you six months after you'd gone."

"Six months?" Lord Dymaris had brought me the water from the Starglass mere days after I arrived in Orican. Not six months. Then again, I've been living in a different fold of reality all this time. Who can say how the years, days, or even hours passed back in my own world?

A bitter taste burns in my mouth. I swallow, and sickness sinks to my gut, settling in a lump. Erolas . . . Lord Dymaris . . . promised to return me home in a year and a day. He promised.

But he never told me that what felt like a year and a day to me would mean many years back in my own world. He never told me I would miss my sister's growing up, never told me I would not return in time to shield and protect her from our father's cruelties. He never told me . . . He let me believe . . .

"Please." Brielle steps up cautiously. She has a quiver of arrows slung over her shoulder and carries a short bow in one hand. Since when had Brielle taken up carrying weapons on her excursions into the wood? Since her sister was stolen by fae monsters, no doubt. "Please, let me in. Give me a chance to explain." Her voice cracks, and when I look closer, I see tears shining in her eyes. The sight is so strange in that young woman's face, but . . . but also so like Brielle.

"It's been such a long time, Vali," she says, her voice gentle but edged with tension. "I've searched so hard, and I began to think I'd never find you. I've been driven nearly mad with frustration! Please, Vali. If you turn me away now, I don't know what I'll do."

My hands trembles on the latch. I feel Ellie and the goblins behind me, watching me. I feel their silent urging for me to slam the door shut, to protect them from possible invasion.

But they don't know Brielle. They don't know the way her mouth twists to one side when she's trying hard to speak without crying, without letting her fear betray her. They don't know the way her hairline comes to a little point on her forehead, or how silky, vibrant locks fall to frame her dainty, heart-shaped face. They don't realize how the little girl still manages to peer through the young woman's face, determined and beseeching and brave and terrified all at the same time. They don't know.

I step back. "Come in," I say before I can change my mind. "Quickly."

Brielle leaps up the steps and through the door, and when I pull it shut behind her, the booming echoes reverberate through the floor and across the spacious hall. Every denizen of the household must know the doors have been opened and shut again.

Turning, I press my back against the moldings, my hands behind me still holding the latch. Ellie and the goblins are nowhere to be seen. They've scattered, hiding from the newcomer, but they're probably still close, watching from hidden nooks and crannies.

Brielle stands in the middle of the huge hall, turning slowly in place, her neck craning as she takes in the grandeur of that space. It's like nothing she's ever seen before. I vividly remember experiencing the same awe blended with fear when I first arrived at Orican. Not long ago.

Or, apparently, years ago.

When she finally drops her gaze and looks at me, a smile breaks across her face, transforming her momentarily into the child I know. But when she moves as though to catch me in a hug, I step away, my nerves jumpy, suspicion humming in my veins. My sister—if indeed this is my sister—looks hurt but puts her hands up and steps back. She looks me up and down.

"You look . . . well," she offers tentatively.

I nod. Then, the word blurting out in a rough sort of bark, "Father?"

She shrugs. "Still alive. Still drunk. Still hating the world. We lost the house a couple of years back. I got a little place for us on the edge of town."

"Do you still work for the Trisdi family?"

"Gods, no! I gave that up ages ago. I'm a huntswoman now. I bring in fresh game for Old Ailmar to sell at market. He pays a fair price. We get by." She frowns, her eyes flashing uncomfortably. "What about you?" she asks slowly, as though fearing the answer. "What . . . Mother Ulla told me you were stolen as a . . . as a fae bride. Are you . . . that is . . . have you . . . ?"

"I'm well," I hasten to assure her. "Lord Dy—the fae who took me needs me to break a curse for him, but he . . . The marriage is in name only. He's treated me well."

Brielle's eyebrow slides up her forehead, and her face sets like stone. "He kidnapped you."

"Yes. I remember."

"And this is where he's kept you? All these years?"

I shake my head. I feel dizzy, sick inside. "It hasn't been that long. Not for me."

"The fact remains. He stole you away from your family and locked you up in this . . . this gilded cage. Don't try to tell me he's treated you well, Valera Normas. I don't want to hear it." She gives me a once-over. "Gods, he's not even given you new clothes to wear! Is that the same dress you were wearing the night you were stolen? Or has he glamoured you to think it's made of fine silks?"

"Oh, no." I look down at my rough work dress, smoothing the front of my skirt. "I . . . I have new gowns aplenty; I simply find this one more practical."

"Practical for what? Are you a servant here? Cleaning? Cooking? Hauling firewood?"

I open my mouth, but no words will come. How can I begin to explain, how can I begin to tell Brielle that I've been blissfully filling my days exploring the possibilities of my own creative urges? What would Brielle think if she knew I haven't been pouring every ounce of strength and will I have into escaping this prison, escaping this world, and returning to my beloved little sister?

As I should have been.

Guilt slashes through my heart like a knife. I should have known better than to relax into this new life, to let my soul settle into these grooves and become comfortable. I believed Lord Dymaris, took him at his word. When he said he would return me in a year and day, when he told me to speak his true name, I'd felt that simmering connection between us and trusted it. When I ought to have resisted, I relented.

And now here I stand, faced with the reality of his lie. How many other lies has he told me? How many other falsehoods has he woven in amid his kind words and his silences?

"Don't worry, Vali." Brielle's voice cuts through the tumult in my mind. "Don't try to answer. None of that matters anymore. I'm here now. And I'll take you home."

"Home?" My head jerks up. I meet and hold my sister's gaze, my mind suddenly whirling.

"Yes. Why else do you think I've come so far?" Brielle takes a step toward me, extending her free hand invitingly. "I tried so long to get through to you. I . . . I can't even begin to tell you all I went through, everything I saw and experienced. I finally learned of this place, and I fought like a demon to reach you! If it hadn't been for . . . but no." She shakes her head, pinching her lips together, then looks up at me again and offers a small smile. "I can tell you all that once we're safely out of this place. For now, we've got to go."

Go.

Step through that door, hand in hand with my sister.

Turn my back to Orican. To the folk of this house. To the memories of fear and delight, of pain and pleasure. To the hope, however tentative and shrinking, that had begun to bloom in my heart.

To leave him.

In his darkness, in his shadows.

Hiding in folds of realities from a darkness deeper still.

My husband.

My hand moved of its own accord and is already halfway extended toward Brielle's, ready to clasp her fingers tight. I snatch it back, pressing my palm over my racing heart.

"I . . . I can't. There's a curse."

"A curse?" Brielle's voice is sharp, her eyes flashing. "On you?"

"No." I swallow and look down before forcing my chin up and making myself hold my sister's gaze. "I told you, on Lord Dymaris. The master of this house. He and his people suffer under a curse, and I'm supposed to break it."

"What kind of a curse?"

"I . . . don't know."

"And who cast it?"

"I don't know."

"And how are you supposed to break it?"

I shake my head.

Brielle flings up her hands, rolling her eyes toward the painted ceiling overhead. "Do you hear yourself, Vali? Do you? This Lord Dymaris has manipulated you from the start. He's told you these stories to keep you happy here, to keep you placid. You're probably ensorcelled to make you believe it. But it's me you should believe!"

"No." I grimace. I know how it must sound to her ears. I know I must seem pathetic, weak—a victim, far too easily molded by my abuser. But that isn't the case. It isn't! I know who I am, what I am.

I know the experiences I've lived these last few weeks. It isn't all lies. It can't be.

Can it?

Brielle moves toward me cautiously, her footsteps soft, but her eyes sparking with fire. "Don't worry," she says. "I'll get you out of this."

"What are you going to do?" I snap, sliding away from the door to put distance between us. Would she try to grab me, manhandle me through the door and into the forest? She looks strong enough to do it. Though she stands several inches shorter than me, her stance bespeaks strength, agility, and wiry muscle.

Brielle puts up a placating hand. "It's all right! I . . . I know how this works. I've learned a thing or two these last eight years. I can't drag you away from an enchantment by force. It'll only hurt you. I've got to break the spell before you can come away safely. It's all right, Vali. Look."

So saying, she reaches into the satchel at her side and offers me . . . a candle—a red taper of fine beeswax with a long white wick.

Though I can't begin to say why, I feel a shudder in my gut. "What is that?" I ask, my voice sharp in my own ears.

"It's how you'll break free," Brielle says. "You've got to . . . Well, I don't know exactly how it works or why, but I was told you have to look at this fae lord of yours by the light of this candle. The moment you see him by this light, the spell he's cast on you will break, and he will lose all power over you. You'll be able to come away with me then."

My heart thuds against my breastbone. "Who . . . who told you this, Brielle? Who gave you this thing?"

"Someone who knows." Brielle narrows her eyes, her brow puckering. "Please, Vali, I can't say more. I might compromise the magic."

Mother Ulla. It must be. Who else would Brielle turn to for help in matters like this? And Mother Ulla fought so hard to prevent the Moonfire Marriage from taking place. Granted, she also made clear that if I chose to step through that door and into the marriage agreement, she wouldn't be bothered trying to help me out of it again. Perhaps eight years has softened her resolve.

I stare at that candle, such a bright, bloody red in my sister's pale hand. "He . . . he told me I could not see him." The words are heavy, like weights falling through my lips. "He said the one rule governing our marriage was that I must not look upon his face."

"Don't you see?" Brielle's voice is tight, as though she struggles to keep her own passion tightly reined. "That must be how he maintains this spell on you. As long as you don't look at him, you remain in his thrall. You believe his words, believe his lies, and you stay here. But don't worry! This candle is ensorcelled so that fae eyes cannot see its light. He'll never know that you've used it, that you've seen his face. Oh, Vali!" These last words emerge in a choking gasp like a sob. "Vali, please believe me! I . . . I can't leave you here. I just can't. If I'm wrong, if there is no spell, the candle will reveal that too. Then you can safely believe whatever he's told you. But search your heart. You know he's lying to you. You've got to feel it deep inside, underneath the magic."

Is it true? I close my eyes, as if blocking out sight of that candle can thwart the desperate temptation to take it. After all, Lord Dymaris has already broken one promise. He said our marriage would last no more than a year and a day. He failed to mention that time's passage differs between the worlds. He lied by omission, but it's still a lie.

What other lies and half-truths has he woven into this world he created for me?

My lashes part slowly. The candle is still there, offered by my sister's hand. And Brielle gazes at me with desperate, longing entreaty.

If there's one person in all the world I know I can trust . . .

"Fine." I take the candle. It's cold in my grasp, but I wield it as though brandishing an assassin's dagger. "I'll do it. I'll try."

"Tonight?" Brielle urges, her voice still tight but now tinged with hope. "Will you try tonight? Please?"

"I don't know. He's been gone for some time. I don't know when he'll return."

"It has to be tonight, Vali," she urges. "I found a path here, but it won't stay open for long. If you wait any longer, I may not be able to return for a long while. It could be years!"

I turn my face away, draw a deep breath. "I'll do what I can, Brielle. I promise."

"That's all I ask. Just do what you can."

My sister moves forward as though to embrace me, but I jump like a startled doe and edge away, still wary. Immediately she draws back, her expression placating. There's so much love and longing in her eyes, my heart breaks to see it. Perhaps I ought to toss this candle aside, take Brielle's hand, and just go, now. While I can.

But no. I can't do that. If I do, I will always wonder . . .

Clenching my jaw, I squeeze the candle, my fingers warming the hard wax. "You've got to go now, Brielle. Is it . . . Can you get home from here safely?"

"I'll be safe enough," Brielle answers, brandishing her bow. Then her stern expression softens. "I'll return in the morning. At daybreak. Wait for me here. The spell should be broken by then without his knowing. I can get you safely away before he realizes you've gone. Once you're back in our world, this *marriage* bargain of yours will be broken. You'll be safe. Safe, Vali." Her voice breaks again. "It's been so long," she whispers. "I've been so afraid for you . . ."

If I listen to one word more, I won't have the strength to stay.

"Go on!" I say firmly. "You can't be here when he returns. I'll use the candle, and I'll see you in the morning. I promise, Brielle. If what you've told me is true . . . I'll see you in the morning."

With this, I open the door, which swings out silently, revealing the deep green shadows of the forest. I wave my hand, indicating Brielle should cross the threshold. My sister—my older little sister—catches my eye sadly as she obeys, stepping out onto the porch. She pulls a green hood up over her bright-colored hair and adjusts the quiver strap slung across her breast.

"Be careful," she says.

"You too," I reply.

She looks as though she wants to say more. I don't know what, and I'm afraid to guess. She nods once, turns, and strides off into the forest. I stand in the doorway and watch her go until the shadows of Whispering Wood claim her, obscuring her from view.

I conceal the candle in the folds of my skirt as I walk through the halls of Orican to my bedroom. Once there I place it in my sewing basket and cover it with scraps of cloth.

The sun has scarcely reached its zenith in the sky. A long afternoon lies before me.

Eventually Ellie tiptoes in, her eyes large and uncertain. She offers me food, and when I shake my head, she leaves the platter on the table and slips out again. The goblin men, who often make a point to leap down my chimney and roll around on my hearth, avoid me entirely.

Do they think me a traitor for allowing a stranger into their home while the master is away? Perhaps. They don't know Brielle, after all. They would have seen only a strong mortal woman armed with deadly weapons. But surely they must have seen how I sent her away again.

Do they know about the candle?

I shudder. Sitting in my chair by the fireplace, I feel as sick to my stomach now as I had in those first terrible days after I came to Orican.

"No," I whisper fiercely. "My *imprisonment.*"

When had I begun painting the scenario in such tame colors? I hadn't simply "come to Orican." I'd been spirited away against my will by terrifying creatures who had manipulated me into believing they held my sister captive. Sure, I now know those creatures as Ellie and Birgabog and all the little host of goblin men. But what difference does that make? Perhaps my comfort with them is simply more proof of the enchantment Brielle claims I'm under.

And Lord Dymaris . . . how many lies has he led me to believe simply by not telling me the truth?

I lay my necklace of lockets on the table and eye it as though it were a snake ready to bite me. Those beautiful fabrics hidden within each locket . . . I've been so delighted with them! Touched by a gift so carefully selected to be a true pleasure to me, far beyond the pleasure of jewels and gowns and riches. I let myself believe such stupid things: that Lord Dymaris cares for me, understands me in a way no one else ever has, and wants to bring joy into my life.

I allowed myself to forget the truth. And now . . .

I slowly release a tight breath, closing my eyes. Now what am

I going to do? I have one night in which to use this candle. If I really intend to use it. But how? Brielle said it's enchanted so that he can't see the light, but that doesn't mean I can simply light it while sitting across from him at the hearth. He would immediately suspect something.

No, it would be better if . . . if . . .

I turn in my chair to look back at my bed. My lips are dry, and I pinch them together, trying to moisten them.

"It might work," I whisper after a few moments of contemplation. "It might just work if . . . if I'm careful . . ."

The day progresses while my mind churns. Ellie doesn't return, for which I am grateful. I eat some of the cold meat on the platter, then step into the bathing chamber. Moving with determined precision, I pour scented soap into the pool, strip, and wash myself. I pat my hair dry, comb it, and pin it up in loose coils that fall across my shoulders. Then I return to the room and open my clothing chest.

The white gown shimmers and gleams as I shake it out and hold it up before me.

How vividly I recall that fevered night following the Glorandal dance, when I donned this gown and waited with bated breath! Ready to risk all. Ready to give all. Full of hope and fear and desire.

That night was nothing like this. Tonight, there is no fever in my veins. Only raw determination.

I slip into the white gown, wrap it across my bosom, and tie it at my hip. Moving to the mirror, I study my reflection. The girl gazing back at me is hardly the same girl I saw all those weeks—years—ago. That girl had been pinched with hunger, wide-eyed with terror, pale and haunted. Now? My frame has filled out and softened after weeks of good food and rest and comfort. Like a fruit ripening on the vine, waiting to be plucked.

My eyes narrow. If that is indeed his plan, I'll soon find out. And I'll beat him at his own game. Just so long as he abides by his own rules.

I adjust the gown's plunging neckline, pulling it slightly apart to reveal more soft, plump curves. The fabric is so fine, so light, it leaves little to the imagination. Perhaps it's too much. Perhaps I risk cutting myself on my own weapon.

No. It will work. It must work.

The room dims around me. The sun is setting; night swiftly advances. I return to my hearth, sit on the edge of my chair, and grip the arms tight. With a word of command, I call the moonfire to life, and for some time I watch the tongues of blue flame dance across the glowing stones.

Then I close my eyes and whisper, "Erolas. Come to me."

I wait. How long, I can't say. I keep my eyes closed, breathing carefully, trying to calm my racing heart.

I hear the door open. Shut again.

I hear footsteps cross the room. A rustle of fabric as he approaches.

Then he stops abruptly.

He's seen me. Seen what I wear.

I feel his gaze devouring me.

My heartbeat quickens, but I don't open my eyes.

"M'lady." His voice is soft, not the deep, rumbling tones I've come to know so well. It sounds almost like a prayer. Full of hope.

Is it just another manipulation? Another fae ruse?

"M'lord," I answer, my voice equally soft. I dare not raise it for fear a tremor will betray me. I hardly dare open my eyes, hardly dare lift my gaze to the shadow standing just beyond the moonfire light. Will he read my plan, the deceit in my gaze? Will he know at once what I intend to do?

I can almost feel a pulsing energy radiate from my workbasket where the candle lies hidden. But I refuse to let my gaze shift that way.

"You've been gone some while," I say at last, breaking the silence between us.

"I . . ." He stops. Is that fear I hear in his tone? "I thought it best," he continues with an effort. "I didn't want you to . . . I don't want you ever to feel as though . . ." He stops again.

Then, even softer, almost a whisper, "Valera."

My heart jolts painfully as that line of connection flares to life between us, sharp as a razor wire but vibrating like the string of an instrument sounding a pure, clear note. I close my eyes, resisting the lure of that note, resisting all the feelings it calls to life in my body. I must be careful, so careful now.

I stand. The soft skirt of the white garment clings to my hips, and the firelight shines through it, rendering the fabric semi-transparent, I suspect. Moving slowly despite the wild beat of my heart, I step toward him, first one step, then another. I stretch out my hand.

At first he doesn't move. I hear his breathing, heavy in the darkness. Then he shifts his weight, leaning toward me. I feel cool fingertips brush mine and the barest trace of long, sharp nails.

"Erolas," I say, "will you sleep with me tonight?"

A powerful surge like a bolt of lightning seems to shoot through his arm and into me, making me quake to my core. "Are you . . ." His fingers close around mine, drawing me toward him. "Valera, are you asking me for the fourth kiss?"

My body trembles so hard, I know he must feel it. But I can't let him see my fear. Or any of the other wild emotions currently churning through my soul.

"No," I answer softly. "I mean only for you to sleep. In my bed. I want for us to lie side by side as though we are truly man and wife."

"But I am . . ." His voice breaks. He tries again. "I am not to touch you?"

I shake my head, dropping my gaze.

"Why do you want this, Valera? Why do you ask this of me?"

Oh, how narrow the bridge and how wide the chasm over which I now tread! One wrong look, one wrong word, and I'll betray myself entirely. But what would I betray? My plan to light the candle, to lean over his sleeping body, to see his face and break his spell?

Or the truth of what I desire with my whole body and soul?

I speak with care each word I precisely practiced in my mind throughout the long afternoon: "I want to know I am safe with you. If I choose to ask for the final kiss, I want to know I will not, with that choice, give up everything. If you lie with me tonight, it is a sign of . . . of trust between us."

Once more I lift my eyes to search in the shadows for some hint of his face. But there is none. Only darkness, a perfect obscuring mask.

"Do you agree, Erolas?" I ask. "Will you sleep in my bed tonight? Will you honor my trust?"

His hold on my hand does not relax. I hear him draw a long, deep breath. Perhaps I should not have worn the white gown. It's too great a temptation. But I want him to know—I want him to believe—that if he grants me this request, the fourth kiss must and will come thereafter.

Will he lower his guard as he lies beside me? Will he fall asleep? Or have I pushed too far? Pushed him beyond the limits of self-control so that he will yield to his darker urges and take that fourth kiss by force? Long hours of night stretch before us. Anything might happen in that time.

"I want you to trust me, Valera," he says. The heartstring hums a sharp, painful note that almost makes me gasp out loud. He means it. I feel the sincerity in his words. "I would do anything to prove to you how greatly I honor and esteem you, how I . . ." He stops abruptly. Then, in a firm tone, he finishes with, "I will do as you ask. I will lie beside you. And I will not touch you save at your asking."

The next few moments pass as though in a dream. I draw him away from the fire even as I have imagined doing more times than I like to admit. I lead him into the deeper shadows where not even the faintest glint of moonfire can penetrate. Knowing the layout of my room well, I do not hesitate.

But when we approach the bed, I pause. It's so high, and I don't like to scramble up into it like I normally do. Not in this filmy bit of nothing I now wear, with him watching.

I turn to him, my eyes still straining in the darkness, though I know it is useless. "You may lift me up," I say.

Strong hands wrap around my waist. I only just have time to grip his shoulders before he sweeps me off my feet and sets me lightly on the edge of the bed as though I weigh no more than a doll. For a moment we stay like that, facing one another. The touch of his hands seems to burn through the thin gown, right into my skin. His shoulders are firm beneath the silken garment he wears. A strong temptation comes over me to find the edges of that garment, to push it back from his shoulders and let it fall down his arms to pool on the floor. To feel the smooth skin and hard muscle my fingers explored with such interest only a few nights ago.

I bite down hard on my lower lip. It's too dangerous. Much too dangerous. I don't trust myself.

"Come," I say, letting go and swinging my legs up to curve beside me. "Join me."

He moves around to the other side of the bed. I feel the change of pressure in the down-filled mattress as he sits. He remains seated, invisible but so powerfully present. He does not relax. But it's not as though I've relaxed either.

I recline onto the pillows on top of the fur coverlet. Lying on my side, my legs slightly curled, I still try, despite everything, to see in the darkness. "It's all right," I say, though my voice quavers traitorously. "Please. Lie beside me."

He shifts onto the bed. I feel the weight of him in the mattress. His legs extend all the way to the footboard, his head resting on another pile of pillows. The bed is large enough that we could lie side by side without touching throughout the night. That should be plenty. That should be enough.

And yet . . .

I move slightly, stop. Then, giving in to an impulse I hardly dare name, I slide close to the warm bulk beside me. He holds still as stone. But when I reach out and touch his arm, he jolts. His skin is pleasantly warm.

"Valera," he breathes.

"Yes?"

He doesn't say anything more.

After a few moments I move my hand up his arm to his shoulder, then slide it softly down his chest. Just as I did four nights ago, I feel his heart thud against my palm. So fast, so frantic. Is this the quickening pulse of the hunter preparing for the kill?

Why can't I make myself believe it?

Slowly, timidly, I shift closer until I can rest my cheek against his shoulder. It feels . . . *right,* somehow. Though not as right as it should.

"Would you lift your arm?" I ask, amazed at my own boldness.

He grunts. Then obediently he raises his arm. I squirm to his side, pressing up against him. His arm comes down around me, cradling me close, and I rest my head on his shoulder, my cheek touching both smooth silk and warm skin.

I close my eyes, no longer straining against pure blindness. My heart thuds in my breast. Can he feel it? Can he guess what I feel? No, that's ridiculous. How could he guess when I'm not sure myself?

My hand resting on his heart moves slightly. My fingertips dance along his skin, exploring the muscles of his chest.

He shivers. "Valera."

"Yes?"

"Please, let me kiss you."

Heat flames through my body. Every sense begs me to give in—nay, to *beg* him for that kiss. I long to feel his lips on mine, long to feel his strong hands on my trembling body.

I squeeze my eyes tight, desire warring with reason, hunger warring with fear.

I slide my hand down his chest until I find his other hand resting on his stomach. There I let my fingers rest a moment, even while my mind burns. I should let him go, should push away from him and retreat to the far side of the bed. I shouldn't play with fire.

Instead, I take hold of his hand and, moving by instinct rather than rational thought, pull it toward my breast. I press his palm to my heart.

His breathing quickens.

I continue drawing his hand down the deep V of my gown. His fingertips trail fire across my skin, and I catch a short, shivering gasp. My eyes flare open, searching the darkness. I can feel his gaze on me, but the shadows are too deep for my eyes to discern even the faintest glimmer of his eyes. Yet I feel the intensity of his study. His fae sight can see me with perfect clarity. I lower my lashes.

"Valera—"

"Hush."

He starts to withdraw his hand, but I tighten my hold, just slightly. Just enough to make him stay, to leave his fingers where they are. My heart rams in my chest, and I know he can feel it.

His hand tenses, relaxes, tenses again. Then, moving with care, he slides one long finger along the inside edge of my garment, up from my breast to my shoulder. He slips the soft fabric gently down my arm, exposing my shoulder. Cold air touches my bare skin, causing little hairs to prickle.

He pauses again. I hear the tightness of his breathing.

My stomach knots. I leave my hand lightly on top of his. Neither guiding nor pushing away. Simply waiting.

As though summoning courage, he continues. Slowly, delicately, he draws one fingertip along my shoulder, across my collarbone. The edge of a claw delicately touches my throat. I bite my lip, trying not to let a sound betray me, but cannot restrain a tiny whimper. His fingers wander down my breastbone and come to a rest above my heart to trace a circle there.

Then, with a sudden growl, he rolls on top of me, his knee braced beside my hipbone, his hands pressed into the furs on either side of my face. My heart leaps, not with fear, but with an excitement equally heady and thrilling.

He lowers himself, his muscled torso pressing against my bosom. His breath warms my shoulder, and I can almost feel the shape of his lips hovering just above my skin. He turns his head, and my neck sparks in response to a touch that does not happen. My eyelashes flutter. I'm not sure I'll ever catch my breath.

"Valera," he says. His voice is almost a command.

I look up. I can't see him, but I can feel him. His face is near. Mere fractions of an inch separate his lips from mine.

I close my eyes again. The precipice yawns before me. I stand on the brink, and one more half-step will send me falling, falling, down into the mystery, down to discover either delight or terror, I can hardly fathom which.

If he would only bend a tiny bit more! Plant his lips against mine, take the moment of decision away entirely! Does he know how weak I am? How my blood races, how my skin burns with anticipation? Does he know how easily I would succumb?

But he remains poised where he is, his breathing ragged.

"Valera," he rasps, "may I kiss you?"

If I give in . . .

If I indulge in the desires even now coursing through my veins . . .

Will I still have the will to pull out the red candle when we're through and lie spent upon our pillows? Will I be able to steal a secret glimpse of my shadowy bridegroom then?

Or will the power Brielle insists he has over me only be strengthened, transforming me into his witless, devoted slave?

I cannot risk it.

"No," I whisper, squeezing my eyes tightly shut and tucking my chin in. I put up one hand and plant it against his bare, heaving chest. "No, you may not kiss me."

I apply a little pressure and for a moment feel his resistance.

Then with a groan, he shifts and falls back heavily onto the bed.

27

I see the shadow of his hand move to his face, as though covering his eyes. I shiver and slip the sleeve of my gown back onto my shoulder, adjusting the front across my bosom. I hold very still on my side, straining my eyes to make something of the indistinct form beside me, my hands clasped tightly against my throbbing heart.

After what feels like an age, he speaks again. "Let me go. You're too kind to torment me."

A dart of pain shoots through my heart. But I shake my head fiercely, squeezing my fingers tight. "No. Stay. Please."

He is silent again for the space of several breaths. Then, in a softer voice: "This is what you need from me? To feel . . . safe?"

"This is what I need, Erolas."

"Very well. I will stay."

How long we lie like so, I cannot guess. Neither of us moves, neither of us speaks, and the cord of connection between us strains tight, ready to sing out if plucked.

I close my eyes. Gods curse my weakness! I'd meant to simply lie here beside him until sleep claimed him. The bed is big enough; we need not have touched at all. I shouldn't have indulged myself so foolishly.

Did I push him too far? Will he not be able to fall asleep now? Have I spoiled my chance?

After what feels like hours, my muscles relax. I sense the tension going out of him as well. The sound of his ragged breathing eases into a more regular rhythm. Setting my jaw, I fight the urge to slide up against him again. It had felt so lovely to be held in his arms. So right. But if once I let him pull me close again, I won't have the strength to resist what will surely follow.

I must be firm. I must remember what I have learned today— that he misled me about the passage of time in my own world, that he never told me the truth of my sister's aging. That his promises to return me home after a year and a day were worthless.

That he may even now have me under a spell, and all those sensations I experienced here in this bed were mere products of his dark enchantments.

Time passes with painful slowness. I doze at last but come to myself with a start, blinking and blind. The moonfire has gone out on the hearth, leaving the room in perfect darkness. Beside me, my husband sleeps as well, his breathing deep and steady.

Moving slowly, I sit upright. He doesn't stir. His sleep is sound, apparently, thank the gods! I shift my weight away from him and slide off the far edge of the bed. My scanty garment pulls as I go, exposing my bare skin to the cold air. Hastily, I grab the skirt and front, yanking them into proper place.

Then, walking on the balls of my feet, I cross to the worktable. I know this room well, after all. I can find my way in the dark as long as I don't let fear drive me to hurry. I must be slow, precise. My fingers find the work basket.

Reach inside.

Touch the candle.

I draw it out and hold it close to my breast, shooting a brief prayer to the heavens. Now, how to light it? It isn't like moonfire that will spring into being on my command. And . . . will moonfire be enough to set flame to this wick?

I crouch on my hearth and quietly speak a small moonfire blaze to life. Though it is scarcely more than a single flame dancing on a small white stone, it seems terribly bright after that absolute darkness. I shudder and glance over my shoulder at the bed. I can just discern the form of my husband lying there. But he hasn't moved, and the sound of his deep breathing continues to fill the stillness.

My hand trembles so hard, I fear I will drop the candle. I hold the long white wick to the moonfire. It sparks . . . and takes. When I withdraw the candle and hold it up before me, it glows at first with bright green light, and a bitter smell sears into my nostrils.

However, after a few faint flickers the green fades, giving way to a soft orange flame. The smell is gone too, vanished so completely I'm not sure it was ever real.

"Right," I whisper.

Slowly, cautiously, I rise from my knees and approach the bed. With each step I take, my fear grows. It isn't too late. Not yet. I can still blow out this candle, stash it back in the basket, and climb into bed beside my husband. I can still wake him, ask for his kiss, and risk everything on the chance that a night with him will be enough to break his curse.

If his curse is even real.

This final thought sears across my brain like a scalding iron. I won't fall prey to fae tricks! Whatever happens, I must know the truth. I must know if he has enscorcelled me. I may not trust him, but I *do* trust Brielle. My sister wants what is best for me. I must believe that.

I approach the bed.

I lift my candle and lean over to look at my husband.

He is . . . incredibly beautiful. And very strange. He lies in an attitude of repose, his lips slightly parted so that the light of my candle glints off points of deadly sharp teeth. But those lips are full and sensual, and though the planes of his face are harsh, they are like firmly drawn strokes from a master artist's hand, perfectly aligned, confidently shaded. He wears a garment of deep red trimmed in gold, open from throat to navel, revealing the powerfully muscled torso I have twice now explored with my hands. His skin is a deep, dusky gray that seems almost lavender in the candlelight, and the hand resting on his stomach is tipped with long black nails that gleam like polished steel.

Two curling horns grow from his brow. Devil horns.

And yet he does not look like a devil.

I stand tense, poised. Waiting. Will there be some electrifying burst as the spell breaks? Or has it already broken, and I don't realize it? Am I suddenly free of his thrall?

No. It must not have worked. Why else do I feel this sudden, powerful urge to lean down, to plant my lips gently against his? To wake him with a fourth kiss. To see those long lashes fanning his cheeks flutter open so that I might discover the color of his eyes.

Maybe . . . maybe . . .

I bend my head.

My candle tilts just slightly.

Three drops of hot wax land on his cheek like spots of blood.

His eyes flare wide, and I stare down into an intense yellow gaze set with hugely dilated black pupils, like a cat's. Those pupils contract under the glow of the candlelight into pinpoint dots.

"Valera!" he gasps.

His sharp teeth flash. With a cry he bolts upright, his arm lashing out to knock the candle from my hand. I can't suppress a scream at the suddenness of the gesture, and the candle hits the floor. The orange glow snuffed out at once, and a bitter smell permeates the chamber as I'm plunged into darkness.

I stagger back from the bed, trip on the edge of my gown, and fall to the floor. My skirts splay out around my bare legs. I am awkward, terrified, exposed. Vulnerable.

I hear him rise from the bed.

"What have you done?" His voice is low but rises in a ragged, wordless cry before turning to a bloodcurdling roar. "*What have you done?*"

28

I cower back, throwing up my arms in defense. But though I'm braced and trembling, no violent assault comes. Instead, a sound like a sob breaks the darkness. It doesn't come from my lips.

"I warned you." His voice cracks, and he struggles to catch his breath. "I warned you that you must not see my face. Valera! Valera, my love! Why could you not trust me? Why? Why?"

I try to crawl, to put distance between us. But my feet catch in my skirts, pinning me in place. I collapse hard on my elbows, staring up into impenetrable shadow.

His voice reaches out to me again, softer now, almost gentle. "Oh, my love, do you fear me still? Was there nothing I could have done to win your trust? I was such a fool! I thought one mistake could be overcome. I thought you would forgive me for bringing you here, if I could only . . . But it's too late. It's too late now. She's coming for me."

"Who is coming?" I gasp.

Another horrible sob wracks the darkness. He moves. I can't see him, and my heart thunders in my breast. My body flinches in expectation of I know not what form of punishment.

Then he speaks again. *"Faugh!* It's *her* magic. I smell it. Impossible to miss that stench! Where did you come by this candle spell? How did it get through Orican's defenses?"

I shake my head. My throat closes, blocking any words, any excuses I might try to offer. How can I tell him the truth? I won't betray Brielle.

I feel rather than see him collapse on his knees before me. His hands close on mine, and I wince, trying to pull away, terror throbbing in my veins. But his voice, ragged with pain, reaches out to me like a caress. "It's not your fault, Valera. I know it isn't. The Pale Queen's enchantments are powerful, and she must have used some trickery to deliver this one. I thought my borders were secure, especially after you managed to ward off her previous attack. But she is insidious. She must have done something—"

A terrible crash cuts off his words, a roar like an avalanche bringing down a mountain. The ground beneath me quakes, shuddering into the deeps. I scream, my voice lost in the tumult, and fling my arms over my head as dust and debris rain down from the ceiling.

When the reverberations pass, I peer tentatively from under my arm. A huge, solid presence looms over me, warm and sheltering. Erolas. He's using his body as a shield, protecting me from falling stones.

"Valera?" His words shudder in my ear. "Are you all right?"

I nod, uncertain whether he can see me in the swirl of dust and darkness.

"Good!" he breathes. Then one of his hands supports my elbow, the other grips my waist. Though I'm trembling so hard I fear my knees will buckle, he helps me to my feet, holding me against him. "There's no time to lose," he says. "She's here. And I can't let her find you. Quickly, my love! Do you still have the necklace I gave you?"

"The necklace?" The words fall out, dull and stupid. My mind whirls, and I can't seem to pull together a coherent thought. Somehow I manage to say, "It . . . was on the table . . ."

He springs to my workstation. The small moonfire blaze I called to light on the hearth still glows through the choking dust clouds, and I can just see his silhouette. A falling stone from the ceiling knocked the table over, scattering its contents, but he quickly sifts through them, then straightens, his hand fisted and upraised. The seven lockets glint in the blue light.

He turns to me, and I see his hand outstretched. "Please, Valera," he says. "I know you've never fully trusted me, never had reason to. Trust me now. All is lost for me and my people, but I have one desire remaining: to see you safe. If I can get you out of Orican before she gets here—"

"Who gets here?" I demand, my voice choking, my throat coated with dust. My gaze shifts from his hand to the darkness where his face must be and back again. "Who is coming? And why?"

He shakes his head. "I can't explain. The curse—"

Another crash erupts in my ears. The walls groan, the ceiling shudders, and the floor shivers and shakes so hard that I stagger. My limbs flail wildly, but then I hit something solid, something warm. Erolas's arms close around me, pulling me tightly to him as he bows over me, making himself into my armor. Through the din of crunching rock, I hear the impact of stones striking flesh. He grunts with pain, his mouth close to my ear.

When the worst of the shock passes, he whispers, "Come. To the gardens. Quickly!"

He steps back from me, and I almost whimper in my longing to return to the shelter of his embrace. One of his great hands closes around mine, and he pulls me roughly after him. I stagger over fallen slabs of stone, broken pieces of my own bed and splinters from the chest and the shattered mirror. We reach the wall where the door should be, and he speaks the command to open. For a moment, nothing happens. I fear the spell on the door has broken.

Then, with a painful groan, it cracks, breaks, and tears apart to create an opening for us. I can see the walls struggling to maintain support. The whole room will collapse in moments.

Erolas grips my hand firmly as he leads me over broken stones through the opening, out into the passage beyond. The windows are cracked, and I see one whole pane shattered. Moonlight streams through the broken place and falls full upon my husband's face. I catch my breath, for the otherness of his features is rendered far more terrifying in fear than when I glimpsed him in repose. His brow is stern and hard over his deep-set eyes, and his horns look devilish and cruel. I almost try to pull my hand free, to flee from him in terror.

Then another shock reverberates through the house, rattling the ground. The windows at the far end of the passage explode in a storm of glass. Then the next window on, then the next, rippling down the passage straight toward us.

I don't have time to scream. Erolas scoops me up in his arms, holding me against his broad chest, and runs. I close my eyes, wishing I could close my ears as well to the sounds of shattering, breaking, and crushing that fill my head. I feel the sting of small missiles against my cheek, but Erolas receives the bulk of the blows.

He bursts from the passage out into the moonlit garden just as the last windows shatter behind us. Even as the shock and roar fades, the ground continues to rumble underfoot. Erolas is panting, and I feel his heart pounding frantically under my hand.

"Seven gods!" he breathes.

I pull back and look up into his face covered in numerous cuts and gashes. More cuts lacerate his shoulders, and his garments hang in shreds as dark streams of blood roll down his skin. But he seems unaware of these wounds. He stares out across the sweeping view of the gardens, his eyes round with horror.

I turn. I see what he sees.

I hardly have words to describe it—the nightmare, so bizarre, so far beyond anything in my range of experience. Darkness looms over Orican like a storm, obliterating starlight and moonlight—a great, living darkness. I see towers, mighty citadels of stone that twist and writhe like living things. I see walls, arches, windows, buttresses, all vast on a scale beyond imagining, crawling straight for us. Breaking through the far walls, swallowing the garden.

"It's too late," Erolas says. I hear his words but can't comprehend them, can't make sense of them through the crazy tumult of my mind. "Her world will devour all of Orican."

Before I can even begin to ask any of the questions choking my throat, he whirls and heads back the way we came, still holding me fast. The walls of the windowed passage are listing heavily, and glass shards litter the ground in glittering, deadly profusion. I hear Erolas grunting, gasping with pain as the glass slices into his feet. But he does not pause. He stumbles, rights himself, his grip around me tightening, and keeps on going. I want to ask him where we will go, where we possibly can go to escape from that nightmare vision. But I can't speak. My tongue is thick, numb with terror.

We emerge into the courtyard. It's devastated, almost unrecognizable. Huge chunks of fallen masonry have smashed the stone floor and crushed the banqueting table to rubble. There is no way through.

"Hold on," Erolas says.

He leaps. I scream and tighten my grip around his neck as he achieves a precarious balance at the top of a massive stone block some seven feet tall. He doesn't pause, doesn't hesitate even a moment before leaping again for another stone a good eight feet across and a little down from us. Nimble as a cat, without even the benefit of his arms for balance, he navigates the destructive mayhem of the courtyard until he reaches a door at the far end.

There at last he sets me down. I'm too dizzy at first to recognize where we've come. My legs feel like jelly, ready to give out under me, and I haven't yet managed to catch my breath. The air is full of dust, and my ears throb with the overwhelming roar of stone against stone as that darkness I glimpsed across the garden bears down upon Orican.

Erolas approaches the fastened door before us. It stands firm in its wall, unshaken by the quakes devastating the rest of the palace. It won't open. The latch refuses to turn, and when he pounds the panels, they echo hollowly. He hurls himself against it, his shoulder hitting the wood with a sickening thud. It rattles on its hinges but nothing more.

"No, no, no!" he gasps, throwing his weight against it again and again. "Will even the gods abandon me?"

I realize then where he's brought us—the chapel. The same chapel I've seen his shadow-self seek for refuge, prostrating himself before the stone images of the gods. He had hoped we might shelter here through whatever storm is coming.

I reach out, touch his arm. "Erolas!"

At my touch and my voice, his whole body shudders, and he

turns sharply, looking down at me. I shrink from the ferocity of his gaze, from the wicked curve of his horns, from the strange yellow, catlike eyes shining down at me through the darkness.

Then his expression melts into one of such sorrow, it could break my heart.

"I'll get you out of this, Valera. I swear it."

He takes my hand, and we're running together now, navigating the ruins of the colonnade. In places the pillared roof is still upheld. In other places, he's obliged to lift me over the fallen stones or carry me across shattered roof tiles. I feel terrified, helpless, stupid with fear. I hate how useless I am. Useless to help either him or myself or anyone here in this moment. Where is Ellie? Where are Birgabog and the goblin men? What of the shadowy figures I've glimpsed through folds of reality? Are they also fleeing as their home falls to pieces around their ears? Or are Erolas and I alone?

He reaches an open doorway leading to some part of the house I don't know. He pulls me swiftly through it, and I'm both surprised and relieved to find the passage beyond mostly intact. But I hear groans in the walls around me and don't trust any of it to remain stable for long.

Figures move in the shadows.

Erolas stops abruptly. I run into him, then grip his arm and peer out from behind his bulk.

A figure stands before us at the far end of the passage. A massive figure, humanoid in shape but far bigger, broader than any man. As big as my husband, bigger even. An open window allows in a stream of moonlight, which lights upon great white wings.

"Sunfire King," a voice speaks. A voice so heavenly, so majestic, it strikes the ears with all the solemn beauty of tolling cathedral bells. It rolls over me, over my spirit, and sends me to my knees. "Sunfire King," the voice says, "your bride awaits."

Erolas braces himself, stepping between me and that figure. "Stand aside!" he snarls. In contrast to that ethereal voice, he sounds like a ravening dog. It almost hurts my soul for his words to interrupt even the reverberating echoes of the winged one's utterance.

The figure at the end of the passage adjusts his stance, wings widening to fill the whole space like a living gate. "I am come to escort you to your wedding, my king." He—she—I can't say for certain which, merely that it is vast and powerful and majestic. Either way, it adjusts its stance, pointing the gleaming point of a lance straight at Erolas's heart. "Come. Come and partake of the marriage feast—"

Before the last word is complete, Erolas is in motion. He springs straight for the lance. For a heart-stopping moment of horror, I believe he will impale himself on it. But at the last moment, the winged one gives a cry—a golden, searing, beautiful cry—and yanks the deadly point out of his way so that the sharp edge merely grazes Erolas's shoulder.

In another instant, Erolas's hands are around the winged one's neck. I hear a single strangled cry, then a sickening crunch.

The glorious being falls to the ground. Moonlight wafts gently against a face of heartrending beauty. Stricken. Dead.

Breath leaves my lips in a half sob. What has just happened? What have I just witnessed?

Did my husband murder an . . . an angel? With his bare hands?

"Valera!"

The sound of my name quickens the heart cord in my chest, drags my gaze up from the fallen one to meet Erolas's eyes. He stares down at me with earnest entreaty. "Valera, please. They are not what they seem."

"But . . . but . . ." I can't think. I can't move. I can't—

"My lord and king!"

I start and whirl around, staring down the passages behind us. Three more heavenly beings approach, their wings flashing bright through the whirls of dust.

"Come, Valera!" Erolas is beside me again, taking my hand. "This way!"

I let myself be turned around; I let him drag me along behind him. My feet stagger, stumble, but he never slows his pace. The walls shudder, the ceilings shake, the floors tremble beneath us. The entire house will fall on top of us at any second. When I cast a glance behind, the dust is too thick to see if we are pursued.

We arrive at a window. I blink, numb in body and soul, but realize after a moment that it is the same window I saw on my first day in Orican, the one overlooking the waterfall and the great landscape bathed in moonlight.

Erolas releases my hand and leans over the windowsill, then pulls his head back in and looks at me. "Do you think you are strong enough to hold onto my shoulders?"

I recall that precipitous drop I witnessed once before and shudder. Then something seems to click into place inside my brain. "Wait!" I say, my voice breathless and choked with dust. "What about this?"

I undo the clasp of one of my seven lockets. The wind garment pours out into my hand, invisible save for the silver buttons and my own small stitches. But its effects are unmistakable as it blows the dust away from us, clearing a little patch of breathable air.

"What is this?" Erolas asks. Am I mistaken to believe I hear wonder in his voice? "What have you been up to, my clever wife?"

I don't try to explain. I don the wind garment and feel its swelling power around me. Power enough to carry us both? I can only hope so. "Hold onto me?" I ask, stepping forward to stand beside him at the window. "As long as you—"

I don't finish. I can't.

For I've just looked out the window on that same moonlit landscape I glimpsed all those weeks ago. But it isn't the perilous empty spaces and vast distances that have stolen the words from my tongue.

Wings fill the sky. Dozens upon dozens of wings. White, gleaming, moonlit wings, like a flock of doves, drawing nearer, nearer.

I pause, one hand still fastening the topmost button of the wind garment, which swirls around me, frigid against my exposed skin. Erolas's arm comes down around my shoulder, his long fingers gripping hard.

"Not that way," he says quietly. "It was a good thought. But I fear we have only one option now."

They're close enough now that I can see their flashing armor, their helmets and cheek plates. I can see the burning of their heavenly eyes.

Then Erolas's arm is shielding me, drawing me away from the window and back down the passage. I still wear the wind garment, which serves to clear away dust and debris, allowing us to breathe more easily as we flee. My eyes search beyond the radius of my personal windstorm for any glimpse of tall figures bearing lances, expecting them to appear and surround us at any moment.

But we reach a large open space. I recognize it: the front entrance hall with its domed ceiling and beautiful mosaic floor. The very place I last saw and spoke to my sister, when she pressed the candle into my hand. The candle, which was . . . enchanted? My head spins, trying to make sense of it all. But I can't. There's too much, too much. And the whole house quakes again with another terrible crash.

Erolas leads me straight to the double doors. He stops a moment as the worst of the quake rolls under our feet, catching me close in his arms once more, pressing my face to his chest.

When the roar of breaking stone passes, his voice rumbles in my ear: "This is not how I would have things end between us. The Starglass was so much truer than I could ever have believed possible. I begged it to show me the face of my true love, and I saw you. I didn't believe it at the time. I thought something must have gone wrong, thought the price I had paid for that single glimpse was not enough. Then I thought, what does it matter? If she weds me, if she becomes my bride, nothing else will matter. The Pale Queen will be unable to claim me before the time is past and my people and I are safe."

"Safe?" I whisper in hollow echo. "Safe from what?"

I feel his head shake, and for a moment his arms tighten. "It doesn't matter now. It's too late. She has hounded me down, even as she did my brother, my father, my uncles. I thought to be clever, but I am not so clever as she. And now the hunt closes in."

I'm quivering so hard I can barely stand. My own ignorance plagues me with nameless, unknown fears. My arms cling to him. I want to hold him fast, to never let him go. If those winged beings are coming for us, to end us, I can only hope the end will be swift and that I will die while encircled in his arms.

But Erolas steps back, holding my shoulders firmly as he puts distance between us. My wind billows his hair around his strange, striking face. He looks into my eyes, his expression unreadable, intent. Then he releases his grip on my shoulders and reaches instead for the silver buttons running down my bosom, holding the invisible garment in place. He undoes them one after another.

"I knew you were talented," he says, his fingers swift and sure. "I never imagined you capable of such a wonder! I believe you could do anything you set your will to with that passion, that drive of yours. You are truly powerful."

"What?" I feel so stupid, so small. Not at all powerful. I can scarcely even comprehend what he is saying. "Erolas—"

He presses a finger to my lips. Then he slides the wind garment off me. For a moment, as his fingers brush the skin of my neck, my traitorous body shivers in response to that touch, despite the fear, despite the horror of that moment. Oh, why did I throw away every chance I had to experience his touch to the fullest? Why did I not realize how little time we had? A year and a day had seemed so long. Now . . . now I would give anything for just one more hour.

"Here," he says, folding the wind garment and handing it to me. "Put this away. Do you still have the shadow cloth?"

I nod even as I hasten to obey. I hide the wind back in its locket, then open the locket containing the shadow, feeling the ripples of nothingness pour free. I can't even see it as it falls to the floor, but Erolas stoops and immediately snatches it up.

"There," he says, draping it around my shoulders. "This will serve. When you're through those doors, Valera, I want you to run. Run, run, run as far and as fast as you can! I wish I could take you all the way home. I hate breaking that promise to you now."

My stomach knots. After all, he'd broken that promise long ago. He broke it when he failed to tell me that time was passing and my sister was growing up by months, by years, while mere days passed for me. I open my mouth, wanting both to accuse and forgive in the same breath.

But then he takes my face in his hands, and I forget all else, lost in the depths of his golden-eyed gaze.

"My valiant wife," he says. "You could have saved us all. I do believe you would have in the end, but now . . ." He shakes his head. "Don't come after me. Forget me, forget all of this. Return home and live in peace, for you are not to blame for what has happened here tonight. Indeed, you may be the only truly guiltless soul in this whole accursed world."

The house shakes again. Something crashes close by. Then a chunk of the ceiling falls and smashes into the floor just to my right. I scream, my voice lost in the noise, the mayhem.

But Erolas takes a lunging step. One arm wraps protectively around my shoulders; the other reaches out, grabs the latch of the double doors and flings them wide. I stare out into a world of green, of daylight, utterly unlike the moonlit world in which I stand. For a moment, the strangeness of it is so great, so terrible, I can't even see it as the escape that it is.

Then his voice is in my ear one last time. "Goodbye, Valera. I've loved you more than I ever believed it possible to love another living soul. May your life be full of joy."

"Erolas!" I cry. I try to turn, to catch sight of him. My hand reaches from beneath the shadow cloth, searching for his hand.

But a great shove between my shoulders sends me staggering through the door and tumbling down the steps. I crash to my knees and feel the folds of the shadow fabric draping around me, covering me entirely. My ears are ripped apart by an ongoing roar, explosion after explosion. Crashing glass and smashing stone, walls and towers crumbling. I curl up into a ball beneath the shadow cloth, my arms over my head, expecting Orican itself to tumble down on top of me, crushing me in an avalanche of ruin.

Other sounds fill my ears—a howling wail, dreadful laughter. A crash and clatter for which I have no name, like some massive engine tearing through the very layers of reality. Once I think I hear Erolas's voice, but perhaps I am imagining it.

Then all is still.

Terribly still.

29

Shivering so hard I fear my bones will shatter, I inhale deep, deep breaths.

I'm alive.

At least . . . I think I am. If this is death, it feels an awful lot like fear-ridden life. Maybe I've fallen deep into one of the nine hells?

Carefully I reach out, feeling for the edges of my shadow fabric. I lift it tentatively and peer out from the darkness, expecting to see stone, rubble, ruin, and dust all around me, the devastation of Orican fallen.

Instead, I see brilliant morning sunlight shining on dew-glittering grass.

With a gasp I sit upright, casting the shadow cloth behind me like a cloak. I stare around, disbelieving. Where is the house?

Where are the broken double doors, the smashed front-porch step, the fallen domed ceiling?

But it's gone. Just . . . gone. Not ruins but vanished. As though it never existed.

I'm sitting in a green glade surrounded by tall, silent trees of silvery white birch. When I twist in place, I see nothing but forest and more forest extending forever on all sides. Of the palace—of the vast house and gardens—of Ellie and the goblin men—of Erolas—there is no sign.

Clutching the folds of shadow cloth around my shoulders, I unsteadily rise to my feet. I feel like a child again. Seven years old and terrified, waking from a nightmare only to realize I cannot call out for my mother for comfort anymore. Because she's gone. Dead.

That same feeling rushes over me, a wave of sorrow so deep, so overwhelming, I'm nearly crushed beneath it.

I'm alone.

Completely alone.

"Erolas?" I whisper, turning in place. I wait for that connection between us to pull at my heart as it always does when I speak his name. But there's nothing. It's as though the cord has been snapped completely. "Erolas!" I call again, my voice ringing through the trees.

No answer. Only a distant echo. Then nothing at all.

I take a step. Stop. Turn, and take a step in another direction.

Which way can I go? It's all the same. Nothing but forest as far as the eye can see. How can I possibly find Erolas? Or home, or . . .

My foot lands on something cold and metallic. I stop and look down, lifting my foot.

It's my necklace. The clasp must have come undone when I fell—when Erolas pushed me—through the door. The seven lockets gleam bright against the dirt, half hidden by curling bits of old leaves.

Erolas's last gift.

I pluck it up, winding the delicate chain through my fingers. For a moment I bow my head, close my eyes. Tears and despair rise in my eyes and spirit, ready to overwhelm me completely, ready to wash all hope away in a flood I cannot resist.

Erolas is gone. Those winged beings claimed him. For what purpose I cannot imagine. Am I wrong in thinking they called him "king?" No, for the words still ring loud and clear in my memory! *Sunfire King*, that winged being had said. *Your bride awaits.*

What bride? Was the being referring to me? No, it couldn't be. It made no sense.

But who else could possibly be my husband's bride?

I grip the necklace tighter, pressing it against my chest. My bare, heaving chest, so scantily clad in the little-bit-of-nothing dress I wore in a bid to seduce and betray the kindest man I've ever known. The man who gave me such joy these last few weeks. The man who treated me with such respect, such kindness. Such . . . love.

The man who'd lied to me?

No. No, I don't believe it. I won't believe it. There is more going on here, more than I've even begun to understand.

Something big and dark and terrible. Something great enough to swallow all of Orican.

Don't come after me.

His words ring in my memory. Almost the last words he spoke to me. Almost.

Don't come after me.

Does that mean . . . does that mean it's possible? That I *could* go after him? That I could find him again? That I might yet unravel the secrets of this curse under which he and his people suffer?

You could have saved us all. I do believe you would have in the end.

I'm dizzy, almost sick from the emotions storming through my soul. Fear, sorrow, guilt, rage . . . but underscoring all is a grimness of determination unlike anything I've ever before known.

"I will find him," I whisper. I lift my head and look into the waiting, listening forest. Then I shout to the leaf-laced sky overhead, "By the seven secret names, I swear I will find him! I will find him, and I will save him, and I will break this curse!"

My voice rolls away, its vain echoes fading, fading. Gone. I listen until I can hear them no more.

And when all is still once more, I whisper, "I'm coming for you, Erolas. Wait for me."

ALSO BY SYLVIA MERCEDES

This arranged marriage romance about a human princess forced to wed a dark and desperate Shadow King is sure to entice!

BRIDE OF THE SHADOW KING TRILOGY

Though she is the oldest daughter, Princess Faraine lives in the background, shunned from court and kept out of sight. Her chronic illness makes her a liability to the crown, and she has learned to give place to her beautiful, favored younger sister in all things.

When the handsome and enigmatic Shadow King comes seeking a bride, Faraine is not surprised that her sister is his choice.

Though not eager to take a human bride, King Vor is willing to do what is necessary for the sake of his people. When he meets the lively Princess Ilsevel, he agrees to a marriage.

So why can't he get the haunting eyes of her older sister out of his head?

The first book in a new fantasy romance series, this sweeping tale of love and betrayal is perfect for readers looking for a touch of spice to go with the sweet in their next swoony, slow-burn romance.

A CLEVER THIEF. A DISFIGURED MAGE.
A KISS OF POISON.

THE SCARRED MAGE OF ROSEWARD

For fifteen years, Soran Silveri has fought to suppress the nightmarish monster stalking Roseward. His weapons are few and running low, and the curse placed upon him cripples his once unmatched power. Isolation has driven him to the brink of madness, and he knows he won't be able to hold on much longer.

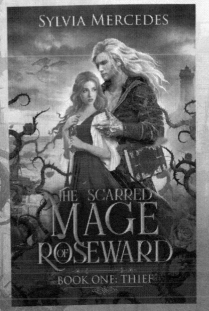

When a sharp-tongued, uncouth, and undeniably beautiful young woman shows up on his shore, Soran resolves to drive her away. He won't be responsible for another death.

But Nelle is equally determined not to be frightened off by the hideously scarred mage. Not until she gets what she came for . . . .

Can two outcasts thrown together in a tangle of lies discover they are each other's only hope? Or will the haunted darkness of Roseward tear them apart?

This romantic series about a mortal librarian and her dealings with a roguish fae prince will keep you turning pages late into the night!

ENTRANCED

PRINCE OF THE DOOMED CITY:

BOOK 1

Clara is an Obligate—an indentured servant of the fae. Serving out a fifteen-year sentence for a crime she doesn't remember committing, she spends her days working in the king's glorious library. Her only hope is to keep her head down, attract no attention, and survive to the end of her Obligation. Only then can she get home to her beloved brother.

But when the conniving Prince of the Doomed City arrives at court, all Clara's hopes are dashed. He is determined to buy her Obligation for his own dark purpose. And he doesn't care who gets in his way.

The only problem? He hates her. More than anyone else in all the worlds. But his hatred just might be the key to discovering why she was bound to this fate in the first place.

Can Clara recover her forgotten memories before the nightmares of her past return to claim her? Or will she be swallowed up by the darkness of the Doomed City and lost forever?

ABOUT THE AUTHOR

SYLVIA MERCEDES makes her home in the idyllic North Carolina countryside with her handsome husband, numerous small children, and the feline duo affectionately known as the Fluffy Brothers. When she's not writing she's . . . okay, let's be honest. When she's not writing, she's running around after her kids, cleaning up glitter, trying to plan healthy-ish meals, and wondering where she left her phone. In between, she reads a steady diet of fantasy novels.

But mostly she's writing.

After a short career in Traditional Publishing (under a different name), Sylvia decided to take the plunge into the Indie Publishing World and is enjoying every minute of it. She's the author of the acclaimed Venatrix Chronicles, as well as The Scarred Mage of Roseward trilogy, and the romantic fantasy, Bride of the Shadow King.

Made in the USA
Middletown, DE
21 June 2024

56135051R00229